Portals to the Vision Serpent

Also by Carla Woody

Calling Our Spirits Home: Gateways to Full Consciousness

Standing Stark: The Willingness to Engage

Portals to the
Vision Serpent

Carla Woody

Inquiries may be directed to:
Kenosis Press
P.O. Box 10441
Prescott, Arizona 86304
http://www.kenosis.net
info@kenosis.net

ISBN-10: 1-930192-03-7
ISBN-13: 978-1-930192-03-4
Library of Congress Control Number: 2013906540

Interior and cover design: Kubera Book Design
Cover art: ©2013 Carla Woody

For those who hold the invisible threads of their fragile traditions.

His prayer:
I call upon My Ancestors, My People, clearly by name and feel your presence,
rising up through time, running in my blood, to my place in the world.

Author's Note

This is a work of fiction. The appearance of any character to a living or historical person is purely coincidental. However, elements of the process that the characters endure or undertake may be familiar to a number of readers. The geographical names are actual with a couple of exceptions. Mother Lode and Johns Wake are imagined. K'ak no longer exists but is modeled upon a village that does. The Hach Winik are also known as the Lacandón Maya. Their plight described here is real, as with other Maya and Native peoples. While a few liberties have been taken to weave a story, descriptions of culture and tradition are largely factual, at least as seen through the eyes of an outsider.

Preston

A LOUD CRACK from the corner of the room jarred his sleep. Then scrabbling, like small claws against bare wood. Preston opened his eyes to pitch darkness and directed them toward the sounds. Did they come from over there or inside his head? He waited for the voices. Silence. Whatever was there had gone—if it had been present at all.

Often at night he had unexplainable experiences. It had always been that way. He'd approach the hazy interlude between sleep and waking and, in the next moment, detect barely audible whispering or muttering a few feet away—as if someone were in the room with him, trying to grab his attention. Flipping on the light, he'd find nothing.

Sometimes he'd smell burning tobacco or resin; the scent never stayed long. Preston knew it wasn't in his room—or not in a way that he could easily explain to others. He didn't smoke tobacco and rarely burned incense.

When he was a boy, he chalked it up to dreams or to Smoky coming to visit him in the night. His mother said Smoky was imaginary. Yet he didn't seem made up. But even now, at twenty-one, Preston wasn't sure what was real and what wasn't; the boundaries often blurred. He'd been considering the big questions lately: What was truth? Reality? If only he had an answer, Preston thought, life would be a cinch, or at least easier to navigate.

He knew one thing: What truth wasn't. Drowsy thoughts of his mother entered on cue. Resentment prickled his skin. He pushed her out of his mind even though she was unwilling to go. Sybilla. Doing what duty called for, the same as the Southern grandmother she was named after. Preston wished the little notice he'd won from her was more than cursory.

He started sinking back into sleep when an image moved lazily across the movie screen of his mind. Mama Luna. Mother Moon. A brown-skinned woman with a black braid down her back smiled broadly at him. He'd loved how her eyes twinkled when she laughed, as though accenting a secret just the two of them held. She had been around so long ago, coming after Mama Flora. Memories of his mother's earliest helper were even more obscure. Mama Luna wasn't her real name. She made up the special name for herself, just as she made up one for him, only to be used between the two of them. He vaguely remembered his mother calling her Maria.

So many times Mama Luna had gathered him to her and chirped, *Ah niño, you are the sun of my life and I am the moon. I reflect your light! Solocito!*

He heard her lyrical voice in his head and loved the silly nickname. How many times had she told him that he was favored? Countless times. *The spirits like you, Solocito! They show themselves to you. Pay attention and they will tell you important things!*

In his mind's eye he saw the familiar gesture—a raised finger to her lips indicating it was their secret. The memory transmitted satisfying warmth through his body. Then the image faded to be followed by dreams.

When he came to again, a rosy light played against his lids. He didn't have to open his eyes to know it was morning. Preston heard purring close by and reached out a hand, burrowing his fingers into a waiting belly. The raspy lick signaled encouragement. Still he didn't open his eyes. Instead, Preston gave himself permission to be just as languid as his cat, Gato, lying next to him on the pillow.

He remembered the events in the night. Once again, he saw Mama Luna from that earlier time. From a spot deep inside him—an empty, hungry place—longing emerged. For what he was uncertain. For Mama Luna? Maybe it was something she represented. He did know that he had an underlying, un-nameable ache, and it wasn't getting any better with time.

Preston could think of no real reason to get up. He rolled out of the tangled sheets and sat on the edge of his bed. He felt rooted there. The house was silent except for the ticking of the clock over on his desk. Alone as usual—but not quite. Gato eyed him intently.

"Okay, old friend," he said, "Let's go downstairs and see what we've got for you."

He gave her ear a slight tug of affection. A few seconds later he was in the kitchen spooning cat food into a bowl while Gato yowled at his feet.

"You just keep getting me up day after day, don't you?"

Gato flipped her tail. He watched her eat for a while and then headed for the shower.

Sometimes piping hot water coursing over his body rendered some clarity if he stayed there long enough. The confusion was never completely gone these days. But water dissolved some of the layers that often clouded his thoughts.

Had he *not* ever felt agitated? Maybe when he was very young and Mama Luna was still there. Preston sensed different factions battling inside him, unsure what the war was all about.

Standing under the shower, Preston looked down at his nude body, a medium frame with a rangy quality developed from years on the school track team. That was over now. He'd tried out for track as soon as he was old enough, quickly attaining star status, not that he cared at all for the personal glory. It didn't bring him satisfaction, just momentary relief. He was too different from the other kids and didn't want to be like them anyway. He viewed most of them as shallow, interested only in the most trivial of things: the brandname of their shoes or how many so-called friends they could collect. His mind wandered over those times and settled on his college coach.

"Son," he'd say, "I never know if you're running to victory or running away from something that's eating you alive! Whatever it is, you keep it up!"

Those words served as praise after yet another race won. But the coach inadvertently pointed out the edginess Preston lived with, setting him apart. People picked up on it and often felt uneasy around him. Preston lingered on the coach's voice calling him "Son." He let the word replay in his head and felt the tugging void in his heart.

He still ran. Sometimes late at night. Often very early in the morning. It was too hot in the central Arizona desert to run during the day in nearly any season. He had to get rid of the strange shimmering feeling that he carried beneath his skin in some way. Otherwise he couldn't sleep at all.

He continued to gaze down at his torso, surrendering to the stinging spray; the shower was doing its trick. He focused on the rivulets of water flattening the hair on his legs that merged into common streams. A parable he'd heard somewhere floated to the surface. Preston didn't remember it completely, but it was something about small life forms being swept along together in a swiftly moving creek. But one of the little guys was curious about the shore and began to notice roots sticking out from the banks as he floated by. One day he decided to go for it. It took an enormous effort to extract himself from the group. But he managed to move a distance apart and looked ahead for a likely protrusion to grab and pull himself to shore. One was coming very quickly. He lunged for it.

In his reverie Preston became that life form striking out on his own. But just at the last split second something gripped his leg and pulled him back. Preston imagined his mother's weighty hold, like a rock tied to his ankle, causing him to sink swiftly to the muddy creek bottom. There he stayed, tethered to the stone, while others rushed by stirring up the silt.

Preston came out of his trance with a start. The shower was cold. He shut off the water. Through the lingering chill he could feel turmoil lodged in his belly, the sediment of hopelessness. His feet searched for something to stand on, but there was no foundation.

What's wrong with you? Why aren't you like everyone else? Why can't you make things easy? You cause nothing but trouble, mister!

The voice continued in a tirade, but a few seconds later another voice erupted.

You are my special one! You are different! Such a gift! Don't listen to anyone else!

The voices got louder, scuffling for control. Paralysis took hold.

Where's the battle? There's your answer! Sounding like the elder brother Preston didn't have, an emissary began to point things out.

He called the harbinger of information Messenger. He was unable to determine if Messenger was part of himself or something else. In

Preston's private world, Messenger could well be something else—not of this world. But he didn't really care or question. When things got really rough, he could count on Messenger to magically appear and offer some wisdom. Even though he couldn't see him, Preston could feel his presence as he offered a sure, measured voice of reason about whatever struggle Preston had at the time. Then he would experience hope, an ephemeral support from spaces unseen. It was a good thing since he felt like a parentless child much of the time.

Listen. Really listen, Messenger directed, *What can you tell me about those voices?*

Now that he was older, there were things he appreciated about Messenger that he used to dislike. Rather than automatically telling him what he was to learn, as a typical teacher might, Messenger asked questions. And Preston found that, sometimes, he was able to get to his own answers. When that happened, he felt a little more confident.

With Messenger present, Preston no longer felt like a ball kicked about between players. He called on himself to bring back at least some of the fleeting experience. Sure enough, it wasn't really gone. It had just moved momentarily to the background. Then a strange thing happened. He wondered why he had never it noticed before.

He growled as he focused on the punishing voice: Sybilla. Since early teen years, Preston used her name whenever he thought about his mother. He chastised himself for all his whining as a child in her frequent absences. He couldn't bring himself to call her "Mother" unless she was physically present, silently demanding it.

He diverted his attention to the soft voice that sounded like Mama Luna. The bitterness in his heart dissipated, lifting his spirits.

Put all that aside and look at the bigger meaning here. What else can you tell me? Messenger guided.

Preston stared into space, but the meaning was still elusive. Then he remembered back to the night before.

Something wanted me to wake up, didn't it? Why did I think of Sybilla in the middle of the night? She's nowhere around. But neither is Mama Luna, he mused.

Then, a fast-forward to the shower he'd just completed.

There's something about that parable I remembered. What is it?
You tell me.

The parable. The voices. It's all about the same thing!

You will always be shown many ways in as many ways as you need—until you understand. Think of these things as guidance, but you take the lead.

While attending to Messenger's lessons, he'd automatically dried himself. Still naked, he stood in front of the bathroom sink and stared at his reflection in the mirror. Dark hair curled below his ears. He had wide-set, ice-blue eyes, straight dark eyebrows and a generous mouth—all inherited from his father. There was nothing particularly distinctive about his nose. He saw that as his own. But the square chin was definitely his mother's, a trademark of the Johns family. It was only these two features that kept him from looking like a carbon copy of his father, at least from the few photos he'd seen.

He glanced at the open door leading out into the hallway. Gato sat there staring at him.

"Something's up, Gato," he said.

— Chapter Two —

PRESTON JOHNS CADELL. He sometimes wondered where he existed in that name. The first two were already worn out by his mother's family. If he had to inherit a hand-me-down, he'd rather it had been Gabe, after his father.

Sybilla used to call him PJ, but Preston put a stop to that years ago. He hadn't been a child anymore and never liked that nickname. The other kids taunted him, calling him PB & J for the sandwich that he always had in his lunchbox. His mother wasn't around, and he'd wanted to show he could take care of himself.

Preston was looking more and more like his long-gone father and knew, at some level, it was hard on his mother. But he didn't care. The part of him that longed for a male influence took a sad pleasure in twisting the knife a little. She was the one who drove his father away. At least, that's what he always told himself. It was easier to think that his dad left for a good reason. Over time, his reasoning fixed in resentment toward Sybilla. He noticed his mother's sadness when, on rare occasions, she spoke of the early years when they were all together. It made him wonder what had *really* happened. She left it a mystery.

Plenty of other kids were raised by a mother, or maybe grandparents, but their father came to see them. Preston's never did. He just vanished. He had a faint recollection of big hands tossing him up in the air, and a deep laugh mixing with his baby one. Those memories were marred by loud voices and banging in the dark. For a while, he was afraid to sleep without a light.

Then the kids at school found out he didn't know his dad. They trilled in singsong voices, "PJ's a bastard! PJ's a bastard!" They trailed him on the playground, singing it over and over until he cried. Even though he hadn't known what they meant, it hurt. A teacher came over and broke it up. But the damage was already done. For the longest time,

9

the meanest of them would hiss "Cry baby!" or "Bastard!" whenever he walked by. That's when he withdrew further from others his age; he stayed to himself.

Preston remembered being a happy kid before then, before he had to go to school. Those were the days of Mama Luna. She always had good smelling things baking in the oven and was forever tickling him, making him laugh.

There were things she showed him that others couldn't see, but he could—after she reminded him how to look. When he looked straight ahead and, at the same time, peeked to the side, Smoky was sometimes there. He couldn't see him exactly. The air was hazy where he appeared, and a slight tobacco smell hung in the air. That's why Preston called him Smoky.

Smoky had definitely talked to him but not like people talked. It was more that he made him aware of things, as Mama Luna had: things about the workings of nature that other people missed. Like how the wind fluttered the leaves to tell of a coming storm, or what agony the trees felt when they were cut down. One time his mother sent him to summer camp up in the mountains. He had walked by an edge of the campground where men from the power company were trimming tree branches that obstructed electrical lines. Suddenly, he was overtaken by convulsive feelings—grief and pain. Through his tears, he saw two majestic pines whacked down to the ground, their insides freshly exposed. Some inner wisdom had told him never to tell the other kids what he saw and felt. Their taunting was bad enough as it was.

Preston had come home from school that awful day and asked his mother in a small voice, "Why don't I have a daddy?"

"Oh honey, you do have a daddy!" Even now, he remembered the pained expression on her face. That was right after the first time she returned from Australia. She had pasted a smile over her sad mouth and said brightly, "He went on a walkabout!"

"What's that?" he asked.

"Sometimes people like your father get a calling. They need to go and find what answers the world has."

Preston hadn't understood what she meant, but it sounded like a grand adventure. "When's he going to come home?"

"He'll come home someday. One day when we're out in the backyard looking out into the desert, we'll see a little dot. It'll get closer and closer and closer. Then when we blink our eyes, he'll be there right in front of us!"

At the time, Preston hadn't detected the false gaiety in his mother's voice. But he remembered that Mama Luna had looked away, as though she didn't want to meet his eyes. She wasn't able to make out everything they said in English, but she understood enough.

From that time he began to build an image of his father in his mind. His mother said she didn't have any photos, but Preston found a couple tucked away in a book. In one he tended a campfire. In the other, he sat on top of a big rock looking into the distance. Preston's early mental picture consisted of an unlikely fusion: a swashbuckling warrior and gentle nature soul. He decided his father must be a very brave man. From what Preston was able to find out from his mother, he knew the aboriginal people set out on long treks without any food, water or clothing. They knew the Universe would give them what they needed along the way. Even back then, Preston liked the idea of providence. After all, where Mama Luna came from, her people didn't have a real store to buy everything.

He had considered the idea of a walkabout for a while, then Preston began to ask more questions. "What's my daddy like?"

His mother would usually get a faraway look in her eyes, and say, "We'll talk about him some other time." But sometimes, she would look warmly into his eyes and tell him how handsome his father was or how they shared the same eyes.

Those rare times thrilled him and created inspiration for the stories he wrote about his father's journey. Since his mother wouldn't talk about him very much, Preston was afraid he'd forget what little he knew. He had kept a notebook where he wrote down clues from his mother and musings of the lost, young boy he was, spinning tales. Those imaginative stories were a mixture of the adventure books he read, stories Mama Luna told him of her own land and the few action films he was allowed to see. Mostly, he shared them with Smoky. Never his mother. When he read them to Mama Luna, she would stop whatever work she was doing, wipe her hands on her apron, and tenderly gather him up in her arms.

Pitiful kid, Preston thought.

Over the years, he'd gleaned enough from Sybilla to piece together some of the family history. He chose to seize upon the parts of it that added to his needs, while ignoring parts that seemed a little unsettling for reasons he didn't understand. At that young age, he was already a sensitive romantic with a vivid inner life he shared with few. His mother was increasingly absent from home. When she was there she was preoccupied, getting ready for the next photojournalism assignment.

The epic that he had chosen as truth read like a melodramatic novel, satisfying on a visceral level, with the same sense of comfort and love he had when he'd wake up long ago to find the little cat Gato, a present from his mother, curled around his head like a vibrating hat. Gato was a welcome friend, finally filling the empty times—loneliness—after Mama Luna, too, had inexplicably vanished.

As Preston thought of that little ball of spiky black fur Gato had been, he felt the sting of tears in his eyes, and came back to the present moment. He found himself sitting on the backdoor stoop, somehow dressed from his shower in a pair of worn cutoff jeans and a dingy white t-shirt. He'd again been on autopilot while his thoughts were elsewhere, a state in which he frequently dwelled. At least some part of him had taken the initiative to clothe himself.

"We don't want to give the neighbors any more fuel for their curiosity. Do we, Gato?" He nudged her belly with a bare foot.

The slow blink of her eyes seemed to say: And why not?

When Preston was at home, Gato was never far away, a guardian. After all these years, her coat wasn't quite as shiny, and the fur was a little sparse on her back legs. She no longer made the big leaps that she could make just a couple of years before.

He knew she'd lived much longer than most cats, but he hoped she'd always be his protector. The emerging adult felt a little foolish, but the little boy found solace. Gato had been there when no one else had, intervening when the night got too dark.

— Chapter Three —

MAMA LUNA WAS THERE. Then she wasn't. Much like his mother, except he always knew where his mother had gone when she left. Anyway, Sybilla eventually returned. Mama Luna never did, following in his father's tracks. He vividly remembered the last time he'd seen her. They were having such a good time.

It was about a year earlier that, periodically, they'd started playing the game. He was barely six and Mama Luna had been living with them about three years. She said the conditions had to be just right for the game. Even at his young age, Preston sensed one of those conditions must be the absence of his mother. He didn't know what the others were. But he did know what they played was very special. So, they didn't do it all the time because then it wouldn't have meaning. He also knew it was something shared just between the two of them. When the game was over, she would put a finger to her lips like she did about the spirits liking him. During the game, she called him by a name from her people. Chan K'in. She didn't use it on any other occasion.

"What does it mean, Mama Luna?" he'd asked her the first time.

"You are Little Sun. You *see* where you shine!" She had gently held his small face between her brown hands, and gazed deeply into his light eyes with her darker ones.

When she'd withdrawn her hands, something had implanted itself in some infinite place inside him, even though he hadn't understood the meaning of what she'd said. Although he hadn't known it then, it was the unconscious memory of that strange transmission that would come back to him in later years as the warmth welling up from an untold space, filling the achy loneliness in his heart. His emptiness would be assuaged temporarily. But eventually it would give rise to tears that he would choke off in his throat, rather than have them escape through their natural passageway.

Even as a young boy, Preston was particularly alert to his surroundings and the people within them. Smoky had taught him to be that way. *This is how you learn awareness and what's so,* Smoky breathed into his ear one day when he was playing in his backyard. *Watch that bird over there. See how that bush pushes its berries out ever so slightly to attract the bird's attention. You might think the bush would try to hide, wouldn't you?* Preston had nodded. When he really focused on the bush and the bird at the same time, he could see a very small movement from the bush, as though it was extending an invitation.

"Why does it do that, Smoky?"

It's part of the natural circle of nourishing. The bush knows that the bird needs what she has in order to live. She also knows that the bird will digest her fruit and the seeds will leave its body. Because the bird is able to fly and the bush has no choice but to stay put, she knows her seeds will be spread much farther than she could ever do herself. In this way she travels.

"Do all plants do that, Smoky?" He was very curious about this strange fact.

Not all of them. Mostly those with seeds. Some plants have to protect themselves. Those are the plants that spread underground through their roots. Just like people, sometimes the animals get greedy, too. They want to take too much. When they take too much, the plant will send a warning to the others. Then all the plants of that kind in the area will make themselves taste bad, and the animal won't eat them, or the plants will make him sick.

So, under Smoky's tutelage, Preston watched and learned what was so. That was why he knew the game Mama Luna played with him was good and nourishing. She took great care in preparation and wasn't greedy by doing it too much. Preston also knew there were things she did that signaled to him when they would soon be playing again.

Mama Luna had a garden in the backyard, perhaps not the easiest accomplishment under the harsh desert sun. Nearly all her years, she had lived in the blanketing humidity of the jungle with its high canopy of trees, not the open blistering dryness. So she went out very early in the morning, or even under the moonlight, to tend her plants. She'd always said she had to have her fingers in the dirt to remind herself of what she was made.

In the corner of the yard that his mother had given her, she grew all manner of herbs, as well as vegetables she put on their table. Some of the herbs she had grown in her homeland down south and brought the seeds with her. She made things with them. Preston didn't know what she did exactly, but she'd sometimes mash them up and put them away someplace secret. He saw one time that she had some hanging in the closet in her room, drying.

Another time, when he was sick, his mother was out on assignment across the world somewhere. Mama Luna had brought a jar of dried leaves and sticks into the kitchen. Preston could see her from where he was lying on the couch. She boiled some water in a pan and turned off the fire. Then she had taken some of the dried plant out of the bottle and, whispering to it, she dropped it into the steaming water. After a while, she poured off some of the liquid into a cup, and brought it for him to drink. It had tasted kind of strange: like dirt. He hadn't liked it much. But he loved Mama Luna and so drank it down.

"Mama, who were you talking to in the kitchen?" he'd asked.

"Oh Solocito, I ask the plant spirits to send you healing. These spirits are happy to help, and we must give them respect by asking!" She'd smiled down at him and put a finger to her lips.

She must have asked in a way that made them very happy because soon Preston became drowsy and fell asleep. When he woke up, he felt much better. The next day he was out playing again. Before he ran out to play, he had kissed Mama Luna. Then he solemnly put a finger to his lips. Mama returned his gesture with delighted laughter crinkling the corners of her eyes.

So one of the things she did when they were soon to play the game was spend time in her garden. But it was different than other times she would dig or weed. It would be late at night and the moon would be up. It was never a full moon but almost full. Preston's bedroom was in the back of the house and had a big window. At night, he always liked to leave the curtains open so he could see the stars and the moon's nightly trip across the sky, if he happened to be awake. Mostly he slept. But when they were getting ready to play the game, something would arouse him very late at night. It was always when the moon was high in the sky. He'd feel himself pulled sleepily to his window, and that's when he'd quietly observe Mama Luna in the garden. She'd walk among the plants in her bare feet, as though doing some kind of slow dance under the surreal silver light. Then she'd turn to one of them, a tall one that came up to her chest, and run her hands up and down its length, nearly touching it. Preston always opened his window and could hear her soft whispering song carried through the stillness to his awaiting ears. Periodically, she would pause, turn her face and hands up to the moon, and murmur some words. Preston didn't understand any of the language but drew comfort from what it generated inside him. Whatever it was must have been transmitted to others who resonated with it, because sometimes the coyotes would answer her offering with acknowledgments of their own, yipping in the night. Once he heard a bird awaken from its roost and return Mama Luna's song.

That was one way he knew. Another way was her weaving. When she'd come home with them, leaving her own people, the only thing she'd insisted on bringing was her loom. It was made of materials that were big and bulky. Even though he'd been very young, the heated argument that ensued between his mother and Mama Luna made an impression on him. His mother wanted Mama Luna to buy materials to reconstruct the loom in their home. She declined, saying *this* loom contained the history of her people. He had witnessed the standoff between the two of them taking place in patched together Spanish. His mother finally backed down when it became clear that Mama Luna was going nowhere unless she had her loom. Sybilla found a way to bring it back. Preston didn't know why it was important for his mother to have Mama Luna come home with them, but his mother's compromise did not go unnoticed by him. Mama Luna's loom graced a nook in their living room just as her garden brightened a corner of their yard during the years she was there. Things grew from her loom just as they did from her little plot of land.

Mama Luna spent as much of her free time at her loom as she did in her garden. She occasionally gave a woven belt to Preston or a colorful shawl to his mother, but usually she wove lengths of cloth and put them away somewhere in her room.

Once when she was busy at her handiwork, Preston asked her, "Why do you weave so much, Mama? You don't do anything with the things you make."

"Oh Solocito!" she laughed. Taking a hand from her work, she stroked his head. Holding one end of the threads dangling from her loom yet to be entwined, she fingered them thoughtfully. "These threads are like things we do. I weave the threads and I see how a life is made. I see my own life. Everyone has these threads. Mostly they don't think about it!"

She motioned him to stand closer. "Look how if I would bring this color in here and wrap it around there, it changes the cloth. It's not the same anymore. It could be good or bad. The cloth shows me how things will be."

He had glanced up at her and met her kind, open face. He had a notion she was talking about something beyond her craft but didn't really get it. His attention span was gone anyway, and he wanted to go out and play.

"Oh! When's dinner?" he had said before he spun out the back door. Her full-bodied laughter trailed after him. She seemed to recognize when he'd had enough, or there was something he didn't yet want to understand.

That year, when they began to play the game, Preston noticed that Mama did her weaving in a special way. She sang lightly as she commingled the threads, but it wasn't the way she usually sang. Her voice had a breathy quality with few distinguishable words, as though she had taken on the sounds of nature: tree trunks rubbing against each other, the flapping of birds' wings, an animal moving through underbrush. It was a repetitive, entrancing tune. The melodic intonations had a strange quality to them; she swallowed them as much as softly expelled them, as if she had two voices singing the same song.

Preston would suddenly awaken late in the night. Something had beckoned him to stand in the darkened doorway of the living room and watch her. In some ways, he felt like a spy because he failed to make his presence known. She never acknowledged him but seemed to know he was there, silently inviting him to witness. He wasn't sure what he was called to see, and he could never figure out exactly what had pulled him from his bed. It couldn't have been the loudness of her voice. It rarely carried to his surveillance point. Even so, Preston recognized it as a sister melody to the one Mama sang in the garden.

She never had any lights on, just a few candles, and her fingers moved automatically. She didn't look at her work so much as gazed at a particular point just above her weaving with a consistent, silent calm. In his budding awareness, Preston had the sense Mama was seeing beyond their living room.

After a while, Preston would return quietly to bed and fall into a deep sleep. In the morning when he came in to get his breakfast, he'd sneak a peek at Mama's loom. Over time, he saw a beautiful cloth growing. The design was unlike any other he'd seen her make. It had corn and canoes and what looked like jaguars and monkeys, all manner of strange things together.

"Mama, what are these pictures?" he finally asked.

"Solocito, this is how the world was made. I tell you this when the time is best," Mama relayed softly.

That was all she'd said, but Preston was satisfied. It was like being patient for cookies to emerge from the oven, and cooled enough so he could eat them. They tasted ever so much better than when he begged for the mixing spoon to lick off the cookie dough. Even at that age, he knew that things had to go through a process in order to be ready for consumption.

So the special cloth grew magically through the nights. During that time, Mama never touched her loom during the daylight hours. Preston only heard her singing at night. One morning, there was nothing on the loom. Instead, he saw the cloth folded up on a low stool next to it.

"You come, Solocito!" Mama Luna had beckoned him over. She shook the cloth open and placed it around him. Her face took on a tender look.

"Time will be soon." She took the cloth from around his shoulders, refolded it carefully and spirited it away to her room.

A few days afterward, he had gone into the living room in the morning and noticed another weaving taking form on Mama's loom. It looked very much like the first one. Its progress was similar to the one that had come before it, growing through the night and resting during the day. Preston thought of the cloth as springing to life, and sensed that something was going on when he wasn't looking, something mysterious emerging that his eyes just couldn't yet see.

Like when he was much younger, he thought the stuffed animals in his room came alive at night, and danced around while he was asleep. Often he would try to catch them by pretending to be asleep. Then he'd open one eye. But they were too clever for him. He never caught them in the act. Sometimes their shadows seemed to move, and he knew he'd almost exposed their tricks. He also thought that Smoky might sometimes inhabit them. He'd heard of people having spirits take over their bodies.

But that was when he was four. He was six when they began to play the game, and knew better about his stuffed animals. He had been very scientific in his determination. He'd sacrificed his least favorite one, the bunny, by carefully cutting open its seams, going through all its stuffing, and found nothing.

The cloth was different. Smoky kept appearing to him in his dreams, holding the completed product. He assumed it was Smoky. Preston would see sooty vapor rising into two tendrils supporting the weaving underneath, holding it out to him—an offering.

He kept the recurring dream to himself as he witnessed the second cloth taking shape. Finally, one morning he had gone to inspect the loom and found it empty. The cloth was done. Mama Luna had taken it somewhere. He allowed the sweet tension of anticipation to build. The time was nearly best.

— Chapter Four —

AT NIGHT BEFORE he went to bed, Preston had marked the moon's cycles and felt an undercurrent of expectancy, barely contained. Mama Luna had kept a nightly vigil in the garden as well, and the loom continued to rest. The two of them shared an unspoken pact as though they were waiting for something to break. Preston wondered if Sybilla had detected the strain of excitement galvanizing the household because, instead of rushing off on far-flung assignments, she stayed home. Periodically, Preston noticed her contemplating him with a fine eye. Other times, she scrutinized Mama Luna going about her daily activities, perhaps trying to tease out something in her actions. For the first time ever, instead of longing intensely for his mother to be there with him, Preston had wished her gone for a while.

Finally, she did go. The assignment to Norway came suddenly, probably too good to turn down. She threw some clothes in a suitcase and left, after giving him a perfunctory kiss on the head and some short instructions to Mama Luna. The moon was waxing. In two nights' time it would be full.

That will be when time is best, he thought to himself. For some reason, he chose to remain silent about this secret thing. Even though he had no clue what the "best time" was about, he knew it was well revealed to both Mama and Smoky but equally unspoken.

If you speak about some things, they lose their power. Smoky gave him this advice some time ago.

"Why, Smoky?" He hadn't quite been able to figure out that one.

It's natural to want to share with your friends. But sometimes people don't understand some things, particularly things they can't see with their eyes. Or things that don't make sense to them. It scares them and they don't like to be afraid.

Preston stared, his lips forming a perfectly round "o."

"Like when I tried to tell Mom about you?"

20

That would be one example.

After Smoky started keeping him company, Preston wanted to share his new friend. He had asked his mother if he could invite him to lunch. She set a place for Preston's guest at the table. But when no flesh-and-blood little boy showed up, yet Preston carried on a lively conversation toward the chair across the table, her brows knitted in confusion. After a while, a slight smile began to play around her mouth. Later he overheard his mother on the telephone to one of her co-workers.

"I wish you could have seen it! It was the cutest thing! PJ jabbering away to an imaginary playmate!" His mother's friend must have had something to say on the matter. "Do you think I should worry about him? His father had problems, you know."

His ears had pricked up at mention of his father, but indignation overcame his curiosity. Smoky wasn't imaginary. He also felt a little ashamed, like there was something wrong with him. So he decided not to ever mention Smoky, even when his mother said to invite his friend to lunch again. He didn't want her to laugh at him. He longed to tell her everything in his small life. But, from that point on, there were some things he made the decision to withhold.

The day his mother left for Norway was a Saturday. Preston had felt liberated. To express it, he played really hard in the back yard, running and jumping straight up in the air, pretending his feet had springs. Indeed, it felt like he could leap right up into the sun. He talked Smoky into a sword fight. Smoky called it "fencing." Their implements looked different, too.

Preston made his sword about a month before during arts and crafts at school. It had a wide cardboard blade and handle. He'd glued aluminum foil over the blade and sprinkled glitter on the hilt. Not too much. It didn't stay glued anyway. Every time he held the shaft some of the glittery stuff came off on his hands. One time he must have accidentally smeared some on his face because his mother noticed and proclaimed it fairy dust. He liked the idea that his sword was magical. He remembered the story about King Arthur. The magic rubbed off on him, just like the fairy dust, and made him wise. Preston relished knowing things other people didn't. After all, he had Smoky advising him on how to notice things, and Mama Luna confided offhand tidbits.

When Preston ran circles around Smoky jabbing the air with his sword, Smoky gave his own arm a sharp shake. A long band of vibrating light emerged from the end of a finger. Preston thought in terms of Smoky having arms and fingers, but it wasn't really like anyone else's. It was more that he could see with his inner vision. Smoky's blade, though, he could make out clearly as throbbing luminous pixels. Smoky had allowed Preston to thrust and yell until apparently he had enough. Then he took laser-like aim with the light particles, and tapped the spot where Preston's hand met the shaft. The sword inexplicably flew out of his grasp and arced over to land several feet away. Astounded but gleeful at the challenge, Preston retrieved his weapon and charged back to win the day. Several times these events repeated themselves until he was just plain worn out.

Red-faced and sweaty with play, Preston huffed and puffed, "How do you do that, Smoky?"

Instead of running and expending his vitality needlessly, a true warrior becomes still. Then he can tell where the openings are for things to go his way. That's when he acts because he knows the truth of his action.

"That's what I want to be! A true warrior!" Preston beamed and waved his own finger in the air with half a hope that light would project.

"Solocito!" He heard Mama Luna calling him to dinner, sticking her dark head out the back door. When he came tearing into the house with a last bit of rambunctious energy, she laughed and exclaimed how stinky he was from his hot play. At least that was the gist of what he understood her to say. But she allowed him to sit at the table with her anyway and fed him his favorite meal: franks and beans mixed with some yellow mustard, carefully sprinkled with sweet pickle relish, and tater tots on the side.

After dinner she bustled him off to take a bath, ignoring his loud protestations. It was their way of joking. With his mother, he'd learned to be quiet most of the time. She usually seemed to have something on her mind.

"Very important tonight for you to take your bath, Solocito!" Mama nodded knowingly at him and closed the door to give him his privacy.

"Oh," he peeped. A light bulb went on. He quickly discarded his clothes and submerged himself in the warm water. He thought briefly about playing frogman, but it seemed bathing had taken on a new significance based on Mama's words. So, instead, he dutifully soaped himself and made sure all parts of himself were sweet-smelling and clean. By the time he had emerged from the now dark-ringed bathtub, he felt the effects of his earlier exertion, a full belly and freshly scrubbed body.

When he came back into the kitchen, Mama Luna was cleaning up the dinner dishes. She took one look at his sleepy eyes and said, "To bed now, Solocito?"

He went through his usual beefing, "Not now, Mama! It's too early! Just a little longer!" Although it was half-hearted and his young body just wanted to lie down, it seemed necessary for him to make the usual show.

Mama Luna nodded knowingly again at him and intimated, "Good for you to sleep now." She appeared to be letting him in on an open secret, and he allowed her to bundle him off to his room.

Preston wondered if the "best time" was imminent. He was intrigued. But his eyes closed almost before his head hit the pillow. He was in a hard sleep when a gentle shaking of his shoulder brought him slowly back to consciousness.

"Solocito. Chan K'in. Solocito," Mama Luna was sitting on his bed steadily trying to wake him.

He said something unintelligible as he struggled to open one eye, and then seeing that it was still dark, he whined, "Oh, Mama! It's too early!"

"Chan K'in. Chan K'in," she chanted softly, refusing to go away.

His eyes suddenly snapped open with a realization that Mama Luna was waking him because it must be the "best time." And she was calling him something he'd never heard before.

"Why are you calling me that name, Mama?" He sat up.

"This is your True Name, Chan K'in. Come. I tell you."

As he got out of bed, he glanced out the window and noted that the moon was high in the sky. He felt a thrilling inside: fear and excitement at the same time. He pulled on some clothes. Something big was about to happen.

23

Preston joined Mama Luna where she waited in the hall. In the dark, they made their way through the house and out into the back yard without speaking. There Mama paused for a moment, standing still, her face turned up to the nearly full moon. He did the same. A beautiful, shimmering, silvery light encased everything, and if Preston wasn't mistaken, himself included. He had a sense that Smoky was off at a distance, to witness what was about to take place, not to participate.

Presently Mama began to move again, with Preston close behind, headed toward her garden. Once there, she stopped.

Looking down at her own bare feet as well as his, she whispered, "Is good. Is good for feet to touch the earth."

Preston nodded silently. It seemed to be the thing to do—to be very quiet. He knew it was about respect and being able to hear. Mama had told him one time.

"It is good to play and laugh. And sometimes it is good to say nothing. Even inside your head. There are those who come to tell you things. If you are loud, you cannot hear them."

That made sense to Preston. As her words came back to him, he recognized this might be one of those times to listen.

Mama entered her garden, and he followed her down the neat rows. She led him to the back where the tall plant stood. Earlier he thought he'd caught a whiff of something. As they got closer, he saw smoke rising steadily. There was a pungent sweetish smell that affected him in a way he would later be unable to describe. When they arrived at the small clearing, he was struck by how it was changed beyond what he saw in daylight. The tall plant wasn't only the guardian, looking out over the tops of the others, but it was also the central focus. There was a wide-mouthed earthen pot on the ground close to the Tall One, as Preston named the plant. The container had a rounded belly and flattened bottom, and a simple face with an open mouth carved on the outside. The source of the smudge was inside the pot. Mama Luna saw Preston gazing curiously.

"This is a god pot," she pointed to its wide opening, "You see gods have open mouths. In respect, we feed them. They like some things we have. Without us to help them, they cannot eat. We burn the copal they

24

like. The *pom*, we call it. It invites the spirits. They come and fill the empty place inside. They give us what we need, too."

Preston nodded slowly, perplexed. He caught a disturbance in the air, a little swirl descending into the clay vessel.

"Come sit." Mama patted a woven cloth placed on the ground. Preston took in his environment and decided that she must have carefully prepared this open-air room earlier in the night. It was special. Mama Luna sat cross-legged on the mat beside him, her regal back straight. It was then Preston noticed she had on one of her own creations, a roomy over-shirt that reached to mid-thigh and a much longer, brightly colored skirt, not her usual attire. Her face gleamed bronze, as if she called on the moon to show off her peaceful radiance, its light to glance off her high, rounded cheekbones, flat sloping forehead and flared nostrils. Preston thought she was the most beautiful woman he'd ever seen, maybe even more than his mother. Mama Luna looked like royalty, yet had a softness that made him feel safe and sheltered.

She took his smaller hand in hers and loosely held it in her lap as they sat together, warm anticipation hanging soundlessly in the air. Finally, she looked down at him with a gentle smile and began to speak.

"I first saw you. You remember. Down in my home. I *see* what is waiting there," she paused for a moment and then continued. "I *see* this in you. But you have no one to open it and to guard your opening. I know you have him," Mama reverently bowed her head in the direction where Smoky watched over the proceedings. "You need one on this side, too. Your mama not know how. Your mama is a good woman and she is also scared. I *see* this."

Preston listened carefully, solemnly drinking in everything Mama Luna said. He wondered what this *seeing* was, and thought it might have to do with Smoky and how his mother couldn't make him out.

"This thing you have is special. I know. I have it, too. This thing must be opened a little at a time with the help of those who know. This is a gift from your father."

At the mention of his father, Preston's eyes quickly begin to fill. Mama Luna noticed and squeezed his hand. As tears spilled over and ran

25

in rivulets down his cheeks, Preston's voice quavered, almost inaudibly, "Mom says something was wrong with my dad. Is something wrong with me?"

Mama had turned and taken both his shoulders in her hands. She put her face squarely in front of his. "Ah, no, my brave one! Everything right with you! I think maybe your papa had no one to guard him. It was not his fault. It is not your mama's fault. She does not come from people who understand these things."

Preston wiped his eyes. She had released him and looked away. Staring into the copal smoke, she was somewhere else, in another place, another time.

"Everyone is born with this gift. Some have more. I think maybe your papa had it much," she looked down at him for a brief second and then returned to the other place. "But for most people here, it goes away for a long time. Does not grow. Things take over from that world over there." She waved her hand in the direction of the housing subdivision where they lived.

Indeed, all the houses nearby did seem to be a separate world. Preston had no interest in anything else and kept his face turned toward the Tall One, and the vapors coming from the god pot.

"These things that take over make the vision sharp. It makes things one way or another way, black or white. People here don't know that to *see* the vision must be soft. They think that soft is bad and get eyeglasses. All those people that got eyeglasses young? They have this gift very strong but don't know it. The spirits try very hard with these people. But with these eyeglasses? They take the *seeing* vision away."

Somehow, this all made perfect sense to Preston.

"Here, as people get older, they began to know that things aren't just this way or that way. They have enough of that world over there to want to know something more. For your people, this begins when they are sometimes forty years. That's when their eyes start getting soft. The spirits are getting louder." Suddenly, Mama turned to him and chortled, "And what do these people do, my Chan K'in? They get eyeglasses! And again they cannot *see!*"

This fact seemed such a huge joke that they broke out in peals of laughter. Realizing it was in the middle of the night and lights might start coming on next door, Preston tried to stifle his giggles.

"Is okay, my Chan K'in! The gods, they like the laughing, too, and they eat it."

Sure enough, for all the noise they were making, the sound waves were funneling themselves into the god pot. Outside their small space was nothing but stillness. Not even a dog had barked.

Mama turned serious again. "Once my people, the Hach Winik—the True Ones—all *see*. Some much more, some less. But all had at least a little of this way of knowing. These things were honored. But a long time ago, those from outside began to come. First just a little. Some called themselves 'God-men.' I think this is not true that they were 'God-men.' They did not respect our ways so much. Some did. But these did not say they were 'God-men.' They did not tell us our ways were bad. They wanted to learn about us.

"Then more and more come. Many want to take our way of life. They want the trees, the jungle. These things are not ours, but these people want us to sell what is not ours," Mama continued, "They don't understand we cannot do this. They come and take. These trees, this land is not theirs either. Hachäkyum, Our True Lord, made the earth strong. He made these trees to keep the sky raised. He made these trees, too, to separate our world from Yalam Lu'um, the Underworld. When these people cut trees, stars fall in the night. And Yalam Lu'um gets darker, too. These people don't care. They take so many trees. Soon the sky of Hachäkyum will be falling on us. And we fall on Yalam Lu'um. The worlds go away. The Hach Winik die. These people don't give us a way of living, and the 'God-men' say our gods are not real. They bring things from their world, that world out there." Once again Mama waved her hand in the direction of the houses.

"My people have less and less. They want something. They are confused and feel bad. These 'God-men' have medicines and food. They say they want to help. But they say to give up our gods. How can we give up what makes our world? What sends the rain and grows the corn? But many begin to follow these new ways and say our gods have left us. Their children must eat. Now many of these with new ways wear eyeglasses. They lose their *seeing*. They forget to feed the gods," she finished sadly. Preston found his eyes wanting to cry again at the lamentable story of the Hach Winik.

"But you, my Chan K'in! You are one in your people who has this gift! You did not lose it. You made yourself safe from many of those who would take it away from you. Your Smoky help you with this. I see that there is hope in you. This is why I have come. This is why I have left my people and come here," she continued and made the same emphasis as before, "These things must be opened carefully and used with wisdom. Now is the start of the best time. You will claim the name that has been inside waiting for you."

"Is this Chan K'in, Mama?"

"This is so. Little Sun. You *see* and this is the great gift. When you call this special name of yourself, the sun will shine where you want to *see*."

— Chapter Five —

CHAN K'IN. CHAN K'IN. CHAN K'IN. Preston could hear a repetitive chant going round and round in his head: Mama Luna's voice from that time in the past. Its insistence compelled him to enter his closet. He dug through discarded clothing and other paraphernalia that littered the floor, and made a half-hearted mental note to straighten things out. There were almost more clothes on the floor than on hangers.

He almost got sidetracked with an old notebook he thought he had lost, containing earlier attempts at journaling his feelings. But Mama Luna's voice got louder, drawing his attention back to purpose. Finally, under old books and lots of dust bunnies, he found what he sought: a battered, green tin box. On the outside lid, he'd long ago painted with his mother's red fingernail polish: Stop! Do not enter! In each corner there was a skull and crossbones that signified the risk to anyone who thought to invade his privacy.

He left the messy closet and sat down on his bed with the box. Popping open the lid, Preston surveyed the contents. There were some old baseball cards, a couple of baby teeth he'd decided to withhold from the tooth fairy, a cork of forgotten origin, a matchbox. He picked up the matchbox. Inside there was a cicada. Only its husk remained. Preston grunted to himself, remembering how fascinated he'd been. There was an invasion of these creatures one year when they were on vacation in an Arizona mountain town. They sang in the trees everywhere. He thought they were magic. When he discovered one dead on the ground, he'd put it in the matchbox to contain its power.

Well, you never know, Preston thought to himself. He slid the box closed and put it back in the tin. Continuing to poke around, he found the two things he wanted. They were under everything else, as if he'd wanted to bury those most secret things, just as the tin box had been cached. He pulled out a small flat stone and blue feather. The brilliance of the feather still remained.

He pressed the stone into the palm of his hand, rubbing it for a while, savoring its perfection and cool smoothness. Placing the feather on top, he gazed down at the two until he felt mesmerized. The constant chant moved out of his head and swirled around him, ushering him back to that earlier time.

Once more he found himself under the moonlight, in the back of Mama Luna's garden, seated in front of the god pot. As the copal smoke rose steadily, he was enveloped in some kind of timeless cocoon. Mama stood in front of the Tall One, whispering under her breath, almost swallowing the words. Preston couldn't make out what she was saying.

It must be her secret language, he thought as he continued to inhale the *pom* vapors. Mama selected three leaves from the Tall One, waiting between each as though receiving instructions. She stood before the Tall One, arranging the leaves in a fan.

Carefully observing her ritual, Preston pondered. They're big. Maybe that's why she took only three. Glancing over at Smoky, Preston remembered a teaching. No. She took only three because that's just enough. No need to take more than you can use, Preston concluded.

Mama held the leaves out to the Tall One in thanks, then offered them up to the moon. If he didn't know better, Preston could swear that a single moonbeam extended and touched Mama's hands. Indeed, when she finally lowered her arms and walked over to him, her hands had an uncharacteristic glow.

Mama Luna squatted on her haunches in front of the god pot. Again, she paused, listening. She murmured in that unusual swallowing way. Preston watched closely. Even as Mama Luna expelled soft words, something spoonfed sounds to her like so much nourishment—and the copal smoke began morphing into form. Then the impression was gone. Slowly, Mama Luna waved the leaf fan over the god pot. In a few moments she turned to him with an exalted expression on her face.

This must be what an angel looks like, Preston decided.

Mama motioned him to come closer. He uncrossed his small legs and moved the few feet to where she stood waiting, wilted foliage in her hands. "We prepare you tonight to take your True Name," she said firmly. Preston nodded his assent. He'd been pop-eyed and open-mouthed most of the evening to make sure he took in everything he could. He made his eyes large and round to encompass all sights; his ears stood out slightly from his head to catch all sounds; and his mouth hung open to invite in the words Mama uttered. He wanted to be fed by the spirits, too.

Preston stood like the Tall One, imitating its stature and strength, while Mama captured smoke from the god pot, scooping vapor with the leaves, and transferring it to him. Wiping him down gently with the leaves, Mama repeated this process until she had moved from the very top of his head down to his toes. Then she disappeared into the garden with the leaves. When she returned, she was empty-handed.

"Now you are clean, my Chan K'in. Now you are ready." Mama smiled broadly at him.

"I *am* ready!" He felt squeaky clean and new.

"Tomorrow night is the best time," she continued and motioned up at the moon. "She says this."

He nodded, eyelids heavy. As excited as he was by this promise, the long night and hard play during the day had finally caught up with him. Mama Luna took his hand. They made their way back to the house and his bed where she sat with him until he started drifting off to sleep.

"*Ki' wenen tech. Ki'i ba' a wilik,*" her voice was barely audible, "You sleep well. Be careful in your dreams."

She slipped silently out of the room. When Preston woke up the next morning he was well rested, having carried Mama Luna's good wishes with him into the night. He took his time getting dressed and looked for Smoky. But he wasn't there. Preston felt different than the day before, a little more grown up, but not too much like an adult. Most adults didn't seem to be having much fun. It was more like he'd seen secret things that others hadn't. When he thought about the night before, he realized how easy it was to step outside the everyday world around him.

"If this is what the 'best time' is all about," he proclaimed outloud, "I want more!"

Preston wandered out to see what was for breakfast. Mama Luna puttered around the kitchen as usual, and by the smell of it, was making something tasty. She made no indication that anything unusual had passed.

"Oh, Solocito! Finally you are up! You are hungry?" She motioned for him to sit down and placed a plate in front of him.

"My favorite, Mama!" he exclaimed.

He devoured thick crisp griddlecakes made with whole pieces of corn, a sweet fruit compote on the side. Preston knew they were having a celebration. This wasn't a meal that Mama made often.

"My Solocito, when you play today, you also get ready for this time tonight. This is good. And you rest later, too, before tonight." She smiled and went about the business of cleaning up. Preston sat and looked expectantly, but no more instructions came. Even though Mama wasn't saying much, there was a note of excitement on the air, and he caught it.

Outside, he made a beeline for Mama's garden. Preston picked his way to the back where the Tall One loomed as usual. But when he peeked at the place they had been last night, there was no evidence that anything fantastic had happened there at all. It looked like an ordinary garden, and even the Tall One didn't look like anything but a big weed. He was disappointed until he heard Smoky's voice in the recesses of his mind.

There are worlds just beyond what most people can see, hear or feel. They are there constantly. The One who made the ways of the worlds understood the need to make them hidden most of the time. Not because there is anything wrong or bad. The worlds are different. The knowledge is for everyone, but only some are ready. And, also, there are worlds to live in at different times.

With Smoky's words, he felt much better. It wasn't a dream after all. And even though there was no sign of the god pot, or even any disturbance to the soil where they had been, Preston sat down in just that place. He faced the empty space where the god pot had rested and became very still. After a while, a slow smile stole over his lips. No, he wasn't imagining anything. There was a slight vibration to the earth beneath him. He glanced up at the Tall One, and it had almost imperceptibly straightened. Preston was satisfied. He got up and walked silently until he was clear of the garden.

Then he whooped and ran in circles. And, as little boys do, began to seek out the diversions that would take him through the day.

— Chapter Six —

THE HOURS THAT DAY were interminably long to Preston; each minute seemed like an hour in itself. But he amused himself until mid-afternoon, when Mama Luna called him to a very early light dinner.

"It's good to go into this night a little hungry. The spirits like it when you are hungry for them. They are hungry for us, too," Mama explained.

He hadn't eaten very much because his anticipation wouldn't let him. Then Mama sent him to his bedroom for a nap, treating him like a little kid!

"You do this, Solocito," she said.

Preston had swallowed his indignation. He laid on his bed and stared at the ceiling. All manner of fantasies ran through his head concerning what was shortly ahead. Finally, he tired of them and slept.

A dream came. But it was so real. He was walking in a place he didn't know. It was green and dense with trees and vines, all heavy with humidity. He could feel wetness on his skin. The droning of flying insects and cries of big birds reached his ears. He knew for certain he wasn't anywhere near his home. Then there was sudden movement in the green a little bit away. Not at all frightened, he waited. A long, narrow, brown face poked through the bushes and eyed him curiously. Preston remained motionless. The animal blinked slowly at him with big brown eyes. When he still didn't budge, it walked gracefully toward him on long legs that ended in dainty hooves. As the animal got closer, the cries of the birds got louder. Were they warning or celebrating? At the very moment it seemed like the animal was going to touch its wet dark nose to his small pug one, Preston startled.

Confused, he didn't know where he was. The sounds were gone. His skin was dry. Then he saw the late afternoon sun coming into his window. He was at home in his bedroom. And he was crestfallen. He got up and went looking for Mama Luna. He found her in the living room, sitting in an easy chair facing a picture window, a sight that he hadn't seen often. She always seemed to be moving. She was looking intently out the window. But when she heard him, she turned her head.

"Solocito," she motioned him over to join her in the chair.

"Mama, I had a dream!"

"Ah! And what is this dream?"

The pitch of his voice got higher as he told her of his experience. "I was there! I know it!"

"Ah, my little one. There is much that happened. It is very good," she mused. "This is your *onen*, your family, welcoming you. Yes, the deer *onen*. This is good."

Preston took great comfort from her words and was no longer disappointed. His family welcomed him, wanted him, claimed him. He sat with this new knowledge and turned his face to match Mama Luna's repose. They sat in companionable silence, watching the shadows outside getting longer until they existed no more. The sun had set. The night was coming. Yet still they rested in that in-between time—motionless.

Mama finally set him on his feet. She arose from their shared reverie and went to her room. There she remained for some time while Preston amused himself with books, close by. When she opened her door and motioned to him, he quickly complied. As he got near, her clean sweet smell entered his nostrils. She handed him some folded cloths with candles piled on top.

"Please, you take this into the room. Then go clean yourself, my little one."

For once, he didn't go into his whining routine. This was the big one. He was sure. By the time he returned to the living room, Mama had readied the room. Some of the furniture was moved back. On the floor next to her loom, she'd spread one of the large woven cloths. Sitting in the middle of the cloth was, not one, but three god pots! The fat candles were placed to form a circle around the loom and cloth, as though protecting what was inside. No other lights were on in the room, creating a surreal, warming glow. Mama had changed into a beautifully embroidered tunic and skirt, the one she had made most recently. She held out a cloth to him with animals and unusual symbols woven into it.

"Here my Chan K'in. This is yours now," she said and put the fabric around his shoulders. "You sit here."

He lowered himself to the floor close to the god pots, making sure to hold the covering around his shoulders. It seemed important not to let it drop. Preston watched her much as he had the night before when she went through her ministrations. She placed little charcoal pieces in the god pots and lit them, then she sat back on her haunches singing a soft haunting song. It was similar to others he'd heard her sing. When she deemed the charcoal smoldering enough, she took the cover from a small wooden box to one side of the pots. Inside was some yellowish quartz-like substance. Mama selected several pieces and placed one in each god pot. In a short time pungent smoke rose into the atmosphere in their small circle.

An afterthought, Mama suddenly got up. From the edge of the room she dragged a chair over a short distance, stood on it and disconnected the smoke alarm on the ceiling. Preston agreed with her. It wouldn't do to have that kind of interruption, or any at all for that matter.

She went to her room, returning with a medium-sized brown glass jar with a pulpy liquid inside. Preston thought it contained flower petals. Unscrewing the lid, she poured some dark red fluid into a waiting clay crock, and set the glass jar aside. She turned to him.

"You ready, my Chan K'in, to meet with the gods who sing your name? Those who call for you to *see* them?"

"Yes, Mama," he assented. He knew this was bigger than anything he could ever have imagined. Although he had no idea what it was, he knew it was special. There was a feeling like fear that jabbed at his stomach, but it could just as easily be excitement. He wasn't sure but decided on the excitement. He sensed Smoky again watching from a distance, approving of what transpired.

"Yes, Mama!" he said again for emphasis.

Mama Luna nodded slightly and turned toward the god pots. Raising her arms, she began a lilting chant, unintelligible to him, that vibrated his internal organs. After a while, she picked up the clay crock containing the red liquid in one hand. An artist's brush with short, stout bristles appeared in the other hand.

"We show the gods the color of our *k'ik'el*, our blood," she said. "When they see this they know we carry life in us. Through blood our life comes again. Through our blood the gods live, too."

Taking the brush, she dipped it into the liquid and painted a stripe from the middle of his lower lip down his chin while she sang her song. She replenished the brush and put a large red dot on each ear lobe. She began to paint spots on the intricate cloth around his shoulders.

Preston looked at her in surprise, but she was already in another world. After she finished with him, she did the same for herself, ending with her beautiful tunic. Setting the dye aside, she stood and positioned him before her. The god pots were in front of him and Mama Luna directly behind him. He was sandwiched between the two. Preston felt her hand reassuringly on his shoulder. With the other hand, she gestured in a circular fashion toward the candles.

"Once there was only the dark. It is hard to see if there is just dark. We use the fire to bring *seeing* from the darkness. It is good to light this path."

Motioning to the copal smoke, she continued, "We use the copal smoke to call the gods to our altar. The gods are always here. But this gets their attention. Just as the fire invites the *seeing*, the smoke lets the gods be with us."

Preston nodded. As usual, what Mama taught made sense to him. She resumed the melodic toning. Every once in a while he heard the name Chan K'in. He thought he heard it not only from Mama but also coming faintly from the god pots themselves. He wondered why he wasn't scared. Maybe Smoky had prepared him for some of this.

Mama sang her song for what seemed like hours. The words were the same, but the nuances varied and took on the sounds of nature. Sometimes her voice sounded like the crackle of lightning, and then as light as rain splashing on moss. In the next moment, she sounded frog-like and transitioned to a lilting bird's song. It reminded Preston of all the sounds ravens could make. Periodically, Preston closed his eyes and felt something vibrating around him. When he opened them, he didn't sense it as much. But the room was taking on an indistinguishable quality to it, like things were losing their edges. Indeed, even though he was still standing there, he no longer had his skin; he was blending with the things surrounding him.

"Chan K'in. The gods give you this name. Call this name from you. This is the name you are born with and you carry it with you now. Chan K'in has been waiting. Has been waiting these years until now."

Mama took on a towering stature, like a large tree. Come to think of it, Preston himself was larger as well. The ceiling had dropped a few feet, or maybe they had grown. Either way, he felt like Alice in Wonderland when she ate the magic pill. Even this didn't scare him.

Mama Luna began moving her hand back and forth, back and forth in the airspace between him and the god pots, like she was clearing something out.

"My Chan K'in, you sing with me." She sang a simple lyric and melody, and continued to clean away with her hand what didn't belong in the space.

Preston's voice cracked from the dryness of his throat, but he was able to follow the song. Presently Mama's voice got softer and softer until she fell silent. His voice followed her own.

"Ah, Chan K'in. It is time for *k'inyah*, the *seeing* of what is," she whispered, "Look here where your eyes see close. And let your eyes travel to where they see far. Move them from here to there and there to here and make your eyes soft. Just let them move easy on their own power. Yes. That's it."

In a trance, Preston allowed his eyes to range from near-sight to far-sight, over and over again. The more he did it, the more relaxed he became.

"Ah yes, Chan K'in. My Chan K'in. This is it. Now as your eyes travel you can see there is a space between the near place and the far place. Yes. That's it. Where the vision gets very soft," Mama instructed him, "When you come to that place that is very soft, let your eyes be even more soft, and leave them there."

He did so, but nothing changed.

"Is okay, my Chan K'in. It comes."

He let his eyes travel back and forth, back and forth. Then they came to rest on the fuzzy place between the two, and he de-focused his eyes further.

"Oh, Mama!" The place where he gazed seemed to be swirling. His body felt electrified, but he wasn't afraid. He kept his eyes aimed steadily at the space, while de-focusing them as much as he knew how. Strangely, his peripheral vision was sharper than when he looked directly. There it continued to fuzz and morph like clouds, until finally a shape began to take form. It was a dark shape, long and narrow.

"Oh, Mama! Oh, Mama!" he exclaimed over and over as the deer's head moved from the middle space until it came so close that he could feel its breath on his face. Then it touched its wet nose to his, completing what had been interrupted earlier—and was gone.

"Oh, Mama!" Preston cried. Huge tears sprang from his eyes, coursed down his cheeks and onto his initiation cloth. He seemed to lose consciousness, but when he opened his eyes he was still standing in front of Mama Luna. The copal smoke was now merely wisping and the candles nearly out.

"Chan K'in. You call this name when you need to *see*. You look in the middle place and you will see what is so. This is the way of those who know."

Mama sat him down in front of the now smoldering god-pots. She kneeled facing him. Pulling a cloth from her pocket, she unwrapped its contents. She uncovered two items—a smooth, round flat stone and a feather, the brightest blue he'd ever seen.

"This stone lived in a place near my home. A sacred place where my ancestors, the Ancient Ones, bathed themselves. They washed to be ready for the gods. This stone lived under a waterfall for all times. It has the power of the water. When I left my home I asked this stone to come with me." She moved her fingers over the silky smooth rock.

"This feather is of the birds who sing the rain onto our *milpas*, our cornfields. This bird is of such power that the Ancient Ones put their feathers on their own heads. They wear these feathers in their god houses."

"Chan K'in. I give these to you that you may have the power of the water to wash clean, and the power of this feather to bring rain on the fields. You keep them with you always. You are opened and you must be guarded." Mama pressed the stone into his small hand and put the feather on top, bringing his thumb to meet it.

Early the next morning Preston attempted to open his eyes, but it seemed to require too much effort. He turned on his side, snuggling even deeper under the covers. Bringing one hand under his pillow, his hand closed over something warm, something that just fit in the palm of his hand. It was comforting. Then the events of the previous night came flooding back, or what he could remember. Much of it seemed like a bizarre fancy. He opened one eye and spied a brilliant blue feather on his nightstand. He put his other hand up to his face and felt the crusty remnants of the blood-paint. Clutching the stone tightly to him, he drifted back to sleep.

— Chapter Seven —

PRESTON SAT ON the edge of the same bed where he'd surrendered to sleep on that morning nearly sixteen years ago. The bedspread covered with riotous red rocket ships had been replaced with a neutral taupe spread, more suited to a young man's tastes. It was the same room but its contents had long been cleared of the childhood toys, books and illusions. Only Gato remained.

Preston reached over to where she lay close by, burying his hand in her fur, allowing her plushy softness to soothe him.

"Even you weren't there until later. Were you, girl?" Gato twitched an ear and opened one eye.

He looked down again at the smooth round stone he held in his palm, the blue feather on top held in place by his thumb. Loss and loneliness arose from the depths of his heart. He found himself moving in an attempt to shake off the emotion. At the window, his eyes were pulled to a particular spot in the far corner of the backyard. His gaze passed through the ghosts of Mama Luna's garden into the myriad memories that he cherished—and some of those he did not.

His mind flitted through snippets of imagery, finally resting on one, becoming steeped in it until he was there once again. It was an evening a few weeks after Preston had assumed his True Name and his *onen* had claimed him. Mama Luna was once again working at her loom, a nightly activity she resumed shortly after his naming ceremony. Preston was arranged on the floor nearby, concentrating on a drawing he was making of his deer friend. Just the two of them were in the house.

Sybilla had swept in from her trip shortly after his big night but left again several days later for an assignment that would keep her in the Far East a month. He was just about to burst with his secret. He'd wanted so badly to share his newfound identity with his mother. But something told him not to do so. It wasn't even that Mama Luna or

41

Smoky advised him to keep quiet. Every time he'd started to open his mouth, in scarcely contained excitement, he saw a picture in his mind of disembodied lips with a finger laid across them and heard a gentle shushing sound. Then he would stop short—his disclosure interrupted. Sybilla noticed a couple of times.

"What is it, PJ?" Sybilla said expectantly.

"Oh nothing, Mom," he would look away.

Each time she'd seemed disappointed. He felt bad about that; he was keeping something from her. Just as he knew he couldn't talk to her about Smoky, he wasn't about to tell her of his True Name, his *onen* or *seeing*.

Sometimes he would be playing and glance up to see her watching him, a sad look on her face. Other times, he saw her contemplating Mama Luna at her work.

Preston loved his mother so much and yet felt a widening gap between them, especially now. It was more than her frequent long absences. He guessed that she loved him equally but also regarded him as something of an alien, perhaps mistakenly born to her. He didn't measure up to some unspoken standard he knew nothing about, and it wounded his little soul. As a result, Preston drew even closer to Mama Luna and her nurturing ways.

Mama was engrossed in her design, shuttling the threads through the weave, tamping them taut. She hummed softly along with her work. Periodically, Preston joined in with her and then tapered off again when his drawing captured more of his attention.

"Solocito, maybe you want to know how the world of the Hach Winik is born?" She glanced over at him and smiled invitingly.

"Oh yes, Mama!" Preston had grown to love Mama's stories. They transported him into another place altogether.

He had been lying belly down on the floor with his artwork in front of him. At the promise of a story, he sat up and bounced cross-legged over to sit directly at Mama's feet. Mama continued to hum softly and move the shuttle rhythmically, back and forth. When he had settled himself, never taking her eyes off the cloth growing beneath her fingers, she began to spin her tale.

"The rainforest is the covering for this world. But there are other worlds, too. They live on top of each other."

"How is that?" Preston's eyes got big.

"K'akoch is always here. Many times ago it is only him and he gets bored. One day he decides to make something to have some fun. And that day he makes the very first sun and moon, the sea and the earth. But they are not like we know them now. They are soft like mud. K'akoch knows he needs to do more, but he gets tired and wants help. Then he thinks something," Mama paused for effect, "He thinks to make the *bäk nikte'*. This flower your people call tuberose. He says to himself that he will make the *bäk nikte'* so beautiful. So beautiful that it is magic. Its magic is in the place where all its petals come together. So this place is like where a woman carries the babies."

Preston's ears perked up, but he didn't ask any questions.

"So K'akoch thinks the *bäk nikte'* into the world. Then he sits back and looks at it. He looks at it so much that his eyes give it the most magic he has given anything. And Sukunkyum comes out of the flower! K'akoch looks some more, and Äkyantho' and Hachäkyum come out, too!"

Preston imagined the tuberose becoming so swollen at its base that it took a big breath and then expelled these beings one after another, as he himself might spit out a jowl full of cherry pits.

"Now these gods are here. And they all knew they had to work because K'akoch wasn't so interested in this sun and moon, the sea and the earth he makes. So Sukunkyum sees the sun and how the sun wants to go across the sky. But the sun gets tired. Sukunkyum is very kind and says that he will take care of the sun. When the sun gets very tired and sinks into the west of the sky, Sukunkyum wants to take him into his own hammock and feed him. That's how the sun can have strength and come up again. But Sukunkyum says he doesn't have a home for his hammock. And Hachäkyum says to his older brother, 'I will make you a home!' So, he makes this dark world under our earth. It is dark so the sun can sleep well.

"But our earth is so soft that it wants to fall down to this Underworld, Yalam Lu'um. That's when Hachäkyum makes the rocks, clay and sand.

He mixes these to make the earth strong and it will hold together. Then he makes the trees on our earth to hold up the sky and it won't fall on the earth. K'akoch is so happy with Hachäkyum that he makes for him maize as a gift. This corn is a very good thing. With corn can be made many things. But Hachäkyum needs the help of his wife because he cannot do it alone. Xk'ale'ox and Hachäkyum learn how to mash the corn and make tortillas and posole because the True People—the Hach Winik—must have food. Now that there is food, they mix the clay and sand together to make the Hach Winik, and they tell them about how to grow the corn in their *milpas* and eat it. They made them of all the *onen*: the spider monkey, the jaguar, the peccary, the deer. All of them. Now they made all the animals from the same things, the clay and sand. Those little pieces that fall from their hands become the ants, the spiders, all the insects. And this is how our world is made, Solocito." Mama gave him a meaningful look.

"What about Jesus?"

"Ah yes, Solocito. Hesuklistos, Jesus, is the son of Äkyantho'. These two look after the foreign peoples."

"Not the Hach Winik, too?"

"These gods all have their own jobs. They each have enough to do with that. Hachäkyum watches over the Hach Winik."

"What about the devil, Mama?" his voice barely audible. His mother hadn't raised him in any religion, but that didn't stop some of the popular doctrine from seeping in surreptitiously.

"Kisin is not the devil exactly," Mama responded, "But he lives in the Underworld with Sukunkyum. Sometimes he gets mad and shakes the pillars that hold up the earth. Then we have the earth quacks."

Preston's trepidation turned to gleeful giggles at Mama Luna's mistaken word. "You laugh at me, Solocito?" She leaned over and began to tickle him. All the while Preston quacked away, a good imitation of a duck, until they were both laughing so hard he thought he would pee his pants.

Passing from his melancholy mood, Preston chuckled at the remembrance. He also recalled other stories she had told him, including the one about how the rains came. Mënsabäk, the rain god, had scooped up copal ashes from a god pot with macaw tail feathers and blown them into the sky. There they formed the heavy clouds and the first rains fell onto the earth. Preston smiled to himself recalling how thunder and lightning was made. Kisin made sport of insulting the Hahanak'u, assistants of Mënsabäk, by bending over and mooning them. The Hahanak'u would get so hopping mad, they'd hurl stone axes at Kisin, making thunder and lightning when they struck the ground.

He particularly remembered Ixchel with whom Mama Luna had such a sisterhood. She was the one responsible for the moon, as well as healing, birthing and weaving. She could often be seen at her loom in the night sky weaving the possible world into being while the sun slept. He put himself out in the moonshine once again with Mama Luna, carefully pointing to Ixchel and singing her praises in beautiful soft tones.

As he thought about Mama Luna, he marveled at her serenity. She had clung with certainty to the parallel worlds in which she lived. In fact, for her, they weren't even parallel. Her life had possessed a kind of fluidity whether she was busy at her daily household chores, or feeding copal into the god pots, and talking to different plants or gods as intimates. Indeed, he recalled how she did the same with people. She hadn't contrived separation between herself and others. Much to his mother's chagrin, Mama Luna had treated her as an equal, whereas Sybilla attempted to maintain what she considered to be appropriate distance from her nanny-housekeeper. Mama Luna had a way of ignoring all Sybilla's airs but not out of rebellion. Preston realized it was more like being patient with a compatriot who couldn't see the foolishness of her own actions. This, of course, frustrated Sybilla even more.

Preston recalled a time when he'd gone with Mama Luna to the supermarket. He must have been about five or six. At the time, he thought those people simply didn't like Mama Luna, and he couldn't understand why. It was only some years later he realized he'd witnessed bigotry for the first time. And he still couldn't understand the stupidity of it all. They had been minding their own business shopping for the week's groceries. He was helping her by choosing from the shelves, putting them in the basket when she called out items from her list. Making a game of their chore, they were having a good time. Then he noticed two women down the aisle standing next to a shopping cart, staring. Preston thought he was being too loud and choked off his laughter.

When they waited in the checkout lane, those same two women got in line behind them. Mama Luna had begun to put their purchases on the conveyor. Preston didn't remember exactly what the women said, but he vividly recalled their hard looks and the cutting sound of their words. They made a show of talking to each other, but everything they said was directed toward Mama Luna and loud enough for her to hear. Preston was shocked and looked at Mama Luna questioningly. She just continued about her business, emptying the cart. He looked at the checkout attendant, who was beet red. She wouldn't look at them. Later, Preston chastised himself for not coming to Mama's rescue.

In the midst of the insults, Mama Luna was somehow even more stately, more beautiful than ever before. When she had finished paying the cashier, she turned and smiled at those two bigots. It was their turn to be shocked, and Preston had delighted in it.

"Come, Solocito. We go home." She took his hand while hoisting the bag on her hip. Nothing was later said between them about the incident. On the walk home, she acted as though nothing had happened. The incident engraved itself in his memory, as a large contrast to their usual happy times together.

Then Preston's mind came to rest on the final contrast. It was nearly a year to the day of his naming ceremony. Not very often, but periodically, they participated in rituals together. She continued to instruct him in *seeing* and the ways of plants, animals and her world of the Hach Winik. Preston sensed Smoky hanging around frequently, but he took a back seat to Mama's tutelage, as if two teachers at the same time would be overwhelming. Inside, he felt more solid. He was finally growing into the spaces in his body that had been empty. He began to think he belonged somewhere after all.

Yet, at the same time, he was even more out of sync with other kids. The distance between Preston and his classmates grew. The internal voice that used to taunt him—Stupid! What's wrong with you?—was now being directed outward more often than not. He saw his peers in a way that he'd formerly reserved for himself. They, of course, intuited his scorn and hounded him maliciously, causing him to withdraw further.

It had gotten to the point that, one time, Preston finally got fed up and jumped on one of the boys who bullied him. It happened in the middle of class. The boy sat behind him kicking at the bottom of Preston's seat. Before he knew it, he had blasted out of his own seat, grabbed the boy by his shirt and slugged him in the face, wailing like an outraged soul. When he came to his senses, the teacher was dragging him out the door to the principal's office. But not before he caught a glimpse of the entire class, pop-eyed and open-mouthed, and his tormentor crying like a snot-nosed baby, bleeding from a split lip. A part of him was horrified at what he'd done, but mostly he was secretly overjoyed.

Most unfortunately, his mother was home when it happened and was called into account for his behavior. After Sybilla placated the principal and assured him it would never happen again, she let Preston have it.

"You cause nothing but trouble, mister!" she scolded, once they were in the car. "What's wrong with you? You better toe the line, young man! How dare you? I've never been so embarrassed in my life! What kind of mother they must think I am! Why can't you make things easy? All I do is work to make things nice for you, and I have to come home to this!" Sybilla's steady condemnations lasted the entire drive home.

Boy, howdy! She's been storing this up.

If Sybilla had paused in her exasperated tirade, she might have seen PJ cringing at her every word, as though she was beating him. She might also have noticed that about halfway through the drive, his pain took on a different stance. Instead of shame, it was transmuting itself to resentful defiance.

What about me? She doesn't care! She's never here! I can't tell her anything! I wish she was dead! Then I'd be free! She's probably not my real mother anyway! Nobody cares about me! Screaming notions circled like a whirlwind until they lodged themselves firmly in his mind, to be recalled again and again when the moment was right.

By the time Sybilla pulled into the driveway, she'd exhausted herself with her outburst, and merely wore a look of irritation. And a sullen scowl, heretofore unseen on Preston's innocent features, was making its first inroads. When the two came silently through the front door, Mama Luna looked up from her cooking; the sudden shift in the air had caught her attention. She took in the slamming door in another part of the house and Sybilla's angry voice.

"You're grounded, young man!"

Mama Luna sighed heavily and returned to stirring the *posole* meant for their dinner. After another two days of tension in the household, Sybilla left for an assignment in Borneo.

Before leaving, she gave Mama Luna strict instructions. "He's to have no television or go outside to play for the next week, Maria."

"You sure, Sybilla? The boy is hurt, I think."

"You seem to forget that he's my son, Maria. Not yours. Do as I say. I'll be home in ten days."

Preston wasn't able to see the sad look Mama Luna gave his mother, but he caught their verbal interchange from his room. He didn't watch much television anyway.

Another sign she doesn't know me.

After the taxi came to take his mother to the airport and the door closed behind her, Preston came out of his room.

"She hates me, Mama!"

"Ah *niño*! Ah no! Your mama love you very much. She just not know what to do. Her mother did not teach her so well. You must be kind. Your mama is very hurt in her life. You are her sunshine!"

"Hmmph! She has a funny way of showing it."

"You be patient, Solocito."

He sensed Smoky in the corner of the room nodding in agreement.

"Okay, Mama."

For the next three days all was back to normal, except Mama Luna complied with Sybilla's wishes and kept Preston indoors after school. He helped her with dinner, and afterward they kept company while she worked at her loom. On the fourth day his life changed drastically. Hers did as well.

The day began normally. She called him out of bed in the morning to get dressed for school. When he came out to breakfast, Mama served him, worry knitting her brow. There were dark circles under her eyes.

"What is it, Mama?"

"Is nothing, Solocito. You hurry. You be late."

Uncharacteristically, she rushed him out the door.

"A snake bite you on the way, Solocito." This was her way of ensuring he had a safe journey to school, also a way they teased each other. But this time laughter caught in his throat, seeing her mouth tightened into a thin line.

When he returned home, the space near the loom had been cleared as though they were going to play the game. He got excited and went to find Mama Luna. His enthusiasm dissipated when he came upon her in the kitchen, even more agitated than when he'd left her several hours earlier.

"Please, Mama. What is it?"

"This is not for you, Solocito."

"Mama, please tell me."

"Ah, this is a very bad thing I dream last night."

"What?" Preston was frightened. Mama had taught him how important dreams were. How they could tell what was going to happen. They could tell you something you were supposed to know. She was forever asking him about his dreams, and sharing hers with him. But he'd never seen her distressed like this.

"I dream the light was put out from the sun."

"I think my teacher says that's an eclipse."

"This is it, Solocito. This is very bad. This mean something very bad happen in our world."

"What, Mama?"

"The dream does not say. It just says very bad. We must do this ceremony tonight and give the gods some good things. They will help us stop this thing."

They didn't eat dinner that night but prepared the room as they had done together several times before. At dusk Mama Luna sent Preston off for a bath. When he returned, she'd changed into a ceremonial tunic and skirt and gave him a tunic to don. She brought out the blood-paint and marked stripes and dots on their clothing and faces. He decided some time ago this was why she did so much weaving and created new clothes. Blood-paint didn't wash out.

Mama Luna lit only a couple of candles. She must have started the charcoal in the god pots when he was in the bath. They appeared ready for offerings. She sat on her haunches feeding copal into the mouths of the god pots as he'd seen her do many times before. When the smoke billowed, she stood but not before drawing him close to her.

She began to chant. Suddenly, she lifted her arms overhead and commenced a long unintelligible speech to the gods. Periodically, she erupted into the trance-inducing, voice-swallowing song that he had grown to love. The melodic offertory filled the spaces that the copal smoke hadn't and created a thick cocoon of ecstasy around them. And they were both lost in it.

Neither of them heard the front door open.

Neither of them was aware of anything but the opening of the middle space, the *seeing* place. Through the morphing clouds, Preston thought he saw big, dark brown eyes imploring him.

Then directly behind them, he heard the screaming, what he thought were evil forest spirits coming to get them. And it cracked their cocoon.

"What are you doing?" Sybilla was livid. She grabbed his arm and yanked him over to her. In his dazed state, all he could remember was his mother screeching the same question over and over, from a gaping mouth with teeth grown large and jagged.

He saw her kick over the god pots and slap Mama Luna hard across the cheek. As if spirited away, he found himself in his bedroom with the door locked from the outside. Crouching in the corner, he listened in fright to his mother's bellowing and Mama Luna's excited shouting, a mix of English, Spanish and Maya. The yelling finally gave way to tight, accusatory voices, abruptly ending with the slamming of doors.

Preston didn't know how long he sat there in the dark. No one came. He finally crawled over to his bed and curled into a fetal position, his tunic wrapped taut around his legs. He must have fallen asleep and been dreaming because he thought Mama Luna was sitting at his bedside stroking his hair. But some part of him knew his bedroom door was still locked from the outside.

"My Chan K'in. I must go. This is our blood sacrifice. We do this so it will be safe. This we do," she whispered softly to him. He could swear he felt her sweet breath on his face and the wetness of tears falling on his head.

"You remember what I teach you. Your Smoky guard you. When you dream of the spider monkey, you see me again, my little one. My Chan K'in."

Then she was gone.

Preston slept late the next morning. When he got up, he took off his tunic and rubbed the blood-paint off his face. After putting on shorts and a t-shirt, he tried the doorknob and found the door unlocked. The house was strangely silent. He crept into the living room. It had been put back in order, but something was missing. Mama Luna's loom was no longer standing in its corner.

Like a knife had pierced his heart, he panicked and ran across the living room to fling open her bedroom door. She wasn't there. In fact, there was no evidence she'd ever even been there at all. And he began to scream in anguish.

Racing around the house, he looked for any trace of her. Finding nothing, he returned to his room, where he discovered his tunic had disappeared. His mother made sure that any outward signs of Mama Luna had vanished. He would only have his memories.

Sybilla

— Chapter Eight —

WITH EVERY RAGGED breath she took, Sybilla's heart wrenched in emotional pain. The most important person in her life was keening with the most horrible lament, much worse than any wailing grief she'd ever heard in the war-torn places she ventured in her work. He was hers. Maybe that's what made it unbearable.

As she tried to pull him to her, his little fists rained down on her in fury. His screaming became louder still.

"What have you done with her? You hate me! I always knew you did!"

"PJ!"

"You took away the only person who loves me! Why can't you just go away and never come back?"

"Oh, PJ. I love you, honey." In the course of trying to pull him to her Sybilla inadvertently grasped Preston tightly by both shoulders. He responded by jerking away sharply, tearing his shirtsleeve.

"I hate you! Go away! Go away! And don't ever call me PJ again! PJ is for babies! You don't know anything about me!"

His normally sweet face was red hot, twisted with intensity. He turned from her and ran outside, slamming the back door. The house shuddered from the fierce impact.

Their struggle knocked the wind out of her; Sybilla sank to the floor. She sat there dry-eyed but bereft. Her heart was a dark empty cavern. She wandered in it unable to find a way out. Her mind alternated between two thoughts.

How could this have happened?

What am I going to do?

Her anguished questions merely echoed over and over again in the cave of her interior. No other voice came back to answer her. Finally she began to cry. The sobs were uncontrollable.

Somehow she got through the day. Just before dark, Preston came home. She didn't ask where he'd been. He refused dinner and went straight to his room, but she felt gratitude as much as relief.

"He really is a good boy," she whispered to herself, noting that he hadn't chosen to stay away and worry her further.

Before going to bed, she tapped lightly on his closed door. There was no answer, but the light shone underneath. She turned the knob slowly and peeked inside. He was lying on his bed curled in a ball facing away from her, a sheet over the lower half of his body. Sybilla walked over and sat on the edge next to him. Eyes shut and breath contained, he held his body frozen like a rabbit trying to hide from a predator. She laid her hand gently on his shoulder and thought she felt him flinch slightly. A tear slipped down her cheek. In his half-closed hand, she saw a stone.

Sighing, she stood and left the room, extinguishing the light. If Sybilla had looked back in the split second before darkness, she would have seen her PJ turning his head silently to catch sight of her, eyes filling.

It was 3 a.m. Sybilla was wide awake. She'd tossed this way and that for hours, finally giving up any attempt at sleep. Staring at the ceiling, she noted the more she gazed into the darkness above, the more the space seemed to recede, trying to suck her into some abyss. Breathing through a stuffy nose, tears trickled into small pools in the cups of her ears.

She became aware of a profound yearning, accepting it as the one lodged perennially inside. She always kept it buried in its furthermost place by remaining on the go, focused on her work, and the greater good she believed she served by her commitment to photojournalism. Now, however, the wash of misery surfaced and splashed over her. In despair, she spoke to the oblivion in a small child-like voice.

"I'm so tired of doing this alone."

There was no audible answer, but something directed her attention into the burgeoning emptiness above her. From a place in her memory a face emerged—his face. A bittersweet pang in her chest identified the source of her longing. She made herself stay with it, to still the image, to engage with it. When times got loneliest, when she most hungered for a loving touch, some comfort after seeing things in her work that brought up vulnerabilities that she steeled herself against, she let his image become visible. This act was always a mixed gift that she gave herself, not knowing if it made things better or even worse. Even so, she'd been allowing herself at least this for nearly five years—after the grief had settled enough for her to stand it.

Sybilla thought wryly how she appeared to her colleagues from the outside. Talented and successful in her field, arising out of obscurity without any formal training, she was in demand. But not claimed where she most wished. The man she continued to love was long gone, just as her mother had prophesied, and she'd somehow alienated the child they'd made together.

She played over the question she'd asked herself earlier in the day and added more definition. How could this have happened to me?

She had to admit that she knew part of the answer to that question. She held some responsibility, as she acknowledged everyone must for their lot. But much of it was still a mystery to her, remaining an impenetrable fog. She allowed herself to slip back in time by ten years. She couldn't believe it had been that long ago.

Back then Sybilla lived in the small town of Johns Wake in northern Georgia, located just a piece down from the point where the state touched Tennessee and North Carolina. She belonged to the first family who settled the area, not counting any of the original residents who were successfully eradicated. Over time, her ancestors cleared the forest on the land they claimed for themselves, and bit by bit established a large cotton plantation. The Johns' became the most prominent family for miles around, owning more than one hundred slaves. The sons and daughters mostly stayed close, and after marrying, either lived in the old mansion or built their own homes on the family land.

Back in the 1800s, Greenville, the town closest to their home, was renamed Johns Wake in honor of her grandfather, several generations removed, who had become a statesman and served the area well. But Sherman's army marched through and destroyed everything. The Johns' family fields and homes were burnt to the ground. Their slaves fled.

By 1865, the Johns' family wealth had been effectively wiped out by heavy investment in the Confederacy and acts of war, a common story of the era. They never recovered their fortune. But Southern pride ran deep, and its memory was tenacious. The Johns' continued to live the illusion of Southern aristocracy, a shabby gentility tied to the past, and the locals collaborated with them. This was the mythology Sybilla was born into, with all the expectations surrounding it perpetuated by the family members and that of the community at large.

It was the summer after high school and Sybilla was eighteen years old. Her mother told her she had the world at her feet. She'd endured being brought out at the requisite debutante balls and found it all pretentious and rather boring.

What interested her more was the camera she'd received as a graduation gift and learning how to capture subjects in changing light. That was exactly what Sybilla was doing early one morning, having ridden a few miles on her bicycle to a particular pasture she'd photographed previously in late afternoon. She was so trained on the scene that she didn't detect a man approach on foot.

"Can you tell me how far the next town is?" He had spooked her. She quickly looked around for his car. There wasn't one.

"Where did you come from? You shouldn't sneak up on someone like that!" She gasped.

"Sorry," he had a low laugh. "I thought you saw me."

"Did you have a breakdown?" She considered him frankly, finding him unlike the young men from around there.

"Not the kind you mean," he chuckled again, "More like a break out. I'm hitching around seeing what the country is like. Maybe finding my place."

"Really?" Sybilla caught herself simpering. Disgusted with herself, she shook her head slightly, deciding she'd like to appear more sophisticated.

"I'm called Gabe." He had a rakish appearance that drew her like a magnet. Startling blue eyes looked out beneath dark hair that fell below his eyebrows and curled around his ears. The color of his dark skin contrasted sharply with his light eyes, creating an otherworldly look, but which world was uncertain. He tilted his head backward, narrowed his eyes in such a way that he seemed to gaze right into her very soul. And maybe he had because that day he seized something of hers.

Like someone walking stealthily room-by-room through her interior house, he'd stolen her heart and captured every other part of her that summer. He was looking for work and Sybilla directed him to a nearby farmer who needed help. Curious, she found her way more and more frequently over to the shed where the farmer let Gabe sleep. It turned out that he knew something about photography and gave her a few pointers.

But that wasn't the reason she went. There was something in her that wanted him. He spun intricate stories of adventures about hitching all over the West and Southwest, times just over the border into Mexico with the Indians, places unknown to her. Vague about where his home was or who he called family, Sybilla was intrigued. He was her opposite.

She'd only been outside Johns Wake a few times, down to Atlanta and once up to Nashville. Plus, her family stretched back generations in the same town. There was too much that was known and demanded. With his influence, she'd begun to realize how stifled she'd felt her whole life.

Even then, Sybilla acknowledged to herself something seemed a little dangerous about Gabe. But maybe she just wasn't used to someone who got so revved up that electricity literally charged the air around him. It ignited her, too. Although he was just twenty-four, at least in her eyes, he had vast knowledge that she lacked.

She hungered for all the education he could give her. So when one day they were sitting in the tall grass of the pasture where they'd met several weeks before, and he looked intently at her, putting his hand lightly on her arm, she'd melted into him not waiting to see if he wanted something different. Sensing his increasing restlessness, she sought to bind him to her physically. Maybe it would keep Gabe in place for a while. With that act, Sybilla drastically changed the fabric of her entire life and veered off course from the one soundly prescribed for her. Paradoxically, she simultaneously began to find and lose herself.

Sybilla kept her visits with Gabe a secret, intuitively knowing that her mother, or any of her extended family, wouldn't like it. Besides, their clandestine meetings heightened the drama, an addiction she was inadvertently catching from Gabe. But Johns Wake was a small town, and there wasn't any hiding. There was no use trying to trace exactly how her mother got wind of her new involvement. One day Sybilla came home after yet another visit to the farmer's shed, making a beeline for her room when she heard her mother's voice.

"Sybilla, come in here. I want to talk to you."

She turned and noticed her mother sitting stiffly in the front parlor that was never used. She must have been waiting for her but continued to stare out the window.

"What do you think you're doing?"

"What do you mean?"

Her mother turned furious eyes on Sybilla. "Don't give me that! The entire town knows you're running around with that nothing. I hate to think where he came from by the looks of him. Do you want to ruin yourself? Nobody to want you after he's done with you?"

After all the years of toeing the line, Sybilla was weary of it. She drew herself up. "He makes me feel alive, Mama!"

"That's nothing! Gone in a flash." Her mother moved quickly, like some wild animal, and held her by the shoulders in a vise grip. "He's not like us. His mongrel looks. Who knows what he is! I forbid you to see him again!"

"I'm not a child! I'm not ending up a dry sack like you!"

Instantly, her mother drew back her arm, open palm connecting with Sybilla's cheek in a sharp retort. Stinging, Sybilla fled the house with her mother's shrill words at her back. "He will leave you! Mark my words!"

Lying in her bed in the middle of the night now, Sybilla heard her mother's voice as clearly as though she was physically there. But the truth was that she hadn't seen her family since then—for two reasons. She couldn't bear to go back to the small-minded place where she grew up. But even more so, she didn't want to witness the triumphant I-told-you-so look on her mother's face. As far as her mother was concerned Sybilla had made herself a pariah, disgracing herself and the family, by going against the rules and suffering the consequences.

IT HADN'T TAKEN Sybilla's mother long to wield her power. The farmer promptly fired Gabe. Rather than putting an end to things, it opened a pathway that may have been taken anyway, albeit not quite as soon. With the town abuzz, knowing where he wasn't wanted, Gabe had no problems leaving.

"Take me with you!" Sybilla had begged, afraid of losing the excitement he'd brought into her dull existence.

"You don't really know me," he cautioned her. "I can't give you what you want."

"That's crazy. Look what we have!" She was relentless, ignoring his defocused gaze, as if he was fixated on another time and place entirely. In the midst of her cajoling, his silence became deafening. Finally, turning back to her, he consented as if he'd presaged things to come and given over to destiny, her words having little actual impact on his decision.

After sneaking home to gather a few belongings, Sybilla met Gabe outside town at the pasture where they first encountered each other. It seemed fitting somehow. From there they blew where the wind took them. They stopped in this town and that, taking odd jobs, finding minimum shelter. Sometimes they camped outside town, sleeping under the stars, going into bus stations to clean up. When they had money they'd get on a Greyhound, getting off on a whim. When they didn't, they'd hitch a ride. They had no stated destination but were definitely heading west in a meandering fashion. Over the next eighteen months, they kept on the move, looking for the right spot and not finding it, never staying anywhere beyond a few weeks.

Having little life experience, Sybilla was willing to follow Gabe without question. Her dormant spirit of adventure was let loose. If she noticed his increasing reserve and off-the-wall irritations directed her way, she quickly shunted them into an area of her mind where she hid anything that was troubling. Virtually everything was unfamiliar ground, including her relationship with him. She let him guide her, or so she thought at the time. But in retrospect, her own directive nature had begun to surface, along with her passion for photography. Her camera was one of the few possessions she'd brought with her. The places they went and the people they saw became her subjects. Sybilla discovered she had a talent for capturing the felt sense of environments they traveled through and exposing secrets folks kept locked away, depositing them onto a two-dimensional surface. Her photography was expressive in a way she was never allowed to be.

There was something about discovering her gift that may have caused Gabe to regress into himself, perhaps thankful he no longer had to do or think for her. Maybe it was his role to be a pied piper, to bring her out into a larger world than the one she'd lived in before. It could have ended at that. Then she realized she was pregnant.

Sybilla recognized that a baby complicated things, but she was thrilled. Her love for Gabe had grown to the degree that the mere thought of him melted her heart—and quelled her growing alarm at the changes in his manner. She found herself surreptitiously watching, always studying him for some sign of the tenderness that recaptured the times when they'd first been together. The glances he'd cast her way back then were of complete adoration and pleasure. That was why, even though he'd said she didn't know him, she did. Remembering soft eyes looking into hers, nakedly, baring his soul. It was seductive—and unforgettable.

They had been in California for a while, moving down the coast, headed over toward the Southwest. Sybilla had successfully hidden the early morning sickness that started to come over her, thinking it was important to choose the right time to tell Gabe. But she couldn't quite find it.

When she finally spoke, haltingly, giving the words hope, he said nothing. Instead, he stared at her in a way she couldn't quite fathom, like confirming something. When he became even more removed than usual the ground beneath her feet grew fragile. Should she walk too heavily the earth might develop cracks she would plunge into, reflecting the uncertainty and growing divide that prevailed between them. Sybilla was afraid to enter into that void with petitions of any significance. Her inner expanse toward adventure was replaced with contraction, not of early labor, but of trepidation.

They stopped in a desert town on the Arizona side near the Mexican border finding a small place, nothing more than a shack really. But the owner was willing to rent on a week-to-week basis. Sybilla was glad to settle in, even if only for a while. They had done well in California, the wages they earned there going far in the desolate, out-of-the-way spots they'd been frequenting recently. Gabe was looking for something, allowing that, if he were to find it, they would have to leave behind the aspects of their culture she considered normal, but he characterized hateful. Hence, the places they rested would barely qualify as a spit in the road, the people they encountered increasingly odd. But probably no more eccentric than they themselves may have become, life on the road encouraging that.

Sybilla got over her morning sickness and was back to capturing the landscape and its characters, rendering interpretation through her lens. This pastime had become her passion, but also her salvation, a distraction from the peculiarities of her new life and Gabe's increasingly strange behavior.

When he first started going out into the night, she thought he was leaving her. She'd wake up in the early hours, reaching for him, finding the place next to her cold, the covers undisturbed. She'd move through their home and discover it empty. Standing at the front door, peering out into the blackness, she'd see the sky punctuated by millions of stars but none providing light for her. Sometimes when Gabe came home near dawn, Sybilla could almost feel him before he entered the house. It was discomforting, the air preceding him filled with bristling electricity. She'd feign sleep, waiting for him to crawl into bed. But he didn't have an apparent need for sleep and would act like he'd risen before her, making the coffee and going outside to drink it. His senses appeared heightened. More than once, he'd winced when she made a dish clatter or spoke a little loudly.

Gabe was restless, unable to be still, only appearing to find any release out in nature. Perhaps the land absorbed what accosted him and gave some relief. In those times, there was an abject innocence and purity that issued through his eyes to hers, asking forgiveness for all the turmoil and withholding. The silent poignancy buried itself in Sybilla's innermost spaces, keeping her there, with him, without question. The vulnerability Gabe made visible at those rare, fleeting moments made up for desolate times, bringing hope for better days.

One night there was a full moon. Sybilla turned in early but tossed and turned. Gabe was in the front room reading, or at least turning pages because she could hear them. Then the front door clicked shut quietly.

Finally unwilling to remain passive and uninformed, she quickly threw on some clothes, and slipped out the back door that led off the bedroom. He was considerably in front of her, headed straight into the open desert behind their house and looked to be carrying a backpack. Under the strong moonlight she could easily follow him but was slowed down by having to watch where she walked, so as to avoid the myriad forms of cacti, and who knew what creatures that came out at night. On the other hand, Gabe skimmed over the landscape, like something transported him, clearly bound toward some rock formations in the distance. Sybilla had seen this form of intensity in Gabe plenty of times; everything else was blocked out except the object of his focus. Even if some part of him sensed he was being followed, whatever was drawing him won out, leaving Sybilla to trail behind without fear of detection.

He disappeared through the huge stones like magic. Eventually arriving at the place she last saw him, Sybilla could only discern a sheer wall of rounded organic forms reaching into the sky. From afar, they looked like otherworldly guardians. Now standing in front of them, she felt a cold shiver crawling up her spine, signaling her to run home, to hide from what she was about to discover. Instead, she found the courage to override it. Sybilla was weary of submitting.

She slid along the base of the rock wall and found nothing. Deciding there must be some access above, she climbed gingerly. Her newly added weight slowed her down. Again she watched her feet, remembering

Gabe's caution. Snakes loved to come out after dark and lay on stones warmed by the sun. Even though the temperature was dropping, as it did in the desert at night, the rocks were still warm. Sniffing the air, she could smell wood smoke. A little farther up, Sybilla spotted what appeared to be a cave. But light from the moon peeked through from inside, indicating an opening in the farther reaches. Carefully picking her way, she slipped into the passageway. Groping along one wall, her heart pounded with exertion—and foreboding.

She saw flickering light ahead. A campfire reached up into the night, playing across the boulders. She crept up to the opening, careful to hang back in the darkness of the tunnel, safely out of sight. Gabe was there below her a few hundred feet, in an open space surrounded by geologic protection, fueling flames that leapt high into the sky. The fire ring looked well used as though many in the past had done just as Gabe was doing now. He crouched, taking something out of his backpack throwing it into the fire. The sweetish smell of herbs reached her nostrils. It crossed her mind that he was calling upon something to join him, an invitation to something unseen.

She remembered him howling with laughter once. "If the Catholics only knew the incense they burn in mass comes from the pagans. Burning it opens a portal! Either side of reality can pass. If only they knew how many disembodied attendants were tucked in among them! They'd run screaming!"

Sybilla shivered in fascination at the scene unfolding before her, not daring to show herself. In the clear desert air sound traveled a good distance. The silver light of the full moon rendered a surreal distinction to everything she saw. Gabe was mumbling something. She couldn't make it out. The murmuring went on for some time while he continued to toss plant matter into the flames. Becoming still, he stared into the fire, perhaps hypnotized, while the blaze popped and hissed. His back to her hiding place, Gabe raised his face to the moon, intoning. His arms were overhead as if to receive something. Sybilla thought she saw movement in the air above him and dismissed it. But when Gabe lowered his arms his frame was strangely larger.

Later, looking back, what transpired next could only have been a few moments, but it seemed like hours. Time was interrupted. Each proceeding nanosecond recorded her terror, rooting her in place. He turned, in slow motion, facing her. He'd known she was tailing him all along! Only it wasn't Gabe she was seeing. Even in the moonlight and from that distance, she was certain. The stranger's face looked carved in stone, deeply etched lines around the mouth, hooded eyes, resembling some ancient Indian, almost cartoon-like. But she wasn't laughing. The creature's eyes pierced the darkness like a heat-seeking missile ferreting out her hiding place and threw a warning. Just below the level of hearing her ears caught a guttural sound.

At that moment, a bat flew out of the darkness, diving at her. The child she was carrying suddenly kicked for the first time, and she felt it, agitated, matching her own state of turbulence. That's all it took for Sybilla to break whatever spell was being cast. Time sped up once more. Her feet flew back the way she'd come until she discovered herself home again, holding onto her belly, the transmission from her hands seeking to reach her unborn child, hoping to extend security she didn't feel herself.

— Chapter Ten —

SYBILLA'S SLEEP WAS fitful, anticipating Gabe's return at any moment. But he didn't appear that night. It was just as well. She needed a head start to digest what she'd witnessed—and what she could even possibly say to him.

What was that? What did I see? Her thoughts whirled. But she didn't doubt her eyes. Sybilla had witnessed something unlike anything she'd ever thought real or possible.

Is Gabe crazy? What's gotten a hold of him? Is that him? Am I crazy? That's the stuff of horror films! What am I doing with him? What am I going to do?

Somewhere in the midst of her fright and confusion, a great power arose. It was the innate, potent energy of a mother protecting her young.

I'm out of here! What's he thinking? He needs help! I can't let my baby be exposed to God knows what!

Standing at the door, she scanned for him. The sun was well up in the east. It was after nine o'clock. He'd never done this before. Even if Gabe went out at night, he always returned by the time she awoke. In the middle of her outrage, Sybilla worried if he was even alive. Deciding she'd better go see, she was in the bedroom pulling on her clothes when the front door opened. She sank down on the bed, waiting.

"Hi," Gabe ducked his head in the door, giving a wave, a small sheepish smile on his face.

She followed him into the kitchen. Silently, Sybilla watched him reaching for the coffee. He was disheveled, more than if he'd slept in his clothes, like something had been wrung out of him. When he turned to face her, it wasn't a Gabe she'd ever observed before. She thought he looked like a lost child. The anger that was bubbling, verging on caustic words, began to soften as he reached out, touching her arm, clearly in apology. Surprised, she'd thought he'd be churlish as he'd been so much of the time in the last months.

"I'm so sorry. You must've been worried," he looked up at her through long lashes, head bowed.

"Where were you?" Sybilla asked quietly, taking in every aspect of him, waiting to see if he'd lie to her or acknowledge her presence the previous night.

"This place. Found it a few weeks ago. Something about it. Been on my mind," his sentences were choppy, words rushing over each other, "Sybilla, you should come with me! Photograph it! It's incredible. All these big stones. So powerful, I think people have been going there for centuries.

"Last night I was reading. Couldn't get into the book. Something kept drawing me back to those rocks. It got so intense I just had to go!" he continued on, his voice getting stronger, like he was defying her, "I thought I'd be right back, but once I got there I needed to stay for a while. It was cold and I made a fire. But I must've fallen asleep. The next thing I knew it was morning. Don't know why I slept so late. It took me this long to get back."

Sybilla regarded him pointedly. She finally decided that, at least from Gabe's remembrance, the story he related was exactly what had happened. He had no recollection of the events he'd omitted from this version, nor was he aware that she'd been at hand. Sybilla couldn't decide if she was relieved or even more terrified. At least it likely explained where he'd been all those nights. It also indicated a growing obsession with whatever the experience brought him.

Finally she spoke, "Gabe, don't take off like that again without telling me. You gave me a fright! I couldn't imagine where you were."

"I know," the little boy again, chastised, "I won't."

Sybilla came to the conclusion that it was better not to say anything to him about what she'd witnessed. There was no sense in challenging him on something he didn't remember, or at least didn't seem to own. She could tell he was preoccupied, though not about her or the baby. Sybilla was so tuned into Gabe that she knew the nature of his silences.

Now he frequently projected inner strain and vulnerability rather than irritation directed outwardly toward her or any situation.

Using this change to her advantage, Sybilla began to carefully drop suggestions that it was time to find a better place. The baby was coming soon. They could just as well stay where they were, but she secretly hoped to snatch Gabe out of whatever otherworld had spirited him away. They needed someplace with more people and an everyday kind of life, not the stark landscape where shadows and legend lurked in the moonlight—because there he would go. She acted disinterested in his invitation to photograph that area to cover her growing dread and unwillingness to imperil the baby or herself.

He continued to disappear periodically at night. Sybilla chose to bide her time, staying silent, putting her attention instead toward preparing for their baby. In her sixth month, Gabe agreed to head toward central Arizona, a place he'd traveled through called Mother Lode in tribute to its affluent mining past. A compromise, he'd said. He described a small town with miles of desert extending to the north—a forest of saguaros, chollas, ocotillos and geologic formations rife with petroglyphs. A place with character, Native people and artists of all sorts! Begrudgingly, he let her know that Phoenix was within reach if she really wanted it. But not so close as to contaminate with the things cities bring. Gabe expressed some excitement, and Sybilla's spirits began to soar.

They found a small place on the edge of Mother Lode. It wasn't much to look at but had a large yard that looked directly into the desert wilderness, protected as a preserve, and all the landscape that he'd described to her before they came. Gabe wanted to be sure that no other housing would encroach. Not too much civilization, to give their child a chance. She got the uneasy feeling that he'd deposited her there for all time, taking care of this one last thing before moving on. But he stayed, growing quieter in his soul, disappearing at night only occasionally.

THE BABY CAME. They wanted a home birth. Gabe had actually insisted on it. "The old way," he said, "Not anything cold to steal our baby's spirit."

Sybilla agreed with him. Not because her values led her away from a hospital birth but to nurture the unspoken alliance that had evolved between them since they arrived in the new spot. Finally. When Sybilla mused about the meandering path it took for them to come to this unexpected place in their coupling, after so much uncertainty, indeed with no grounding that she could count on, she had the welcome feeling of having come home. This, even as she projected herself several years ahead—it being her nature she simply could not help but do—she intuited Gabe's absence. She knew the time was coming. He would have passed through a room of her life, leaving just his scent forever lingering in the air. From that she would draw bittersweet memories. So the time that was left became precious indeed, something to preserve against what was to be—for their child and herself.

As the baby grew inside her, Sybilla experienced a newfound sense of self and the promise of what was developing within her. When Gabe took the stand on a midwife, she deferred, having no qualms. He rewarded her with a steady gaze of love that he had never spoken in words. Sybilla took it in and held it dear. In times to come she would seek out the affirmation he'd transmitted, find it nestled inside, reminding her that it was real. Not something she'd desperately manufactured.

Gabe wasted no time in finding a midwife, a Maya woman living in town who knew the ways of the earth, the Mother, he said. He'd excitedly told how she came to midwifery through a dream. The gods chose her back when she was young and still living in Guatemala. Sybilla cocked her head in question. He was talking so strangely these days: things she didn't understand. But she determined to wait and judge for herself whether this was the woman who should be entrusted with the birth of their child. When Doña Flora came the next morning for a consult, Sybilla immediately felt at peace. Doña Flora invited tranquility. Sybilla was sitting in their small front room reading when she glanced out the window. A short, matronly brown-skinned woman approached the house. Her loose, brightly colored dress was simple, a woven belt cinched at the waist accentuating the comfortable folds of middle age. Her long black hair was caught in a braid down her back. The woman paused outside. Sybilla heard a lilting voice, a short intonation in a tongue she didn't know, perhaps a prayer.

Gabe answered the knock and ushered her in proudly. Doña Flora immediately clapped her hands together in delight at seeing Sybilla. When the midwife gestured toward her burgeoning front and raised her eyebrows in question, Sybilla couldn't help but give her the permission she requested. Doña Flora laid hands on Sybilla's belly, closed her eyes and was silent for what seemed like an eternity. Opening, her eyes looked directly into Sybilla's, transmitting a deep sense of appreciation.

Nodding her head sagely, in heavily-accented English, she stated matter-of-factly, "This one will be gifted, Mama. One who will be guided."

With that pronouncement, they heard a long exhalation, a rush from breath contained. They'd forgotten Gabe in the room, so involved were the women in their communion. Including him with her smile, Sybilla saw immediate relief projected on Gabe's face. Doña Flora's prediction appeared to be what he'd been waiting to hear. Doña Flora went on to school them both in what would be needed for the home birth and advised she would come by every week.

Ultimately when the birthing came, it was relatively quick and easy. Sybilla didn't know if it had to do with all the prayers Doña Flora undertook during her labor, but she found it comforting to hear the melodic voice petitioning the spirits she believed in. Gabe was her assistant, maybe not culturally correct or usual, but Doña Flora praised him afterward and gave him the honor of cutting the cord of his newborn son. After the baby was cleaned and swaddled, she gently deposited him in Sybilla's arms.

"His name?" Doña Flora asked.

Exhausted but proud, Sybilla smiled up at Gabe and stated firmly, "Preston after my grandfather. Preston Johns Cadell."

"Ah…but he has another name. It will come to him. But not now," Doña Flora spoke softly and extracted a small object from her skirt pocket. Placing it in Gabe's palm, she closed his fingers around it, "You keep this in a special place for your son. There is a time when it will speak to him."

Gabe opened his hand and found a small flat stone. Looking closely he saw its naturally raised ridges resembling the symbol of the sun.

— Chapter Twelve —

SYBILLA TOOK TO motherhood like she couldn't have imagined. Surprising her, Gabe was right by her side. He got up in the night nearly as much as she did when the baby cried. Even though she'd heard how exhausting it was to care for a newborn, Sybilla discovered a new strength and vitality she'd never had. She had put away her camera when things had gotten so tense on the road. She brought it out again photographing PJ, as she began to call him, at nearly every turn. Gabe fussed over him, sometimes talking to PJ in low tones she couldn't hear, perhaps relaying wisdom only for his ears. Within a couple of months, Gabe made a practice of taking him outside, lifting him up like an offering to the sun, a proud father and laughing baby.

Doña Flora continued to come by every now and then, checking that all was well. She brought a gift one day, a large oblong multi-colored weaving that she'd made herself. To carry the baby, she said. And showed Sybilla how to wrap PJ in such a way, and then tie the cloth over her shoulder, so it was possible to carry him on her hip or sling on her back and go about her business. Sybilla couldn't get the technique down pat. Gabe was a natural though. Doña Flora didn't quite reconcile a man hauling a baby in the traditional Maya way meant for women but finally gave in and smiled encouragingly. The wrap gave Gabe new mobility with PJ in places where a stroller couldn't go. When he asked to take PJ out into the desert behind their home, just for a short while, Sybilla hesitantly acquiesced. Gabe seemed so much more stable in the last months. He was never gone too long or when the sun was strong. She finally determined he was just bonding with his son. It gave her a break, too. She needed time in her makeshift darkroom. She started submitting some of her prints to magazines. One was accepted, which made her think she could possibly make a living through her passion. And Gabe established a handyman service, word getting around that he could take care of anything that needed fixing. They traded off caring for PJ. Thus was the rhythm they established, a relative flow of domesticity and their child was thriving. Gabe was even periodically tender with her—and Sybilla allowed herself to exhale. But soon she began to notice the old edginess creeping in. The silences returned. Gabe would spend long evenings, after the baby was put to bed, out in the back yard, gazing at the sky or at some point in the desert. Then came the times when Sybilla would open the door to check on him and he'd be gone, with never a word to her, returning some hours later. The sense of dread re-entered Sybilla's life, the inevitable she knew would come to pass. PJ was nearly two years old.

GABE HAD NEVER disclosed much about his origins but did say he'd never known his father. He was estranged from his mother and refused to talk about the reason. One time early in their travels they were wilderness camping in the Colorado mountains on their way farther west. She had retired to the tent early, not long after dark, and fallen asleep immediately, snuggled deep in her sleeping bag. Sometime into the night she awakened to a loud, insistent screeching directly overhead. Groggy, she heard the sharp crack of wood popping and smelled smoke. Reaching next to her, no Gabe. Panicked, Sybilla unzipped the tent and witnessed Gabe feeding a fire too large for the small clearing where they'd set up camp, its flames leaping into the air. He appeared to be transfixed. In the glow, Sybilla could just make out a large bird flitting from one branch to another, shrieking at the blaze, calling a warning to the rest of the forest.

"What are you doing?" Sybilla called.

"Nothing. Sorry. I didn't mean to wake you."

Her voice startled him and shook him from his trance. Gabe backed away from the fire and sat down heavily in a camp chair. Throwing a blanket around her shoulders against the night, Sybilla joined him. They sat in silence, drawn into the undulating flames; shapeshifting images offered an invitation to the obscure. Reaching into a small bag, Gabe threw in some plant matter and Sybilla smelled the comforting scent of sage and other herbs burning. The bird quieted and flew away, gone to roost, having abated danger.

Gabe spoke quietly, "You don't know what it's like, do you? Not to have roots. Not to know your people. Not to know who you are."

She'd never heard him sound wistful, yearning, uncertain. Thinking about her mother, all the aunts, uncles, cousins, Sybilla snorted. The Johns family line stretched back in time and reached out from history with the tendrils of some suffocating vine, squeezing all the life out of her, as far as she was concerned.

"No, really. Your people have been in Johns Wake forever. They settled it. You grew up surrounded by family."

"You've got that right. And I couldn't wait to shed all that."

"But look at it this way. You know your tribe. At least it gives you grounding."

Sybilla had to admit that as much as she despised the small-mindedness that seemed to flourish in the very soil of her hometown and all the expectations laid upon her by family, it constituted a pretty clear path. She was glad to be able to strive against it. In a strange way, it did give her something to move from—and go back to if she was ever crazy enough to do that.

"I guess you're right in a way. But what about you? You came from somewhere."

It was Gabe's turn to snort. "Grace. Graciela, she likes to call herself. Said her people called her that. Problem was that 'her people' changed with the wind. Still does, I guess."

"How so?"

Gabe picked up a nearby stick and poked at the glowing logs, sending sparks flying up into the night. Save the crackles of the fire, silence filled the air. Finally he shook his head and went on. "She must have been starting her Christian period when she had me. So I ended up with the name Gabriel. But that phase didn't last long. She was always kind of evasive about my middle name Bol. Something like a family name from my father's side. Put all that together with Cadell and you've got a mouthful."

They had lived on the road most of his life, largely in the States and a little along the border on the Canada side where his mother had family. But they'd usually skirted her relations.

"She always said they didn't understand her and it wasn't worth trying again. I guess the family was pretty straight-laced and you could say Graciela was a bit wild by their standards, a throwback. With our lifestyle, I think they looked on me as some oddity raised by a she-wolf. So I didn't like them much either what little I saw."

"Why do you call her Graciela when she's your mom?"

"That's what she wanted me to call her. I guess she had trouble reconciling her image as 'Artist' and 'Rebel' with being a mother. It was odd. Like she couldn't quite shake where she came from. I guess that accounts for the times like her Jesus period. She'd try something on—like she was auditioning for some role. Then we'd be living like regular people, if you call it that. But she just couldn't pull it off," Gabe made no effort to temper the sarcasm in his voice.

How long they stayed in one place depended on the weather, what art she could sell or a whim. If Graciela was bored and heard about more interesting people or a more lucrative pasture, they'd pull up stakes.

"There was this one place out in the Arizona desert. Crazy it was. In the middle of nowhere and not even a town most of the year! Graciela heard about it and off we went," his laugh was more like a sharp bark. "We had this beat-up red pick-up and a little white trailer we pulled. That's what we lived in. Sometimes it was hard to find a place to sleep in there because of all the stuff she collected. She did sculpture and collage out of 'found objects' and back then it was cactus skeletons, snakeskin, dried pods, hummingbird skulls. You name it. We were always stopping to go on what she called scavenger hunts. It was like she had a sixth sense for finding these things. I have to admit she made some pretty interesting stuff and did okay selling it.

"Quartzite. People started showing up with their trailers and RVs around November and stayed through about March. That was the town, hardly anything permanent. The rest of the time it was scorching hot. There was a gem show in January and February. That was the real reason people were there, and why we went. To sell things. It became a huge flea market going on all hours. We got there in October, early enough to get a prime spot. And Graciela pulled out an awning from our trailer and set up a studio and shop right there."

Gabe was twelve that year when they stayed in Quartzite, old enough that Graciela didn't keep tabs on his whereabouts. He had the run of the large encampment and found that a majority of the folks led lives like theirs—nomadic. Perhaps because of that, most seemed used to

77

making fast ties where they landed. For the first time in his life, Gabe found himself part of a big, noisy makeshift family he began to think of as grandmothers, grandfathers, aunts, uncles, and cousins to make up for what he never knew. In the evening, campfires dotted the place here and there warding off the chill of the desert night, sending an invitation for the inhabitants to gather. And most regularly did after all the potential customers finally left for the day. Gabe sat with them, after Graciela would wave him away; his asking for permission just served as a distraction from her work. He sensed he was an interruption to the heated debates she liked to engage in one-on-one there in her studio with whoever dropped by, usually about "big life questions." After a while Gabe quit asking. One time Graciela joined him in the nightly circle, and someone asked about Gabe's dad. Gabe glanced up hoping she would reveal his whereabouts, or anything really.

"Oh, you know. Gone on the wind," she shrugged it off. Gabe picked up a stick and stabbed at the fire perhaps more diligently than needed, his eyes remained lowered. Later, back in their trailer, he attempted to bring up the subject again.

"Why don't you ever tell me anything about my dad?"

"Not much to tell."

"Tell me something! I have a right to know about my father! You owe me that."

"Look, you're better off without him. He came from a backward place with backward people. I don't have anything to do with them and you're not either. They're not civilized," she made a sharp downward gesture cutting him off.

"Like we're civilized! I don't even go to school!" Gabe went to bed, jerking the covers over his head. His mother was obviously hiding something.

That night he had a dream. But it seemed so real. The first thing he was aware of was the pungent smell of decomposing plants. Then his senses activated in waves. Soft, light rain hitting arms and legs, cool against warm skin naked to the air. Squishy ground on bare soles. Gentle tap-tapping sound. Vision washing into play, misty drizzle ran off foliage so thick there was little light. Leaves large enough to find shelter under and tree trunks stretching up to the sky. This was not a place he knew, totally foreign. Yet he wasn't scared. A slight rustle and a deer's face peeked from around a tree close by and showed itself a bit more. It wasn't afraid either. They watched each other, both stock-still. A sweetish, heady scent wafted in, mixing with that of the humus. And a strange thing happened. The deer's face shifted to near transparency revealing a brown-skinned man with long black hair cut straight across at the eyebrows. A fleeting glimpse and then Gabe awoke—a disoriented, intense longing emerged.

"That's the dream. Over and over. Sometimes it changes a little, like I'm walking down a path instead of standing still. But the main elements are the same. Forest. Rain. Smells. The deer and the man. The man appears and the dream ends. I can go for a year without having it, or it happens several times a month. But that's the dream—for years," he mused.

Gabe ended his monologue, it being the most Sybilla had ever heard him talk at one time. He returned to staring at the flames, closing himself off, until finally Sybilla got up and returned to the tent, laying a hand lightly on his shoulder as she passed. He had given her some insight into the complexities of his origins and a hint at the painful hole he lived with. But later what knowledge she gleaned from his disclosure did nothing to give her peace of mind.

— Chapter Fourteen —

SYBILLA WAS WORRIED. Several times over the last days she had to repeat herself loudly to get Gabe's attention. He'd startle as though being pulled back from some far off place. If he wasn't entranced then he was restless, moving, pacing. Often muttering under his breath, glancing over at something she couldn't see, he carried on a conversation—but not with her. Sybilla thought she should be petrified for PJ. Their child, rather than fearing the strange way his dad was behaving, had an ability to enter wherever Gabe was, get him chuckling as they both spoke in undertones that sounded like another language altogether and acknowledged unseen presences.

Sybilla told herself PJ was just mimicking his father. So whenever he'd point to thin air and give a delighted baby laugh, she'd clap her hands together in approval and peal laughter, too—a game that was becoming common.

A shrine of sorts materialized overnight in their back yard, just at the edge before it merged into the miles of desert beyond. Sybilla noticed it through the kitchen window when she got coffee in the morning. Gabe hadn't shown up before she retired and hadn't slept, at least not in their bed. Wandering out to inspect it, the installation of stones, cactus skeletons, wood ravaged by the elements, laid carefully, spoke of something Sybilla didn't understand. The only times Gabe appeared settled were when he was sitting cross-legged in front of it, burning herbs in a terracotta pot, the smoke curling in wisps toward the sky. PJ was often beside him sitting quietly; normal child's play vanished. Sybilla wondered what Gabe was doing, and whether she should be concerned for PJ. If she ventured near, she felt like an intruder. So she was willing to leave them be, as long as she could keep them both in her sights. And when she had something that took her away, she called PJ inside to go with her. Sybilla felt brittle. It was impossible to ignore the strong wind approaching, one she knew would blow apart her carefully constructed reality.

Sometimes Doña Flora sat with Gabe. Heads together, they talked earnestly. Things she couldn't hear. At other times Sybilla heard repetitive prayers, the singsong of her soft Native voice, body rocking slightly while Gabe sat eyes closed. The smoke of incense was dense, creating a separation from the world around them. Once she bent over the top of his head and appeared to blow. That time Doña Flora sought her out, leaving Gabe outside.

She gave Sybilla a sad smile, "Ah, dear one. I think he has not told you. His dreams are very strong now. This is something for him. Something you will not know."

Tears sprung from Sybilla's eyes, the tension to hold them back finally too much. "I've been so scared. I don't know what to do. It's like he's gone and I don't know where he went."

"There is nothing to do. It comes like this for some and they have to follow. If that not happen, their soul goes anyway."

"Is he losing his mind?"

"Not like you think. But his longing is deep and he is a special one. In my village the elders recognize things early, and those young ones are prepared. Not so for Gabe. He is feeling this now so much like he is lost. No ground under his feet."

"But what about our son?"

Doña Flora smiled broadly, misunderstanding Sybilla's question, "Yes, that one is special, too."

"I meant that he needs his father. I need his father," she cried in anguish.

"Your boy is protected, dear one. There are those who protect him. No worries. One will come." Doña Flora laid both hands gently on Sybilla's cheeks, gazing directly into her eyes. And even as tears continued to stream down Sybilla's face, she felt a wash move through her, lessening her apprehension, sending some relief.

Patting her on the shoulder, Doña Flora started to leave but turned back. "Dear one, sometimes it is good to let them go. Sometimes this is best to not carry the wound."

Sybilla stood looking at the spot where her midwife had stood, long after she heard the soft closing of the front door.

— Chapter Fifteen —

SYBILLA WAS SEQUESTERED in the darkroom all day, hesitantly entrusting PJ's care to Gabe. She'd been sorting through her black and whites, developing old film, poring over contact sheets, all from the times they'd been on the road. With an undercurrent of quiet excitement, she realized just how professional looking a number were. Scrutinizing which were the most dramatic: soaring monsoon skies, vast landscapes, those that spoke to what a small place any human had in the universe, or curiosities, oddities she'd encountered, craggy-looking people that reflected the rough environment, abandoned buildings laid victim to the elements, shots that told a story. She scribbled down notes, setting them aside in separate piles with images attached. Ideas bubbled up so quickly it was like a dam had burst, spilling out what had been cordoned off and contained. She felt a grounding that had been absent since she'd made the decision in Johns Wake to take off with Gabe.

I can really do something with all this, she thought happily. First a portfolio. Stories with photos. No telling where I can go.

This feels really good, she noted. Bursting with energy, light on her feet, Sybilla gathered up her piles, flicked off the lights and stepped out of the darkroom intent on getting dinner prepared. Cocking her head, dead silence greeted her. Her buoyancy instantly deflated, replaced by the now-familiar sense of foreboding. Calling through the house, no Gabe, no PJ. Glancing into the front yard, then rushing out back, both were empty. Hastening to Gabe's outdoor altar she scrutinized the rock-lined circle and its accoutrements, hoping against hope that the contents would tell her where they were. Touching the terracotta incense burner, it was cold, no lingering scent in the air. Sybilla's heart raced as an argument ensued inside her head: He would never hurt PJ. Maybe not knowingly…No telling how long they've been gone. No telling where they went. Where's my boy? Her chest tightened.

Turning, she scanned the desert landscape, squinting against the strong rays of a late afternoon sun that sought to blind her. Every distant rock outcropping or cacti took on the potential of a man accompanied by a small boy heading home. But finally Sybilla had to admit she saw no movement and ran inside. Grabbing the phone she dialed Doña Flora's number. When she answered, Sybilla asked in a rush if Gabe and PJ were there. No. She babbled her worries, words spilling over each other. Doña Flora responded in a soothing voice saying she would come right over. A short fifteen minutes later an old beat-up truck pulled up to the curb, and Doña Flora got out of the passenger's side with a covered pot in her hands. Leaning inside, she said something to the driver and turned toward the house. The pick-up pulled away. Sybilla waited in the doorway twisting her hands.

"Hello, dear one," Doña Flora greeted her with a smile, cocking her head toward the disappearing truck. "My nephew. My sister's family is visiting."

"I'm so sorry! I didn't mean to interrupt your Sunday. I'm just so scared!"

"This is okay. No worries. They are here for a week. Let's go inside. I brought something for the dinner."

Doña Flora led the way to the kitchen, putting the pot on the stovetop. "Now let's sit and you tell me."

They pulled chairs out from the kitchen table. Doña Flora took Sybilla's trembling hands in hers, resting their arms on the tabletop. Sybilla took a big breath. The mere touch of the Maya woman's hands conveyed comfort. She was able to go over the day and speak her concerns with less anxiety.

"But it seemed fine. Gabe and PJ were putting something together with legos. He said he'd watch him and to enjoy myself. I never should have left him for so long. I just lost time. I should have known better! I'm a terrible mother!" Sybilla ended, berating herself miserably.

"Ah no, dear one. You must do these things for yourself. This you must do," Doña Flora clucked her tongue and offered a slight incline of her head for emphasis. "Now, let's see how things are."

She gave a reassuring squeeze to Sybilla's hands. Gazing past her, the *curandera's* eyes became de-focused and then closed. When Doña Flora began to chant in the sing-song voice she recognized as prayer, Sybilla closed her own eyes. She had a strange sensation, like being taken along somewhere even as she remained seated in the chair at her kitchen table. She noticed that her trepidation had evaporated. The chanting stopped and they sat in silence for timeless moments. Sybilla felt another slight squeeze to her hands and opened her eyes. Doña Flora was looking intently at her, a face set in kindness. In that instant Sybilla noted the glow she emanated, every line erased from her face, belying her years. Why, she looks like a young girl, a beauty, thought Sybilla. Aware of her surroundings again, she realized night had fallen. Her breath caught.

"No, no, no. It is okay. You can calm. Your boy is okay. We wait. They are coming," Doña Flora patted her hand again.

Seven o'clock. An hour later Sybilla still endured the wait. The temperature outside was dropping rapidly in the fall night. In the desert there could be as much as a forty-degree difference from day to night. Sybilla paced. She just knew Gabe hadn't taken PJ's jacket. Unable to stay inside, she went out and peered into darkness. The moon hadn't risen, and the stars weren't yet visible. Nothing. She stalked back to the kitchen and glanced at the clock. After eight o'clock. All the while Doña Flora had busied herself in the kitchen, heating up the contents of the pot, making rice. A savory, spicy smell filled the house.

"This is the *kak'ik*," she called over. "This is a soup we make with turkey. I think you'll like. Do you have tortillas?"

"I can't think of food right now!" Sybilla had to stop herself from snapping at Doña Flora. She was strung tight as a drum. "I'm sorry. No."

"Ah no, dear one," Doña Flora walked over and put a hand lightly on her shoulder. "It is okay. They come soon now. We must feed them. They are tired. You just sit."

Sybilla almost slapped Doña Flora's hand off her shoulder. I can't sit! I'm about to jump out of my skin! Doña Flora shrugged slightly and returned to her preparations. Sybilla planted herself at the sliding glass door that led to the back yard, brooding.

A few minutes later, she noticed out of the corner of her eye that Doña Flora was setting the table. Only three places, it distracted her.

"Not four places?"

"Ah no. My nephew knows to come. He is here in a few minutes."

How's that? Sybilla didn't want to ponder the fact that she hadn't seen her call him and shifted her gaze back to the night, where she was greeted with black emptiness. But then she detected something where the shrine was situated. There was a shimmer like waves of heat radiating into the night air. Sybilla blinked her eyes a few times thinking she'd been staring into darkness too long. But no, something was happening. Her mouth hung open. Sybilla started to call Doña Flora but stopped. Mist now surrounded the entire shrine. Through the mist, light flickered as though it came from a campfire. But there was none. She was rooted. Her breath stalled, mind vacant.

Then Gabe and PJ were just there—appearing out of nothingness. Gabe held PJ in his arms wrapped in something and started walking toward the house. In a split second Sybilla wrenched open the sliding door. Her feet flew the fifty yards between them and roughly snatched PJ from him.

"How dare you! Where have you been? What's the matter with you?" she bellowed with rage. PJ woke from sleep and cried out. Her words became unintelligible, screeching out all the anguish she'd held inside for so long, finally freed. She clutched PJ tightly to her chest as he continued to howl. The next-door neighbor flicked on the back porch light and stuck his head out his door. Sybilla turned on her heel and stomped into the house, leaving Gabe standing silent, arms hanging loose at his sides. He hadn't uttered a word in the midst of her onslaught.

"It's okay. It's okay, my baby." Stuffing her own terror, Sybilla whispered to PJ over and over, in the process attempting to reassure herself. Laying him on the couch, she checked him over all the while softly saying the nonsensical things a parent says to a young child. He felt hot and damp. She put a hand to his forehead. No fever. Sybilla buried her head in his neck. He smelled like something she couldn't place, almost earthy. PJ was quieting and otherwise seemed untouched. She turned her attention to the strange whitish covering around him. Its consistency was like thick, hand-made paper only much stronger and more flexible, a little scratchy. Doña Flora came over and put her hand on top of PJ's head. The child became calm, eyes growing heavy.

Gabe slipped silently inside and stood at the perimeter of the room. He nodded at

Doña Flora in silent communication, an acknowledgement of some sort. Something had been accomplished that excluded Sybilla. A hesitant knock sounded at the door. "There he is, my nephew," Doña Flora smiled. "I will just go now."

"Thank you for coming," Sybilla said woodenly. She sought to regain composure. "And the food."

"Of course," Doña Flora turned.

The sound of the front door closing came a moment later. Sybilla threw Gabe a murderous look, daring him to come any closer. He remained where he'd first entered. Gathering up the now sleeping PJ, she went to put him to bed.

When she returned, Gabe was sitting at the table eating the soup Doña Flora left. He didn't acknowledge her and remained focused on his bowl. Sybilla had planned to tear into him. But now she just lost all energy. She stood arms crossed, leaning against the kitchen counter glaring at him, stony silence electrifying the air, conveying her convictions without words. When Gabe finished eating he took his bowl to the sink, his face untroubled, bearing no indication that her accusations had reached him. Without appearing to know Sybilla was present, he opened the back door and exited into the cold night. Sybilla's fury bubbled over. She expressed it through the clattering of pans and dishes as she cleaned up.

— Chapter Sixteen —

SYBILLA OPENED THE bedroom door noiselessly to check on PJ. He had kicked off his covers. Tucking him in again, she noted a little snore punctuating deep sleep. Exhausted herself, she decided to get ready for bed. She ignored the draw to go see what Gabe was doing, or if he was even still around. Her anger still simmered.

Some hours later she awoke with a start. Without reaching out her hand, she sensed Gabe's absence. Listening, there was nothing but silence. Sybilla started to turn over and go back to sleep when she heard the penetrating, unearthly cry of a coyote pierce the quiet then low, muffled murmuring. She leapt out of bed and made a beeline for PJ's room. He was there but tossing in his sleep making soft, unintelligible noises, not loud enough to have awakened her. She didn't have to have a sixth sense to determine the source of the sounds. Down the hall a flickering yellow glow bathed the back part of the house. Fire! Her nerve endings responded. But no smoke greeted her, no smell.

Sybilla rushed to the back door and, for a moment, her brain couldn't register what she saw. The entire yard was filled with lit candles, right up to the door. The installation at the back was going up in flames. Gabe was clearly visible standing in the middle of his sanctuary, throwing herbs into the blaze, wearing the strange white garment that he'd wrapped PJ in. It looked like a gown of sorts and came below his knees. She cracked open the door and his voice reached her. No longer murmuring, she could hear, without making out any words, an underlying intensity in the entreaty he directed to the fire. Sybilla quickly slid the door shut and stepped back.

He's gone crazy, she thought. The neighbors are going to call the police. This is it. I've had it. I'm done with this. Backing off, she was resolved. He's a danger to PJ. He's no good for me.

Leaving the room, she glanced at the clock; it said 2 a.m. Sybilla closed and locked the door to PJ's bedroom from the inside and then slid into her son's small bed, curling her body around his. If Gabe came for PJ, he'd have to get through her first. She lay there for a long time attending to any signal that he'd entered the house.

Sybilla didn't know where she was. It seemed like their home, but it was different. Looking around, things were missing, and others had taken their place. She didn't recognize the clothing she was wearing and couldn't feel her body. She started to panic and cry out. But her voice wouldn't come. Then she saw Gabe. He was standing outside looking at her through the kitchen window. He was saying something. She tried to get over to him but each step was like slogging through thick mud. With each hard-earned footfall he reciprocated the opposite, diminishing in the distance. His face was lined with sorrow, looked older. I'm so sorry, he mouthed, then just disappeared. She cried out in anguish, struggling against unseen hands holding her back. A whitish, ovoid shape appeared near her, hovered silently. She began to calm.

When she opened her eyes, Sybilla saw it was quite early. The soft light of dawn played in the room. Not quite awake, disoriented, she remembered the strange events of the night. PJ was in a ball next to her. The bedclothes were twisted. The bedroom door was ajar. PJ moved in his sleep, uncurling himself. Sybilla saw something tucked into his hand—the sun stone Doña Flora had given to Gabe at PJ's birth, entrusting him to hold it for his son.

Sybilla came fully awake and sprung out of bed. First, checking in their bedroom, it was empty, the rest of the house as well. She went to the back door. Everything was as it had been—except the ashes and charred remains of the altar.

Gabe was gone.

SYBILLA LIGHTLY QUESTIONED PJ about where he had gone with his dad, not wanting him to feel undue pressure. But when he excitedly told her about being on a river, flying through the stars and being in a wet place where people wore no shoes, she decided he must have slept through it all. He dreamt the tale he told her. The thought came later that Gabe might have fed PJ a hallucinogen then dismissed it. That's something he wouldn't do.

For a few years Sybilla had been waiting for the other shoe to drop. Now she knew it had. When that invisible part of her reached out, against her will, to anticipate Gabe, he was not to be found. Emptiness prevailed in the space that he had filled. Her body told her, with a sensation, that she'd landed—with a thud. She was no longer in limbo waiting for something to happen. For all the dread, the anticipated longing for something lost, that had permeated her days, she instead discovered a sense of relief. Sybilla had the unusual experience of becoming reacquainted with herself. The self that had stepped out of the picture, been put on hold, regained footing. Sybilla's natural drive and curiosity once again seeped into her life.

She was faced with two things immediately. As the days went by, PJ questioned her frequently about his daddy. She heard the increasing yearning in his little voice as he asked her, "When is Daddy coming home? Why isn't he here?" What could she tell him when she didn't even understand herself? So she told PJ that Gabe had been called away on an important trip. While that bought her some time, she knew she'd eventually have to offer him something else to hold onto.

Perhaps more troubling in the moment was how to put food on the table. They lived quite frugally, it being the way Gabe preferred. However, he had been in demand with his handyman services and worked long hours. Gabe was well paid and managed to sock away a decent amount.

Sybilla checked on their account, but he'd taken none of it with him. Finding there was enough to cover needs for a few months easily, she sent him a silent prayer of gratitude. In her heart, she knew he'd intentionally laid in provision for them. The future was an unknown worry, but in the moment she had some ease. The mere thought of asking her mother for help made her nauseous. Besides, she'd severed contact. If or when she saw Johns Wake again, she intended to return with successes under her arm.

A week went by, and then late one morning the doorbell rang. Sybilla opened the door to Doña Flora holding a plate covered with a dishtowel.

"Ah, dear one. I brought you some fresh tamales," the Maya woman offered. "How is our little one?"

Sybilla had not contacted Doña Flora after Gabe left. They shared an unexpressed knowledge that he was no longer in the region. Sybilla thought Doña Flora might be giving her wide berth for any part she may have played in, what Sybilla thought of as, Gabe's deterioration. But she held no anger toward Doña Flora for something that had been inevitable and uncontrollable. She looked upon the kindly face and invited her in, offering coffee.

PJ had been playing in his room but came rushing out and threw himself into Doña Flora's ample arms. "My daddy! Do you know where my daddy is?" His voice broke and tears slipped down his cheeks. Sybilla's own eyes filled, the pain of watching her son's hurt was too much.

Doña Flora gathered him up. "Little one, it is okay. Let's sit." Sybilla took the tamales to the kitchen and returned to find her holding him close on the couch, rocking rhythmically and speaking softly in dialect. It had a calming effect on PJ, and his sobs turned to snuffles.

"But Mama Flora, why doesn't my daddy come home?" This was the first time Sybilla heard PJ call the midwife by that name, but she didn't begrudge it. After all, she helped bring him into the world.

"These things are sometimes hard to know. Your papa? He has heard something. This thing he hears calls to him and he goes to find it. He must do this for himself. But, little one, even more he does this for you. It's because he loves you so much. And he is not gone because he is with you."

PJ's eyes got wide. He looked around the room hopefully. "No, he's not!" he said indignantly, "You're playing a trick!"

"Your papa always thinks of you with great love. This feeling is a sacred connection. You will know this more in your own way. He is not gone from you. And whenever you think of your papa, he feels it, too. This is alive."

"Will I see him?"

"He will come to you. You must be patient and wait."

PJ looked doubtful but seemed to gain some reassurance. His tears dried up, and he yawned. Meanwhile, Sybilla felt disquieted. She didn't know whether to be upset with Doña Flora for getting PJ's hopes up, or re-activate her own mixed feelings at the potential of Gabe returning.

They sat silently for a while. PJ shifted, stretched out and lay with his head on Doña Flora's lap. She stroked his head lightly. In a short time, he fell asleep. Doña Flora looked up at Sybilla searching her face.

"And how are you doing in this time?"

Quietly, so as not to awaken PJ, Sybilla confided about her relief, the guilty excitement, sadness, anger, all the internal conflict. It allowed her peace of mind just to be able to speak what had been whirling inside, bottled up since Gabe left. Finally she whispered her worries about the future, how she would make a go of it.

She finished with, "What exactly did you mean, all the things you told PJ? Do you know where Gabe is?"

"No, I do not know exactly where our Gabe has gone. But he told me about his dream, and I looked. I see a place and some people from the south. Hundreds of years ago such people lived in northern mountains of my country. This is thick jungle. But these people came from somewhere else. They are not like my people. I have heard stories that they crossed the river and left Guatemala. He receives a calling from them. He cannot refuse to answer. If he does, he will die inside. It is true what I say to the little one. His papa does this for him, too. It is important for both of them."

"Is he coming back?"

"Maybe not in the way you think."

"What else do you see?" Sybilla was skeptical, and Doña Flora knew it.

"This is all except, the white cloth he wrapped around the little one? They wear this cloth." She would say no more.

SIX MONTHS PASSED with no word from Gabe. Sybilla's time filled with caring for PJ and planning a future that left no time for nostalgic sentiment—real or imagined. In fact, she preferred to focus on the bad times with Gabe, the frozen clutch her body held walking on eggshells around him, and she found the memory spurred her on. The side of Sybilla that would later be described as shrewd and hard-nosed began to emerge. She consciously sought to re-invent herself from who she was raised to be. And certainly beyond the one who obediently followed Gabe's lead on their cross-country odyssey, intermittently opening up to the wonders she experienced and contracting when faced with uncertainty.

At night, after she tucked PJ into sleep, Sybilla would sit outside and stare into the desert at its ghostly shapes, her eyes not searching for Gabe as they'd done so many times, but allowing the desert to open a vast inner landscape. Then she'd raise her gaze to the inky sky and find stars winking a message of inspiration. This ritual became her practice, a source of strength. She contemplated the woman she wanted to become and viewed that person as her opposite. She would be, Sybilla decided, someone who was fearless and lived by her passion, whose work was respected and life meaningful—and began the process of stepping into that potential. She kept the vision to herself—held it close—away from others who would think it romantically unrealistic and lofty. But who did she have to tell anyway? She'd cut off her family without regrets and had made no close friends. Gabe was gone, and he was the one who would have understood. But then it was quite likely because he'd vanished without a trace that her determination was showing itself, having been there all along—waiting patiently.

Sybilla was touched, not by ambition, but by the thought of making a difference. She paid attention when Gabe had spoken of glorious things he saw in his travels, and the worst injustices. She'd heard Doña

Flora when she bemoaned the plight of her people and what was being done to their land in the name of progress, really just plain greed. Sybilla wanted to document such things, wake people up, show them what's important. Just like she was awakened when Gabe came into her life. She did thank him silently for that but didn't dwell too much on the important role he'd played, aside from being PJ's father. If she did, then the worry she'd roughly cast aside would cozy up to her and find a tight companion, and the hollow feeling she'd tucked into a hidden pocket would discover a way out. So she busied herself instead with how to provide for PJ and, at the same time, live up to her vision. Sybilla found it a challenge to juggle everything and give PJ the care he needed. At the end of most days she just felt exhausted, until she could take a breath of the night sky to fortify herself for the next day.

Sybilla began to consciously shed the Georgia inflections in her speaking patterns. She mused that being seen as a stereotypical Southern belle would do nothing to help her career goals. She wasn't able to do anything about her striking patrician features or petite frame. She supposed her green eyes to be an asset in any world, unless she wanted to go unnoticed. Just as Sybilla was undergoing a metamorphosis so was the face of Mother Lode. Long the home of artisans, a smattering of Native people, and a plethora of off-beat characters who fit in nowhere else, a well-read national magazine had run a story on the small town in the desert. They called it a mecca for artists and new thinkers—the "Village" of the Southwest, likening it to the one in New York City. Opportunists opened galleries, quick to see an advantage. Trendy cafes sprung up which, in turn, attracted curiosity seekers from out of town—and people with means who bought art. Some of those visitors stayed and took up residence. The locals grumbled about interlopers but found they prospered in the wake of the intrusion. Sybilla was one of them.

After spending long hours poring over hundreds of black and white images she'd shot over the last few years, she selected the most expressive for her portfolio. It took but a few inquiries to get accepted at a small tasteful gallery just off the main street, an area becoming known as the arts district. Sybilla felt she'd fallen into a wellspring after learning the owner also had two larger galleries. If she sold well in Mother Lode, then she was promised placement in Tucson and Santa Fe. Investing some of her dwindling funds in mats and simple frames, she also wrote prose, a short tale for each image, sensing people would be more likely to take her work home if they connected with it. She convinced the gallery owner to display the descriptive passage beside each piece. Her intuition served her well.

A part-time job opened at the town newspaper, and Sybilla wrangled for the post. She took it on, seeing the chance to dip her toe, somewhat safely, into the waters she sought as her lifework. Her task was to write a weekly human-interest column and to shoot any accompanying photographs. She wrote about the old-timer who lived half the year on the edge of town; the rest of the time he vanished into the Bradshaw Mountains to live alone in a tent and pan for gold. He wouldn't say where his claims were. Then there was the couple with a rescue sanctuary for burros, and a dowser who was known to have a sixth sense about finding water sources in dry land, as well as lost objects. Between penning the column and keeping the galleries stocked, Sybilla found that, while she wasn't getting rich, she was able to eke out a living. When she stopped to exhale, she looked back with satisfaction to see how far she'd come from the girl she'd been. Small successes built upon each other. And before she realized it a year had passed since Gabe had gone.

Sybilla didn't feel successful where PJ was concerned though. She was lucky she could work at home. Even so, she was guilt ridden about not spending more time with him. There was always some deadline. I'm doing all I can, she told herself. And he's such a quiet child and has his own inner world. One day she recognized just how much PJ had started resembling Gabe, had taken on some of his mannerisms, and it gave her painful pause. Why he looks just what Gabe must have at his age! There were times when he gazed so intensely at her with those ice-blue eyes that her breath would catch; she'd see Gabe all over again. How was it that her child could see into her soul? More than once she'd take a break to check on him and find him talking to thin air, immersed in a conversation—and she worried. She knew that lonely children made up playmates. Soon, he would enter pre-school, but Sybilla didn't anticipate things would change. PJ already shied away from the neighborhood kids. The only person he lit up for was Doña Flora who still came by regularly. Truth be told, Doña Flora was the only person Sybilla felt close to. Over the last months she'd become family, providing a sounding board and childcare that was increasingly needed. It was she who Sybilla consulted about her son.

One morning Doña Flora stopped by with fresh tamales, the comfort food PJ craved on a weekly basis. He grabbed one on his way out to play. Sybilla brought coffee over to the kitchen table and watched her load it up with sugar. Sybilla liked her own coffee strong and black. She learned to provide a sugar bowl and a little pitcher of water for her guest, so that she could dilute it to her liking.

Stirring thoughtfully, Doña Flora gazed silently at the dark liquid. Sybilla joined her in silence, sipping her coffee, watching PJ sitting on the ground out where Gabe's sanctuary used to be. He was gesturing into the air. When the midwife finally raised her eyes, they were filled with sadness.

"What's wrong, Doña Flora?" Sybilla couldn't bring herself to drop the title of respect, even though her friend had asked her months ago.

"I have very bad news from my home. Many bad things are happening," she went on, shaking her head slowly, "I say these things can't be true. They are supposed to end with this new government in my country since five years ago. There are too many stories coming!"

Sybilla urged her on with a dip of her head. She knew that Doña Flora fled from the Guatemala highlands in the mid-1980s with some family members after government soldiers cut a swathe through Maya villages, massacring large numbers. She was particularly marked due to her status in the village as a healer and midwife; her safety was in peril, even though she went underground while still in the region. Fortunately, Doña Flora had a cousin who emigrated some years prior, eventually settling in Arizona and becoming a citizen. He sponsored her when she sought political asylum for herself and the few family members who accompanied her.

"I got a letter from my sister. A month it takes to get here! And she say that a spiritual leader in the next village is killed! That some men come in the night and drag him from his home! So terrible I cannot tell you! I know this old man," tears came into her eyes, "He is a good, kind man and healed many people. He helped my father when even my mother could not help. And it is said that three healers are missing from other places not so far from there! People are scared in their own homes, my sister say. People think it is either the government or the new church that is coming into these areas! Maybe they are the same people. Ah, you see that these spiritual leaders, these healers, have the trust of the people, powers that those bad ones want. What can I do? I am here."

Sybilla felt the weight of Doña Flora's distress. It certainly put her own concerns in perspective considering what she just heard. When she opened the door to Doña Flora, she'd felt relief and had planned to speak to her about PJ. He said Gabe was appearing to him in his dreams. And she'd experienced odd occurrences herself that she couldn't explain. Several times she'd heard Gabe's voice, unintelligible snatches rising slightly above the wind, or humming along just above the music from the radio. It was easy enough to dismiss as her imagination, except it was happening too frequently. Then there was PJ and his nighttime stories. But after hearing Doña Flora's news from her homeland, she decided to raise her worries another time.

"And you know there are other things. In the north they are logging the rainforest and these people go in and look for oil. I think these are greedy people. They don't think what they are doing to the Mother Earth, to the world. How can they not know? The animals and birds are disappearing! The trees and plants are gone! So many medicines come from these! All these things make me sad. I ask always, what can I do?" Doña Flora ended her monologue, not conceding defeat, but entreating the forces that guide her for answers.

A possibility popped into Sybilla's head. But it seemed so insignificant she hesitated to voice it, especially since it could appear self-serving in the face of Doña Flora's anguish. Such subject matter was exactly the kind of topic Sybilla hoped to cover on a regular basis, not to say she didn't appreciate the human-interest stories she pursued. She just wanted more dramatic ones. Her most secret self held up Rachel Carson and Margaret Bourke-White as role models. She intended to put herself in places where she could pull off exposés, be on the front lines—eventually anyway—and catapult change.

"I have an idea," Sybilla offered haltingly, "Why don't I write a column on you and how you came to be here, how some of these things are still going on? More people need to know these things are happening. I didn't know until you told me your story. It could be a human rights and environmental piece."

Doña Flora raised her eyebrows, then broke into a broad smile. "Yes, this is a thing we will do."

Sybilla's excitement knew no bounds. Somehow she sensed this was her break. She overrode a gnawing doubt. How was she going to convince Mr. Devry, her editor, to run this story? She didn't have license to include any political statements in her column or do any hard reporting.

— Chapter Nineteen —

SYBILLA DECIDED THE best tack to take with Mr. Devry was to focus on Doña Flora's midwifery skills and how she had adapted to living in the US, so different from her homeland. That way she could still weave in some copy about circumstances that had caused Doña Flora to come to Mother Lode. If she was clever enough she could leave readers with an understanding, if not an outright call for action, toward the horrific situation in Guatemala, between the words, and couldn't be chastised for being too "progressive"—or worse yet, have the article yanked before it saw print. The region's mores in 1996 were still backward in as many ways as they were forward thinking. Not nearly as bad as Johns's Wake though, Sybilla noted. Still, she was learning to walk the line between the two factions. At least for now, she promised herself.

She was a couple of weeks ahead in her column submissions. So she had the luxury of taking more time than usual interviewing Doña Flora. They agreed that Sybilla would come to the midwife's home to gain a flavor of how she lived. Although she'd been invited before, Sybilla hadn't accepted. Too much to do, she always told herself. But the truth was that she was uncomfortable out of her own environment, around people so different than she was. She was secretly ashamed. She hadn't yet been able to shake her upbringing. But now she pushed herself, having good reason to step outside her comfort zone.

Doña Flora lived on the far edge of town in a neat adobe with her husband and their daughter's family. As Sybilla approached, children played with noisy abandon in the front yard, and the family dogs all began barking. Putting her hand on the gate, she smiled tentatively at them. A young girl scooted inside calling, "*Abuelita!*"

Her friend emerged through the door, wiping her hands on a towel. "Ah yes! Come! Welcome to my home. Here are my grandchildren. Maria, Alberto and this little one we call Grillo because like a cricket he jumps a lot." They all stared inquisitively at Sybilla with huge brown eyes, then immediately resumed their boisterous game. No shyness there, Sybilla noted.

Doña Flora ushered her inside where it was comfortably cool, thick walls providing a natural buffer from the scorching heat outside. "Everyone is at work and the children will play outside. So we will have our time just as we like. Maybe you like some lemonade? I make it fresh. We have our lemon tree in the back."

Sybilla settled herself on a wide couch and noted her surroundings, while Doña Flora went to get refreshments. The room had a comfortable lived-in feeling, equally as neat inside as outside despite the young ones living there. Against one wall there was an elaborate altar with candles and religious statues. A sole flame was lit. Icons hung on the wall above. A few small bowls containing items she couldn't see sat in front of the candle. She didn't want to appear too nosy, so pushed aside the desire to inspect the contents close-up. Her host returned carrying a small tray with two glasses of lemonade and a plate with small cakes that she set on a low table in front of Sybilla.

"I think you will like to try this cake. It's traditional in my country. The children especially like it!"

Sybilla took a bite of the sticky, moist cake and could see why. "Delicious!" she proclaimed. "I'm really anxious to get started. I think this will be an interesting article. Not the usual thing the paper publishes. And I hope we can bring some things to light. Is it okay to record?" She removed her notebook and a small recorder from the bag she carried.

"No problem for me if you want to record." Doña Flora sat in a well-used loveseat a few feet away.

After Sybilla set the device up on the table between them, she took a big breath and realized her heart was racing, just like when she'd interviewed for her first article. Maybe it's because this piece is so important, she thought.

Doña Flora smiled affectionately at her. "We are just friends talking."

"Yes, of course." Sybilla relaxed a bit and picked up her tablet, scrutinizing the notes she'd jotted down over the last week. "Why don't we start with how you came to be a midwife?"

"This is perfect for me," Doña Flora leaned back and settled in to tell the story. Gazing down at her lap, she silently smoothed her skirts, perhaps brushing aside the present. Finally she looked up, nodding to Sybilla but rested her eyes at a point just beyond, one through which she saw the past.

"My mother and grandmother were midwives in my village. As far back as I knew there was one or two in each generation of my mother's family who had the calling, and received special ways of healing and Sight. This is the way it is given. It's not only for the women to have the gifts. Men can have them, too, coming through their mother's ancestors. They don't do the childbirth healing just for women, but they can have the way of speaking to the gods and ancestors. This they can do. And the people will come to them for their powers when they want help.

"But my mother had eight children and I was the seventh one. She never talked to me about this possibility and I did not think it was for me either. And my grandmother had ten children. So there were many others and a boy cousin already received the visions very early. Such a calling is from the gods. No one just decides. When it comes there is much responsibility, much work. I saw this for my mother and my grandmother. They were away from home to care for other families and long times in prayer to prepare. It was sometimes hard for them and my father and grandfather, too. When the signs come that person must say 'yes' or there will be sickness and accidents." Doña Flora took a long drink of lemonade.

Sybilla's eyes rounded and her mouth hung open as Doña Flora warmed to her subject. An innocent opening question had taken her into totally unanticipated territory. Now how in the world am I going to write about this? This stuff will never go over with Mr. Devry! Once again Sybilla's heart was thumping. Do you want to take a risk or not?

"Uh, tell me what you mean about 'sickness' and 'accidents,'" Her eyebrows knitted.

"Well, you see, in the ways of my people the gods send this invitation. But I think this is so for everyone. The gods send something, maybe it brings alive something that has been asleep inside, a thing that came

100

through from the Other Side at birth. And the person must know it and serve this calling. If they deny it, then there is a wound."

Sybilla nodded slowly. She understood what Doña Flora said with regard to herself. Something had opened inside her. It wasn't ambition that compelled her to work long hours, but something holy that she couldn't put into words—her innermost expression bursting to be known, in a way that somehow, to someone, would make a difference in the world. At the stillest point in the night, when the noise of the day no longer held back the worried voices in her head, the ones that questioned what she was doing, and why she didn't scuttle back home to Georgia, she found the strength to soothe herself and send a promise up, like a prayer, to remain true to this element she so recently discovered—one that had no words. If she didn't, then she knew she'd wither away inside, even if, from the outside, her shell looked basically the same.

"My people know this to be true in a way that they don't know it here," Doña Flora paused for effect, "Yes, there was a woman in the next village who received the dreams, but it is said that her husband had no respect. He treated her badly and wouldn't allow her to help when women came to her. She got sick with terrible pains and nightmares. But the doctor at the clinic there in the village could find nothing wrong. Finally, she went to the *curandero*, what you would call a curer or shaman. He told her that she would die if she didn't serve the people like the gods wanted. Still she didn't do it because her husband wouldn't let her. She was afraid—and her illness got worse. Then one night she had a dream that she must take all her children and go visit her sister in the next village. The dream was so strong that she did it. The night after she went to her sister's, the husband said the dogs woke him up barking outside. And when he woke up, his bed was on fire! He said his wife's grandmother was standing in the doorway with a torch. But this was not possible because the grandmother had gone to the ancestors years before! He put the fire out, but it scared him so bad that he left the village and never came back. The people didn't like him anyway, you see. When his wife returned with the children, she didn't deny her gift anymore. Her sickness went away, and she helped birth many babies. I think she still does. She was better off without him anyway. He was a bad man. He had no respect. This woman's family didn't suffer because the people gave her what she needed for herself and the children. She birthed their babies. This is how it is done in the ways of my home."

Sybilla sat mute, eyes still round, which Doña Flora took as a sign to continue.

· "For me, it started like this. When I was thirteen years old I had a dream. I was walking through my village like I was going somewhere, and I needed to be there fast. But every place I passed, it wasn't the place I was supposed to be. Then suddenly the road wasn't dirt anymore. It turned into a creek, and I was floating along, being taken with the waters. But it was gentle. I wasn't afraid. I could see there were many fish in the creek swimming all around me. And still the water took me past many houses. My mother was there when I went by, and she smiled at me. I saw my grandmother, too, and other women. More and more came and stood by the banks of the creek as I floated by, until I was no longer in my village." Her eyes grew moist.

"Something woke me up then. I opened my eyes. And the room was glowing—a beautiful blue! I wanted to tell my sisters, but I saw they were asleep. And then in the corner of the room, I saw a woman in a long dress. But it was hazy, like I was seeing her underwater. Her hair was wrapped in a cloth. There was white light all around her and when she moved, this light moved. She came over to my bed right there and reached out her hand like she would touch me. And the light came from her hand, and I felt it with my whole body, like such a love came to me that I have never felt. I feel it now when I tell you this. And we stayed like that, she and I, for what seemed to be a long time. Still my sisters slept. And I knew something was happening just for me. Slowly she disappeared, and then the blue glow left. It was just the bedroom again."

Doña Flora's eyes shone, her face serene. Her body radiated, the very act of recounting her calling activated a luminescence that only became stronger with the silence she now held. Tears leapt from Sybilla's eyes but, transfixed, she didn't reach to wipe them away. After a time, Doña Flora shifted in her chair and spoke softly, "Yes, this is how it first happened."

They both reached for their drinks, breaking the spell. Sybilla took a bite of the cake, chewing thoughtfully. Not knowing what to say to this fantastic story, she said nothing but was deeply touched, even the panicky voices in her head stilled. Doña Flora looked at her, nodding slightly.

"Yes, I know. With my people it is common to have dreams that tell things. But like you right now, I didn't know what to think about this. This was a very strange dream. But the woman? She was not a dream. I kept this a secret for many years. The dream came many times after that over the next few years. Many times it was the same but sometimes a little different. Like one time the creek waters took me to a house just outside the village. When the door opened it was my mother, and she took my hands in hers and filled them with mariposa flowers. So, sometimes a little different like that. I finally told my mother but only about the dreams. She said I was being blessed, that I should go see the *curandero* about this. But I was a young girl, and I didn't do it. Then the dreams stopped."

"Do you know why they stopped?" Sybilla queried.

"You know I was a young girl, and I had things on my mind. Not these crazy dreams," Doña Flora chuckled. "When I look now, I see that I was being told something. Maybe about my future, but I wasn't ready at that age. I had many things to learn yet, and I wanted to be like any young woman! By then I was seventeen and thinking about who would be my husband."

"But that's so young!"

"Not so young to think of these things! You did that, yes? But in my home the girls do marry at that age, even younger, and begin to have babies. Some people thought something was wrong with me because I didn't hurry to be married. Well, I knew I wanted a special man, and sometimes that takes a while to find. It was important to me that this man would respect me. Even though I didn't want it then, I knew that my time would come for something, and I couldn't refuse. This much I knew from the dreams."

The children came bursting through the door sweaty from their romping and squealed when they spied the cakes. Doña Flora laughed.

"Not so much now! Just a little bit. We will have dinner soon! Your mama will be home."

Sybilla glanced up at the clock, shocked. The afternoon had flown by. She began to gather up her things, remembering she had to pick up PJ from her neighbor Sonya Whitehead, who'd said she'd watch him. "I didn't realize it had gotten so late! We covered so much ground. Thank you so much for these stories. But there's more, isn't there?"

"Ah, dear one. You are very welcome. Yes, there is much more. And next time you bring PJ. He will play with my grandchildren."

They made arrangements for Sybilla to return in two days. She smiled brightly at the children who were beaming at her, crumbs on their faces, and stepped out into the late afternoon sun. She was bursting with excitement and couldn't wait to get home to listen to the recording. Although, she wasn't at all sure yet how to write the article for her column's readership—given what Doña Flora had shared with her. Getting into her car, she began to mull over that bit of a nut.

SYBILLA AND PJ arrived mid-morning at Doña Flora's home in the softer heat of the summer day and found her finishing up the breakfast dishes. The children greeted them both with delighted cries, and PJ crowed as they swarmed over him like happy puppies. Sybilla had to admit she felt welcomed as a member of the best kind of family. She soaked up the warmth from the exuberant acknowledgment and couldn't help compare how different they were to her own kinfolk. PJ joined right in like he belonged in this brood, Sybilla noted with some relief, never having seen him do so with such abandon. He hadn't found his place amongst the children in their own neighborhood. It's good for him to spend time here, she thought, setting aside any previous uncertainties about leaving him at Doña Flora's home for childcare instead of having her come to theirs.

"Okay, dear ones. It's time to leave us and go play," the midwife shooed them out good-naturedly. The boys dashed out chattering, while Maria put her hand in PJ's. Like an older sister, she led him outside.

"They must be a handful! And I'm amazed how you can keep everything in place. I've only got PJ, and I can't do it."

"They are my heart, these precious ones. It was not so easy for my daughter to have these. We prayed a lot, and she took the herbs. So we have been blessed."

Sybilla took up her previous position, setting up her equipment as before. The sole candle on the altar was still lit. She made a mental note to ask about it later. Doña Flora swept into the room carrying a tray. Sybilla suppressed a smile when she saw two small pitchers, one with coffee "mud," as her friend called it, and one with hot water. Her friend had remembered her preference. They poured and stirred to their own taste, Sybilla's being without any additives.

"I have so many questions. What you've shared with me is rich, and I know there's more. I'm wondering about some things in general." Doña Flora nodded encouragement.

Glancing down at her notes Sybilla asked, "How common is it for your people to have the calling you spoke of—healing? I mean are there many healers in the villages like there are many doctors here?"

"No, it is a bit different. Your doctors go to the university. There are many of them, and they decide to do it. In my culture, there are not so many *Indígena* healers and maybe not one in each village. So the people may have to go farther. Although, these healers may have special skills they are given, just like a doctor goes to school to learn a certain thing. So some talk to the ancestors, or help with the babies and work with herbs or the sweat bath, like I said. But there are others who just set bones, heal through singing rituals, or other ways like this. The big thing though is that they all have the dreams and visions that bring them. And this is how they learn to do their work, too."

"What? There's no school?" Sybilla was incredulous.

"It is a school," Doña Flora smiled. "But not how you think about it. I think maybe I'll continue with my story and you'll see."

"That would be good. Last time you said the dreams ended when you were seventeen," Sybilla prompted her.

"Yes, well, they did not end exactly. They took a long pause for some years. And in this time I found my husband. His name is Xun but now he goes by John because it's easier for the people here to understand. He was from another village, a few years older than me, and his wife died in childbirth a couple of years before with the first child. The child died, too. We met at the house of my aunt when he was visiting my cousin Eduardo. When I saw him, I knew he was for me! After that he came to my home many times to see me. He didn't think I was too old, even though I was twenty. I didn't tell him then about The Lady because I told no one still. But I decided to tell him about the dreams I had when I was younger. It must be fair for him because I thought he would ask my parents soon if we could marry. He is a special man. He understood that the dreams were special. He agreed that we could live at my parent's house instead of his. This is what I wanted because I thought it was important for me to stay close to my mother and grandmother. So we did live there for a while until our babies began to come. Xun built us a home close by because it was already crowded in my family home. So I was a married lady and now a mother with three babies that my mother delivered from me. And the dreams returned. I was twenty-nine, and my daughter and sons were not babies any more. I was glad of this because I knew that if the dreams came again like this I must soon accept. But first, there was more that came.

"One time in my dream there was a stone that jumped into my hands. Now when I looked at this stone it was ordinary, but when I turned it over there was a raised line like a snake. I could see that it was the umbilical cord that came from the stone like a placenta. All of this in my dream. In the next day I had to wash the clothes at the river. I was scrubbing the clothes on a big rock and there was a song that came softly on the breeze. But there was no one around, and somehow I knew the song from somewhere. But I couldn't remember, and it was puzzling to me. Then when I turned to rinse the clothes in the river, I saw something shining very bright in the water even though it was a cloudy day. I reached my hand in and felt a hard thing stuck in the mud. I pulled it out, and it was just a muddy rock. But I washed the mud off—and I could see that it was the smooth placenta stone of my dreams! It had the umbilical cord, too! And I heard that song. It came from this stone! Then I remembered, too, that I heard this song in my dream."

Sybilla gasped, "No! How is that possible?"

"Well, these things do happen," Doña Flora nodded sagely, "I couldn't understand the words of the song. I'm not sure they were words. Or, if they were, it was to a language lost to us."

Doña Flora got up and went over to the altar. Gently she picked up a small wrapped bundle and, returning, placed it on the low table between them. Taking her time, she carefully pulled away the cloth, simultaneously whispering prayers in her native tongue, to reveal a stone nestled in pine needles and resin pieces of some sort.

Sybilla leaned over to take a closer look, which generated a sharp intake of breath—and the hair along her arms and the back of her neck raised. The stone emitted an inaudible vibration that she caught, just as a deaf ear may recognize music. And yes, there was something like a snake ridged along its top. She sat back abruptly. There's no way she was going to touch it!

Sybilla had no reason to believe that Doña Flora was telling anything other than the truth; she'd always displayed complete integrity. Sybilla's own personal beliefs about the ways of the world had been stretched thin before by what she'd experienced with Gabe. With the contents of Doña Flora's tale and the object that sat in front of her now, the membrane that held her convictions together was being systematically perforated. Sybilla was ungrounded.

Doña Flora reverently re-wrapped the stone, returning it to its place on the altar. And Sybilla got up and took a bathroom break. The niggling voices that worried about how to present this information in a mainstream article got louder. But she silently shushed them, because by now Sybilla was equally enthralled and morbidly repelled by the material, just wanting to hear it all. I'll worry about all that later, she thought, exiting the bathroom.

"Shall I continue?" Doña asked.

"Yes, of course," Sybilla attempted to erase any skepticism from her features.

"One day my mother sent me to a certain place on the mountain near our home to collect an herb that she uses. I was busy looking when the placenta stone begins to sing in my pocket. After it came to me, I always carried it with me, you see. This stone is singing the prayer that we say when we purify ourselves at the sacred lagoon near where I was hunting the herb. I understood the singing even though it isn't the way you think about singing out loud. And I knew the message of the stone is that I must go to the lagoon. So I did. I was washing the water over my face and hair when the stone sang very loudly. And when I looked up The Lady was there! She was moving across the top of the water to me from the other side! Just like before, she stopped close to me and reached out to me. But this time she filled my hands with mariposas and closed them like in prayer! Her light came to me and wrapped me in this great love! I felt so much gratitude that I couldn't say anything. And then I couldn't see her anymore, but the feeling stayed. It's still here—always for me to call on. This is what guides me every day in my life," Doña Flora whispered the last bit, then sighed deeply before going on.

"I am sharing with you that this was the calling I knew would come. It was my time to accept, but I wanted to be sure. So I went to the same seer who told my mother about herself. He was very old then, maybe almost one hundred, when I saw him. Even he wasn't sure how old. I cannot tell you how he did the ritual for me because that's a secret in our religion. We don't talk about these things. But he said that, yes, The Lady had touched me, and it was now the time for me to take on the responsibilities of the midwife. This is a most sacred thing in my tradition, to help the women and communicate with the gods who send the babies to be born. And this thread with a midwife and the babies she helped to bring? It stays all her life.

"Now this old man tells me that I must pay attention. There were things that would be put in my way that were for me to learn how to do what I must. And that when I was to deliver the first baby, I would be told. And he was right. My dreams began to show me how my work would be, ways to let the gods and ancestors guide me, how to talk to the unborn child. I was shown the herbs to gather, when to collect them and how I would use them. The prayers to say were placed in my soul. Yes, I knew something of this from my mother and grandmother. But through my dreams it was complete.

"This happened over several months. Then one day I went to collect water from the river. I was walking on the path and the stone started to sing loudly like it wanted my attention. So just like when The Lady appeared, I knew to look around carefully. There just on the side of the path, almost hidden by grass was a small knife. I picked this knife up and saw that it was one that is used by midwives to cut the umbilical cord! That's how I knew it was time for me to deliver my first baby. I put the knife in my pocket with the placenta stone. Then I went home and told my mother and grandmother. They were sitting at the table waiting. Later, they told me they knew it was my time. That's when they told me that a young woman had come to them asking for me a few weeks before. This woman said she had a dream that I was to deliver her first baby, even though she wasn't pregnant yet. They had waited to tell me until I had the sign. That's how it happened. In a month this young woman was pregnant. I have delivered many, many babies since that time thirty years ago. Your PJ, too, of course," her friend smiled fondly at her.

"That's just a wonderful story! Is that the way it always happens for a midwife?" Sybilla chose her words carefully.

"If she is a traditional *indígena*, then yes, something like this. But if the woman let her ways go or she is *ladina*, then she may not be able to hear it. She may just get a feeling and go train at a clinic in the city. But this is more like a nurse in the Western way."

Sybilla realized then she hadn't questioned Gabe at all when he brought Doña Flora to her. She'd assumed she had bona fide medical training! She was horrified now. It appeared that she'd put the welfare of her baby in the hands of someone who did not! She couldn't write an article about a charlatan except as a warning to others! She attempted to hide the slow burn of anger forming against Gabe's foolishness, and her own, by clearing her throat. "But what happened when you came to this country? Because you deliver babies here. Surely you must have taken clinical training?"

Doña Flora recognized in the reddening of Sybilla's face that she was mightily upset. "Dear one, you must know that I did everything I needed to do to make it legal here. When I came I looked to see. Here it is possible to go to a school or apprentice with a midwife. So even though I delivered babies at home for many years, I did this apprenticeship to make it acceptable in this state. Her name was Anne Owens and she was a good woman. We became good friends. She's gone now but sent people to me if they were open to my ways of tending. She had traveled in Central America and knew about our ways. We had respect for each other. We did what we needed to do so I would be accepted here."

"I see. That's good to know then," Sybilla was visibly relieved. Her article wasn't in jeopardy, although she still chastised herself for not doing more checking before her own delivery. "I noticed your altar over there. What can you tell me about it? And that there's one candle lit? Is that usual?"

"Yes, we have this altar to remember our connections. It is a common thing in our households. But that one candle we have lit as a vigil for our people at home for what they go through and, too, for the spiritual leaders that have been killed in these last months."

Sybilla reviewed with Doña Flora the areas they had discussed weeks before: the atrocities against local healers, the dangers her people faced from the government, the influx of aggressive religions, and the crimes in the rainforest against the whole world by the oil and logging companies.

Sybilla snapped her notebook shut with satisfaction and patted the recorder. "I think I've got plenty of material. I can't wait to start writing!"

"I'm glad for that. Now, why not some lunch before you go?" The midwife went to call the children.

— Chapter Twenty-one —

SYBILLA SAT BACK, satisfied. She'd scrutinized her finished column not able to find anything that Mr. Devry could redline. Setting aside all the really juicy contents of her interview with Doña Flora, Sybilla was confident that she still got the crux of her subject matter across, albeit with much skimmed off the top. That way, too, she was testing the waters. Maybe she could do similar pieces, surreptitiously introducing something controversial, planting a seed. If this one flies, then it opens a door for something much more exciting, she thought happily. Besides, Sybilla knew that some of what Doña Flora told her was for her ears only, like The Lady, and she was honored with that trust. So instead she wrote that Doña Flora came from a long line of midwives and that it was common in her tradition for people in her role to dream about it. But she left out the dreams themselves, and certainly the visions. She told, in general terms, why Doña Flora had come to Mother Lode and how some of those same dangers still existed in her homeland. Sybilla ended very tidily by citing the number of babies she'd birthed and her legal certification, noting that Doña Flora had delivered her own child PJ—for that added bit of human interest. Sybilla held her breath and pressed send, emailing it off to her editor. The next morning a return message waited in her inbox. Mr. Devry had made only a few minor changes and blessed it for the next week's column. Exuberant, Sybilla popped from her chair and, arms thrust overhead, did a twirl. Yes! She'd flown beneath his radar.

The article had been out a few days when she dropped by Doña Flora's again with PJ. By then it had generated a number of positive letters to the editor and only one that Sybilla couldn't even consider derogatory. Somehow the piece had gained attention outside the local area, the missive was from the president of the Nurse-Midwives Association in Phoenix cautioning against untrained midwives, which had nothing to do with Doña Flora. Sybilla had covered herself there.

"You know I have received some calls? I have three new ones that their babies are coming," Doña Flora nodded approvingly. "And, too, some people even outside the state that come from my homeland. They said their relatives here sent this article from the Internet. They tell me about their families in Guatemala and the hard times. This saddens me. I am here. What can I do? They are there. What can they do? But we make this connection and can pray together. Sometimes I think this is not enough." Doña Flora was silent in her reflection. Sybilla didn't know what to say and so sipped her coffee. But an idea was forming.

Over the next weeks Sybilla did her research online. She was looking for just the right periodical or magazine: one that published about cultural integrity but didn't avoid the politics that may accompany it, one not too obscure that had a good, even somewhat mainstream, readership. When she took an outing to the local mega-bookstore and surveyed the racks of journals, she knew she had it—*Thrive: A Journal for the Planet and Her People*. Its publication offices were located in nearby Phoenix. Flipping through, she remembered there was an old issue at home, tucked away in a pile of possibilities when she was ready. I'm ready now, she thought. Carrying her newly purchased copy, Sybilla went home, not wasting any time.

She'd already written a draft query message, which included a link to her column on Doña Flora. Now that she'd chosen the journal, she made sure to include key attractors she'd gleaned from the contents of the editor's own magazine, intending to gain at least some interest if not a full foothold. She proposed to write an in-depth article using material she had not used, offered some teasers and threw in her professional photography experience. To have photos published, too? That would be a dream come true. After letting the final version of the query sit overnight, Sybilla examined it one more time. The deep breath had worked last time. She repeated the ritual and hit the send button, then took up the excruciating wait. The submission guidelines said one to three months.

But two weeks later she received an answer: *Call me. I'd like to talk to you about your proposal.* It was signed: Jay Turner. His address block included the title Editor-in-Chief. Sybilla's heart was in her throat.

— Chapter Twenty-two –

THE ARTICLE SYBILLA wrote for *Thrive* honored Doña Flora's natural gift and traditions, and exposed the dangers to spiritual leaders in her country in such a way that there was an outpouring from the readers. For months afterward, she still received fan mail forwarded to her. It turned out that she'd chosen the magazine wisely. She later discovered that Jay Turner, an environmentalist and supporter of Native traditions who had cavernous pockets, was not only the editor-in-chief but owned the publication. He wasn't afraid to be controversial and took a hands-on approach when it came to *Thrive*. When he personally offered Sybilla a place in his stable of writers, she was giddy and thought it a fluke but certainly didn't turn it down. The night of his offer she took up her ritual position under the sky after she'd gotten PJ off to sleep. She swore the stars were winking particularly bright, affirming her place in the world. For the first time, she had a real sense of what lay in front of her, the task she'd chosen, what that could mean—and how complex her life might be. How would she accomplish it all? Could she?

In the midst of excitement about her own future, she was worried about her friend Flora. Yes, after all they'd done together, she'd finally felt comfortable dropping the title of respect even with the vast age difference between them. A couple of months after the article was out on the street, Flora and her husband made the decision to return to her home village. Flora had said she just couldn't stand by any longer. She must go home to her family and people. One brilliant Mother Lode morning, they shared a tearful farewell at the midwife's home. PJ was especially upset. Even though Flora plied him with one of the sticky cakes he loved, he hung on her skirts, inconsolable.

"Just like my daddy! You're leaving!"

Flora knelt down in front of him and held his hands, "Ah no, little one. You know even if you don't see me all the time, just like your daddy, I love you and I'm with you. Now you know this." She held him close. When Sybilla and PJ were leaving, Flora hugged Sybilla tightly and spoke softly in her ear. "You will do well, my friend. You remember your son and his gifts. There will come a time when he needs teaching by one who knows about these things. I am sorry I cannot be here to do it. But there will be one who comes."

Emotions welled up for Sybilla: guilt, loss, worry. "Flora, your friendship has meant so much to me. You've been so kind to us both and to Gabe when he was here. And I'm afraid that I may have put you in danger by writing about you!"

"My friend Sybilla, we all take a road we must. I have been praying for many months, you know. I feel this protection. And there are no worries for your writing! Who from my country would have seen it? You take care of yourself and your boy. The Lady is with me always," Flora finished softly.

After Sybilla returned home with PJ, she made herself some coffee then sat at the kitchen table. She re-imagined the countless times she'd sat there with Flora, she with her coffee so strong she could chew it, hers watered down and sugary the way she liked it, discussing the mysteries of the last few years, parenting PJ or even such everyday things as what to plant in the garden. Where would she again find such warmth and solace? She felt just as bereft as PJ. In the moment, only her writing and potential future in that realm offered any comfort.

— Chapter Twenty-three —

AT JAY'S SUGGESTION, Sybilla began to research logging in the rainforests of Mexico and Guatemala. Yes, they were on first name basis. Jay had seen promise in her and taken her under his wing, providing shelter in the sometime cutthroat business of publishing. His idea was that, for the time being, she would maintain a focus on threats to Native lands and peoples, it being smart to hone her skills in one area of interest before becoming a generalist. Her instructions were to formulate an in-depth article that conveyed a broad understanding of the issues but also personalize it enough that their readership would gain a stake in what happened in a faraway land. She was to insert the effect on a particular village or even a family unit.

Sybilla was overwhelmed. She couldn't understand Jay's confidence in her. She was such a rookie. It was one thing to interview people she knew or dig up local characters, another thing entirely to ferret out some focal point of interest in a land two thousand miles away, most of the places she'd never heard of and certainly hadn't been! But she hadn't wanted to disappoint her benefactor, particularly not this early. So she spent time first perusing the archives of environmental publications to familiarize herself with the logging operations going on down south: the effect on the ecosystem, trespass on indigenous lands and the corporations involved. She needed to understand the overall issues. Her article would cover more than the cursory mention she'd given the problem in her piece on Doña Flora.

Her bedroom now doubled as her office. She wasn't very good about keeping work and home separate; toiling in the corner of the living room in their small house became unmanageable with all PJ's things littering the floor and hers, too. Research material and notes, already including spin-off ideas, gave birth to other stacks until it looked like there had been a population explosion. The visual mess finally got in the way of her thought process. So Sybilla took one weekend and set about organizing. Moving the small worktable to her bedroom, she placed it in front of the window. From there she could envision herself gazing out into the desert landscape, allowing it to deliver to her just the right language she needed to illustrate her subject. Pushing aside her clothing, Sybilla turned half her matchbox-sized closet into a filing system using labeled milk crates. Not pretty, she thought. But I know where everything is, and the living room is relatively clear. She kept the sliding closet door open when she worked to let her know she had what she needed at her fingertips, and it gave her assurance. The isolation worked for her, and she could still cock an ear to listen for PJ, often playing alone elsewhere in the house.

One night, long after PJ was sound asleep, she was at her computer. She stared at the screen, immersed in what she had found, not noticing that time had passed. Her face was bathed in its eerie glow, the only light in the otherwise dark house. Sybilla kept promising herself she'd stop and go to bed, but her research had taken her on an unending hypnotic trail from one web page to another. Now something of great interest caught her eye. It was a scholarly entry from the 1970s talking about the interlacing rainforest waterways that emptied into the Usumacinta River that served as a natural border between a good portion of southern Mexico and northern Guatemala. The photograph that accompanied it did well in capturing dense growth rising high toward a bright cerulean sky with wide majestic waters cutting a swath through the middle.

Breathtaking, Sybilla noted. A thought niggled at the back of her mind, something Flora said that was eluding her. She continued reading. The author avowed that, even as early as the late 1870s, large logging companies started extracting valuable hardwoods from the area, floating them down these jungle channels to the Usumacinta River and on to large settlements. From there the destination was foreign markets. There was mention of an unusual-looking tribe that made the deepest recesses of the forest their home, thick humid places no one else would go full of jaguars and the most poisonous snake in the world, the fer-de-lance. Ghostly looking natives would step out of trees onto the riverbanks as loggers went by offering to trade monkey meat, tobacco, bows and arrows in return for tools, salt and cloth, then fade back into the mists as though they'd never existed at all. Their language was indiscernible and the loggers were frankly scared of them. There were rumors of cannibalism they'd picked up from other natives downriver. The writer said that encounters with the lumbermen were disastrous for these Native people they called the Stone Worshippers. Exposed to foreign diseases, increasingly when they did show up to trade, there was evidence of illness among them. Then they ceased making an appearance at all, causing the foreigners to think either they'd died out, or retreated even deeper into the miasma of time. For nearly forty years they weren't seen—until five of them were displayed like animals in 1938 at the National Fair of Guatemala held in Guatemala City. It said the men were kidnapped from the jungle and brought in cages. The article ran on to discuss devastating changes and deforestation as a result of the logging over the years.

But only one thing any longer held Sybilla's interest. Frowning, she leaned in. The National Fair of Guatemala held a link. She clicked it. As the page began to load an image appeared, and the breath left her body. She felt faint and sat back, shaking her head in disbelief. The age-stained photo marked 1938 showed five figures with long dark hair past their shoulders wearing whitish shifts, their broad brown-skinned faces handsome to a one—and held features not unlike Gabe's.

— Chapter Twenty-four —

SYBILLA SAT STUNNED. This cannot be true, she repeated over and over in her mind. But now the elusive memory of her discussion with Flora after Gabe had disappeared surfaced and clicked into place. She'd said to Sybilla that she'd "looked" at his recurrent dream.

...I see a place and some people from the south. Hundreds of years ago such people lived in northern mountains of my country. This is thick jungle...I have heard stories that they crossed the river and left Guatemala. He receives a calling from them. He cannot refuse to answer... the white cloth he wrapped around the little one? They wear this cloth.

Sybilla obsessed over the recollection, which only served to reinforce her shock. She had summarily dismissed what her friend said at the time as a hallucination she'd somehow shared with Gabe. Now she was faced with the potential that, not only might Flora's "seeing" be real, but other more fantastic possibilities could split her world apart if true. Could Gabe have come across these same people on the Internet and incorporated them into his fantasies? Sybilla rejected that interpretation. Gabe had always prided himself about "not being seduced by technology" and had never surfed the Web to her knowledge, in fact didn't know how to operate a computer. A book? It was quite doubtful he would have found such subject matter in the Mother Lode library or their only bookstore. It was too obscure. He'd only started to have those dreams about a year after their move here.

But the final most frightening thought had to do with the white cloth. After Gabe vanished, PJ insisted on keeping it in his room draped over the back of a chair near his bed. Sybilla crept into PJ's bedroom. He was sleeping soundly. As she picked up the folded cloth from its resting place, he mumbled something she couldn't understand. Waiting a moment, she decided he was talking in his sleep. Sitting on her own bed stroking the rough material in her lap, Sybilla tried to make sense of her discovery. How could Gabe have gotten this cloth? Could it

119

somehow have made its way all the way up to one of Mother Lode's secondhand stores Gabe had occasionally dropped into? She attempted to settle herself down with this explanation. But then remembered PJ telling her about where he went with his daddy that night they'd just reappeared out of thin air in the middle of Gabe's backyard altar: *We were in a wet place and the people didn't have shoes.*

She'd passed it all off as a silly dream. Yes, but when they reappeared PJ was wrapped in this cloth! Sybilla buried her face in it. She was incredulous and a foreboding question exploded in her brain: What does this mean? If only she had Flora to consult! But that line of communication was gone.

What sleep Sybilla got was fitful. For hours she lay awake staring at the ceiling with her mind racing. Full moonlight played through her unadorned window, surreal light against shadow. Once she thought she saw movement beyond the foot of her bed in her peripheral vision and, on high alert, switched on the lamp on her nightstand. Nothing. Just the white cloth there where she left it folded at the end of the bed. Finally she must have slept. She heard Gabe's voice faintly calling her name as though from a great distance. Sybilla sat up in bed, listening. There it was again, somewhere outside. Going to the window she peered out into the silver night. The landscape began to whirl, as though she was in a tunnel whose walls began to rotate as she stood still. She felt light-headed and held her palm against the windowpane, steadying herself. Her stomach swirled in time with the landscape. Bending slightly, she took deep slow breaths. The dizziness and nausea subsided. Straightening up again, she froze. The vista was no longer sparse desert but dense, wet foliage. And there was a palm mirroring hers on the other side of the glass. Sybilla hesitantly raised her eyes to behold Gabe's calmly gazing into hers.

She awoke with a start, electrified. Just a dream, just a dream, just a dream, she gasped and turned her eyes to the window across the room. Nothing there. The silver light had dimmed; there were clouds moving in. Her breath decelerated, and she started to turn over on her side to rid herself of the nighttime images. That's when she realized she was clutching something in her hand all bunched up against her body. Feeling the familiar scratchy surface, she launched it to the far corner of the room in a panic. After a few minutes, she went over to the spot it landed and stared, shuddering. Picking it up between her thumb and forefinger, she held it away from her in distaste, marched out to the back door, yanked it open and pitched the bundle outside. I'll take care of this tomorrow, she told herself.

The next morning Sybilla arose before PJ was awake and retrieved the cloth. Touching it still gave her the willies, and she thought about throwing it out entirely. However, intuition told her it could be useful to her in the future. In the light of day she felt a little silly about her jitters. Knowing that stranger things had occurred over the past few years, she humored herself and folded it into a large shipping envelope, hiding it on a shelf in the garage behind other items. She knew where it was but didn't want the thing in the house.

However, PJ seemed to know something was amiss immediately. Later in the day, he asked Sybilla where his "Daddy blanket" was. She told him that she'd taken it to the dry cleaners when she'd run errands earlier when he was with Sonya. He looked at her doubtfully. A few days later he asked again and she told him the dry cleaners lost it.

"My daddy! My daddy!" he wailed like a lost soul, "You took my daddy from me. I want my daddy!"

He was angry with her and despairing for days. Sybilla felt wretched and guilty, but she stuck by her story, saying there was nothing she could do. She hated to admit the possibility that the cloth held some kind of power, perhaps provided a portal of some sort. Her very rational mind rejected the thought, but she couldn't explain away her own experience logically enough. She remembered PJ's stories of nighttime visitations from Gabe, the ones she'd chalked up—again—to dreams. So, in a manner she could deal with it, she'd literally shelved the issue. Sybilla assured herself that this was the best thing for PJ. Over the following weeks, she noticed his night stories of Gabe ceased. If they hadn't, despite her misgivings, the "Daddy blanket" would have magically been found. He did awaken her sometimes at night crying out. But at entering his bedroom, she'd find him still asleep.

— Chapter Twenty-five —

THE IMAGE OF Gabe's face so close, looking into her eyes, observing her, would not leave her alone. It found its way into her consciousness at unexpected times, even in the midst of her busiest moments, insistent. If she gave in and went with it for even a moment, she'd feel the coolness of the windowpane on her palm, separating them. And when that would happen, the angst of tearing loss would overtake her until she roughly thrust it back into the depths she'd placed it. More than a window that ever separated us, she told herself. She found anger an effective ally against her misery and threw herself back into her work, repeatedly.

Sybilla continued her research, finally knowing she had enough material to pen a knowledgeable article on the devastating effects that many decades' logging had on the Mexican and Guatemalan rainforests. Once one vast, life-giving organism literally creating breath for the planet's people, it had now turned into a checkerboard of cleared land, more so every day. But she was well aware she had none of the human-interest aspect that her piece must contain. She kept thinking about the insult levied upon the Stone Worshippers when they were kidnapped from their home and displayed in a sideshow all those years ago. The article stated they were especially terrified because, they'd said in very broken Spanish to their captors, that the place they'd been taken was the end of the world; the real world was made of trees that held the sky up. She also wondered what happened to those five men after the fair was over. An idea began to play at the edges of her mind. If she was able to get a modern-day angle on these people, it would make her story quite intriguing. But she may need a research assistant. She made an appointment with Jay and went into the city to pitch the story face-to-face.

Jay listened intently as Sybilla outlined the parts of her proposed article that she was able to document and the gaps she couldn't, in fact were still a mystery. When she finished he swiveled in his chair, his back to her and faced the window. From previous experience, Sybilla knew he wasn't being rude but contemplating. She'd learned that, much like her, the scene from his own office window, albeit desert mountains marred by Phoenix high rises, ushered in provocative notions. When he finally faced her, Jay leaned back, looking over steepled fingers, a slight smile playing about his lips.

"Go down there."

"What!"

"Sure, go down there. Think about it. Some of those people must still be living somewhere. Find them. Ask them about their worldview, their lives, what changes have they lived through because the trees are disappearing and the sky has fallen down. If you're not readily able to uncover something about this tribe, then this is fresh ground. Someone probably knows more, but our readers don't and neither does the wider world."

Sybilla was thunderstruck. She had only asked for a research assistant, someone Spanish-speaking who could be her go-between to make phone calls to government agencies in Guatemala, bean counters who kept track of people and maybe some in-country anthropologists whose names she had. Neither of them spoke. The silence was pregnant with potential. Sybilla attempted to quell her bubbling excitement in order to sound professional.

"I see where you're going with this. I'm just wondering how to get there," she mused out loud.

"First do what you said. You'll get your assistant and translator. How about Javier? He can make those phone calls. Give him a list. Then when you've lasered in on a location for the Stone Worshippers, go down there. Javier can accompany you as translator, assuming they speak Spanish. He's had field time unless you can think of someone else you'd want."

"No," she shook her head slowly, "He'd be ideal." Sybilla couldn't believe this was happening. This could be another huge break for her, almost unheard of for someone her age.

Be careful what you ask for, the voice in her head counseled. She didn't want to think of the complexities complicating the opportunity.

What if the Stone Worshippers *were* actually the same people who called Gabe? What would that mean? Would she stumble upon *him*? PJ! What am I going to do with PJ? She lamented once again that Flora was no longer there.

"Is anything wrong?" Jay queried.

"Of course not! I'll get right on it." Sybilla pulled herself together and left Jay's office. He looked quizzically after her.

— Chapter Twenty-six —

IT TURNED OUT she didn't need Javier as much as she thought, at least initially. He'd contacted the director of the census bureau in Guatemala City, a very nice woman who spoke English. Sybilla took over and queried her on what she knew of the 1938 national fair and the people she sought. Senora Alvarez promised to research it and get back to her.

"It was not a good moment for Guatemala that it was allowed to happen," Senora Alvarez said. "I am sorry to tell you that there is no documentation on the people you asked about or what happened to them afterwards. I don't know if the five men were freed, or if they returned to their home. You know, back then there were very few roads, if any, in parts of the jungle. So our government had no way of keeping track of people there. And there was little enforcement of the borders between my country and Mexico. People could pass freely."

Would that it was like that everywhere still, Sybilla sighed. It looked like a dead end.

"But I did come across the name of someone you might talk to if you can find him. You might call him an archeologist or anthropologist. Back then I think he was considered an adventurer more than anything. But he explored those areas in question and spent a lot of time there in the 1950s, especially at Piedras Negras. That's a Maya ruin in the north. He might know of these people. But he would be quite old now, in his 80s I think, a man from your country. His name is Davis Mitchell."

"Thank you! You've been very gracious, and I appreciate your help," Sybilla brightened. She faintly remembered that name mentioned in passing in a journal she dug through. Maybe Davis Mitchell held some clues, if he was still around, and perhaps bore more importance than it first seemed.

"*Da nada.* I hope you find what you're looking for."

That's a loaded statement, Sybilla thought as she hung up the phone.

It wasn't hard to find more on Davis Mitchell. He'd written a book detailing his long ago explorations. Sybilla tracked down a copy of *Maya Mysteries* through a rare bookstore she found online and then impatiently awaited its arrival. Thus far, she'd found nothing else about the Stone Worshippers anywhere after many hours digging. When Mitchell's book arrived she devoured it, hoping to find that he'd encountered them, even pinpointed a location and who they were. It being pure research she hadn't expected to enjoy the read. The jungle of El Petén and ruins with exotic names like El Mirador, El Zotz, and others she couldn't pronounce, came alive. He had a knack for storytelling in what could otherwise have been bone-dry material. Even so, she had to stave off disappointment as the narrative wound through the northern Guatemala sites where Mitchell participated in digs, deep in a jungle where machetes cut the only paths that disappeared again in a few days, overtaken by vines and other vegetation. Mitchell wrote about the people who lived in the area, most often hired to help with excavation and cooking, offering the suggestion that their ancestors had built the ancient temples obscured by time and whatever devastation had brought them to ruin. But his description of those natives didn't match the ones she searched for.

— Chapter Twenty-seven —

SYBILLA WAS NEARLY to the end of the thick volume when her luck turned. Mitchell described a two-man expedition with a local guide leaving Piedras Negras to float down the Usumacinta River. After several months at the dig they wanted a breather and headed downriver, leaving the rest of the crew behind to continue the tedious work. Sybilla got caught up in the description of the journey: wide rolling waters moving through dense jungle, humidity, a warm breeze somewhat intervening against the sun that beat down mercilessly on the travelers' heads. Periodically they passed ceiba trees. She knew from research that this was the World Tree sacred to the Maya, often depicted on ancient murals and sarcophaguses—and the one that the Stone Worshipper had told his captors was the central axis separating the Underworld and Upperworld. Even today when the rainforest was cleared and decimated, any ceiba would be left standing; the mythology persisted. Sybilla had seen pictures and could easily visualize a naked trunk a hundred feet high with huge buttresses and its branches gathered at the top, reaching up to the cosmos. She imagined seeing one just so as she herself drifted down the river of her mind.

Mitchell and his companions had thus been traveling much of the day when they spied the roof comb of a temple barely peaking above the canopy, resembling perhaps the headdress of a king or antenna to the gods. He'd heard of this place the natives so revered, where people were thought to receive visions merely by walking through the area, moving through dimensions of time. This ritual site, located on land jutting out into the waters like a horseshoe, was called Yaxchilán.

Guiding their launch to the water's edge, the guide threw out a rope to secure it to a tree close by. They jumped onto Mexican soil and all gazed up the steep bank to the jungle above. The site appeared to be close by, but there was no indication that humans had been this way, at least recently. The guide used his machete and hacked rude steps into the natural mud walls that separated them from their destination. The men clambered up with the help of vines and small bushes as handholds. Still no sign of human presence. They moved in the general direction of the roof comb, now unseen, the machete swinging in front of them to clear a way. Slow going. The guide was preoccupied with making a trail and didn't notice that Mitchell and the other archeologist had suddenly stopped behind him. An arresting sound broke the commonplace undertones of the jungle, the buzzing of insects and twitter of birds. It came from the direction they were headed. The sound grew—a primeval roar, a dinosaur come to life or a jaguar on the prowl. But the men weren't stopped by the cries, those of howler monkeys, which they knew well in a rainforest environment. Their eyes were drawn ahead to the sight beneath where the howlers gathered in the trees, the mossy crumbling stones of some high ancient wall. The closer they came, the louder the howlers, it being hard to tell if they were drawing them in, or outraged that Mitchell and his friends had shown up. A small beaten path was visible coming from the left, leading up to a narrow slit in the wall. The men paused at the opening and peered into blackness. Mitchell knew from his Maya informants that such man-made structures, plus caves and sinkholes, had meaning, gateways to the Underworld where shaman-priests journeyed to fight demon-gods and rescue lost souls. Nothing was visible. No telling what awaited them. Mitchell shone his flashlight and revealed a passageway, but no light came from the other side. It turned to the left some ten feet ahead. Single file, they entered, careful not to touch the slick walls. Who knew what had taken up residence there? Mitchell led the way. The dank passage twisted and turned like a maze, the uneven ground wet. Around a corner, the flashlight disturbed bats at rest. They beat their wings and filled the passageway. The men had to bend over and cover their heads. Finally there was a glimmer of daylight ahead, and they broke out onto an overgrown plaza.

The band of howlers had dispersed farther into the site and could be heard still in the distance. The explorers stood stock-still taking in what lay before them, at least what they could readily see. Used to the grandeur of places like Tikal, this ancient Maya city was more a fairy kingdom in comparison, shrouded in vines and mist, blanketed in humidity. Enraptured, they picked their way into the clearing. The guide halted abruptly and grunted. Throwing up a hand to signal a stop, he pointed downward to moving grass a few feet ahead. They'd nearly blundered over the dreaded fer-de-lance. The men waited until it slithered away, unperturbed by their presence. Mitchell saw eyeholes and a gaping mouth peeking at them. Brushing away plant litter revealed a mask carved into a stone façade covered with codices, the transcript of ancient annals. The men grew more excited, talking in hushed voices. As their eyes became accustomed to looking just beyond what was apparent, the stone treasures hidden there appeared. Temples and intricately carved slabs languished all around them. Mitchell caught movement in his peripheral vision and turned just in time to see a figure dash between trees, to dematerialize into the undergrowth. In those split seconds he couldn't tell the gender. Curious, he thought. Too large for a woman but wearing a white dress.

Sybilla sucked in her breath, and the skin on her arms tightened into chicken skin. Suddenly she was present, as though she'd slid right into Mitchell's body looking right through his eyes, experiencing the sudden rush of his blood.

Then very faintly a sound came through the rainforest canopy; their ears picked up thin chanting. After a minute the intoning became more robust as other voices joined in. They crept over in the direction of the singing and came upon narrow, overgrown pathway stretching up toward the sky, the endpoint hidden. The men all looked at each other silently. Joint nodding signaled agreement, and they started upward unable to see very far ahead.

As with the Underworld, so with the Upperworld, Sybilla thought, the metaphoric meaning not lost on her, even though such loss of control was out of her comfort zone.

The steps were irregular and slippery, victims of decay. The explorers labored on, careful not to make noise. The chanting continued from above, repetitive, trance-inducing if they'd allowed it, and became louder as they got closer. Until finally a roof comb came into view, then a temple, and above the last level of steps they saw a pillar standing upright, a lookout frozen in time, protecting a holy place. Just beyond was a small group of four figures, backs to the explorers, with long dark hair down their backs and shapeless white shifts that fell to mid-calf. They were bent over tending to some smoking vessels, their song accompanying them. A sweet, intoxicating scent reached out to the men in their semi-hidden place below. Then another figure broke into the clearing, interrupting, jabbering, pointing. And the faces of those in the ceremony turned to those on the steps. They looked dazed, men shaken out of their ritual, their white shifts sooty, hair wild. The scout continued to gesture vehemently and shout, finally picking up a bow and arrow nearby. The elder of the group commanded something in a strong voice, and the younger man reluctantly laid the weapon back on the ground. Then the elder took a step toward the men below who had frozen in place and opened his hands in their direction, in the universal sign that offered peace and safety.

The natives standing behind the elder looked frightened, ready to flee. But the elder stood calmly, his gesture of peace held. He said something in a language unintelligible to any of the explorers. They shook their heads slightly to show lack of understanding.

"Where? Your people?" the elder then said in halting, broken Spanish.

The guide signed a leap of the river with his hand, his chin extended in a slow upward thrusting to signal the direction they'd come from—a long trip.

"Ah…humm," the elder considered the communication, eyeing them intently.

No one moved.

The elder continued his appraisal. The terracotta vessels on the ground persisted in pumping out smoke and the stimulating smell. Then finally signaling to them, he said, "You?"

The explorers nodded.

"Me," the elder brought his hands to his chest and then pinched up skin on his forearm. "Eat?"

Mitchell and the other two looked at each other to see if anyone understood what the old man meant. Suddenly, the frown of confusion lifted from Mitchell's face, and he broke into laughter. Waving his hands back and forth, he chortled in Spanish, "No! No! We won't eat you!"

"Ahm...humm," the elder allowed. His companions now appeared less anxious.

Mitchell had remembered the rumors that abounded in these jungles, tribes ascribing cannibalism to each other. Whether the propaganda came from a long ago memory passed down through generations, or as a cautionary tale to keep their own at home and the village intact, he didn't know.

Pinching up his own forearm, Mitchell offered the same question to the elder, "You eat us?"

The elder broke into a wide grin. All of his *compadres* slapped themselves in laughter, a big joke.

"Who are you?" Mitchell asked now that it was established that none of them were after the others' flesh.

The old man beat his chest, "We are Hach Winik. The True People."

— Chapter Twenty-eight —

MITCHELL'S REMAINING ENTRIES on the Hach Winik were scanty. He and his companions were invited to stay while the ritual with the smoking pots, each one displaying a different crude face, and prayers was completed. Then the Hach Winik broke out big hand-rolled cigars and offered the smoke and dried monkey meat to their newfound friends. Mitchell reciprocated with a gift to the elder, a pocketknife with a bone handle. Mitchell was amazed at his appearance. He was less than five feet tall and the lines in his face spoke of advancing years, but his movements and coal black hair were that of a much younger man. He oozed an aura of power—of the sort kindly administered. However, Mitchell had the certainty that, should there be a need, his stature could grow in appearance to that of a giant.

Attempts at conversation produced information. The Hach Winik didn't live near by but deep in the rainforest at some untold distance. They came to this place to make offerings to one of their gods. It was a most holy place.

As the natives wrapped their pots to leave, out of respect Mitchell asked permission to stay.

"Yes, yes," The elder nodded vigorously, shaking his long curls. "It is possible your own god may be visiting."

"This is so?" Mitchell asked.

"Uhm…hummm. If you see, yes." The elder's eyes twinkled. They all clapped each other on the back in farewell, and the Hach Winik made their way down the steps, disappearing from sight.

Mitchell and his friends pitched a camp before dark and kept a fire going all night, especially mindful of the creatures that came out at sunset—in this place potentially even those who didn't wear skin. They stayed on through the next night, poking around the temples, making notes and drawings. Mitchell's camera jammed and refused to work in the excessive humidity, or maybe the god who lived there wanted to hold onto his secret place a while longer and did what he could to stop documentation. When they pushed off from the shore to head back upriver they told each other they'd return one day soon.

At last! Sybilla thought she would jump out of her skin in anticipation. *I've found them, or at least I'm close. But this was forty-something years ago and I still don't know their exact location. Maybe I can find Mitchell,* she mused. *Maybe he went back.*

But he wasn't easy to track beyond his book. Her first attempt was through his publisher, but the press had folded back in the Sixties. The Internet turned up nothing, just a few very old notations. Then she made a foray into archaeology and anthropology circles and was referred on from one to another of their colleagues. She learned that Mitchell was considered a minor player who hung around the edges of the boon earlier in the century. He never published anything else. There was some indication of a scandal so long ago no one knew the details, just that something had occurred. Whatever it was had caused Mitchell to abandon his work and society in general. No one was sure if he was still alive, or if so, where. Her questions about the Hach Winik also returned vague answers. Yes, they were known to live somewhere in the Mexican rainforest but kept to themselves, leery of outsiders. And the land was so inhospitable that little mapping had been done. She did learn that the Mexican government declared the region a protected environment, one of the few rainforests in North America able to support the jaguar and other endangered species. But it was just lip service. Loggers had eaten away the edges and made ventures inward, an illegal activity—while the government did nothing, perhaps even sanctioned it.

Sybilla was tightening the focus of the exact land and people for her article. She had Javier call the state-run logging company, with ties to US markets, rumored to be making forays into the preserve. He identified himself to the public relations manager he finally reached as a journalist and first asked casual questions about any encounters with the Hach Winik, then moved on to more pointed queries on the numbers of acres damaged by illicit tree-cutting. He was stonewalled on both accounts. Meanwhile, Sybilla finally reached someone who held some knowledge of Davis Mitchell. Diego Montez was a young man, only nineteen, when he attached himself to a dig in Piedras Negras, the same one Mitchell wrote of, hoping for a mentor. Now he was a respected archaeologist himself. She reached him via phone where he lived in Flores, the closest town to Tikal. Sybilla identified herself and the reason for her call.

"Yes, I knew Davis," he said in heavily-accented English. "Please call me Diego."

"Thank you, Diego. I'm interested in interviewing Mr. Mitchell about his encounters with the Hach Winik. He seems to have dropped out of sight years ago. Do you happen to know if he's still alive and where he is? Or do you know something of the Hach Winik yourself?"

"I don't have the experience myself with the Hach Winik. Even today not so many do. They had bad experiences with people like us, you know. If you see them at all, you might catch a look at them outside the Palenque ruins over there in Mexico. They will sometimes sell their crafts there and go right back home. They won't stay long in the place where the world ends."

"What do you mean?"

"Well, they believe that in places where the trees have been cut down the world is in danger of caving in on itself. Where they could be plunged into a tumult and lost forever, an Underworld with only chaos and no escape."

"Yes, I remember reading about the ceiba and its role in Maya creation stories. So the Hach Winik believe that, too?"

"I would say so, yes. And I have heard that the few who have ventured into our world have a difficult time, which lends to their belief that the True World stops at the edge of the rainforest. So, ours is a make-believe world, and they cannot live in it. They go home," he said. "We have no ceiba trees, however you want to take that."

"So it's hard to get closer to them?"

"Normally, yes. Now Davis was a different story. I heard he developed a relationship with the elder who was a leader in one of their villages."

"Oh, so there's more than one village?"

"Just a few, I believe. As I said, I don't really know too much. But there aren't very many of these people—and at one time they almost died out. That's, of course, one of the big reasons they avoid the rest of us, other than we're aliens to them."

"I see. So the elder he befriended was the same one in his book?"

"This I don't know. But perhaps you could ask him."

Sybilla came to attention. "He's alive then? You know where he is?"

"Yes, I think so. If anyone knows for sure, it would be Ricardo Delgado. He has a compound near Palenque. Now you must know a little something of Davis. I was very young when I knew him, and I was a little afraid of him, this American. Sometimes when men who aren't born into it stay in the jungle too long, it gets in their blood. Some say that Davis went mad after a time, haunted. That was a little later than when I knew him. But then you could say he was quite eccentric, and perhaps that was the beginnings of what occurred later. I won't say more because I don't know the complete story and don't want to be talking out of school, as you Americans say. But if you do talk to him sometime, you should not expect someone warm and friendly. Unless he has changed in his old age, expect someone rather acidic. So now I will find Ricardo's information for you."

After several minutes he came back to the phone. No phone number or email, he gave only a mailing address to a post office box in Palenque. "I am sorry I don't have more. I haven't seen my colleague Ricardo in a very long time. So this is about ten years old, but I think it will still be good. We don't move around like you Americans," he chuckled. "Señora Sybilla, I wish you all the luck in your search."

Sybilla thanked him profusely and hung up. One step closer, perhaps. She was elated and also heard the warning Diego relayed. Something told her that, if Ricardo Delgado did know the whereabouts of Davis Mitchell, her message would need to be carefully worded, a concise accounting of why Mitchell should welcome speaking to her. Over the next few days she gave her letter the same amount of careful attention she would if querying a potential editor with a proposal.

She sent it off and resolved to an indeterminate wait and, after all the long hours, was satisfied that she'd done as much as she could to that point. She also needed to turn her attention back to PJ. I've neglected him, she thought with a pang. They'd been in the same household, but Sybilla had been preoccupied with her work, sometimes short-tempered. PJ had withdrawn from her and carried on ever more lively conversations to the air, much to her concern, but also irritation. She set about to make her amends.

Chapter Twenty-nine

SIX WEEKS PASSED. Sybilla was fixing lunch for PJ when the phone rang. A gruff male voice on the other end said, "Sybilla Johns?"

The line crackled and sounded far away. "Yes?" she said.

"This is Davis Mitchell and I hear you want to speak to me." No friendly tone there.

Sybilla felt her knees go a bit watery. She sat down abruptly at the kitchen table. "Yes, Mr. Mitchell. I do."

No response but static in the line. He's not going to make this easy, Sybilla realized. My next few words will make or break this contact.

"Yes, indeed. I am a journalist for *Thrive* magazine. I don't know if you've heard of it?"

"No."

She gave him some background on the publication to show it wasn't built on fluff but invested in serious environmental issues supported by the funds and integrity of its editor, then went on to essentially repeat her letter proposing to tie in logging with any effect on the Hach Winik themselves.

"That's all well and good. But what makes you think I should talk to *you?*" Mitchell growled.

Sybilla took a deep breath and plunged ahead. "Well, Mr. Mitchell. I've read your book, and I believe you cared very much about that land and those people. Am I right that you became quite friendly with the elder you wrote about?"

"Perhaps."

Sybilla realized she had to tell him something that would hook him into tolerating her questions, some personal angle from her. To herself, she had played down the potential that Gabe's people may be in that region, or Gabe himself. But such things suppressed during the day often came out at night. Increasingly when she awoke in the morning, she would fleetingly remember portions of dreams where he played a part—and she would feel the ache of loss, which she quickly tossed off. So she didn't even consider this admission. Instinctively, she knew such a divulgence would drive Mitchell away: an abandoned woman on a sentimental search. No, she had to come from another place entirely.

"A Native midwife from Guatemala helped birth my son. We became good friends," she said. Sybilla went on to relate how, through Flora's stories, she had come to care about what happened to places and people who were intertwined to nature in their traditional beliefs and physical survival.

"So, my research led me to your book, and then to the complicity between the Mexican government and logging companies, and the negative impact I would imagine is happening to the Hach Winik themselves. I also know that US consumers are benefiting by this travesty called fair trade. I want to expose all this and my editor is firmly behind me. I believe you hold a key to reporting it accurately," she finished.

Silence stretched, then a short answer. "I'll get back to you."

An abrupt click on the line. Sybilla held the phone away from her ear, looking at it incredulously. Acidic is an understatement, she thought, remembering Diego's comment about Mitchell. Nothing to do now but wait. And Mitchell did keep her waiting.

Ten days later the telephone ringing at her bedside woke her up. She groped for the phone. "Hello?"

"Come to El Paraiso near the Palenque ruins. Be there in two weeks." The caller's words were slightly slurred.

"Where…" she flipped on the light and sat up. Click. The line went dead. Sybilla looked at the clock, nearly midnight. She muttered under her breath. Piece of work. But she scribbled down the site Mitchell had given her, no need to determine the caller. She'd recognized the gravely voice. Elation spread. This is it!

She was up half the night excitedly making a list of all she needed to do to get ready. And then her shoulders dropped with a realization. What am I going to do with PJ?

SYBILLA DREADED ASKING Sonya Whitehead to take PJ while she flew off to Mexico. Who knew where else she'd end up or how long it would take. Increasingly, she'd had to ask the favor since Flora had gone home. Sonya lived only a block away, far enough that she hadn't been privy to the strange goings-on in their backyard when Gabe was still around. They'd met one day when Sybilla and PJ took a morning walk and Sonya was gardening in her front yard. She readily disclosed her background, a recently retired elementary schoolteacher who was divorced and lived alone, her children grown. With a sunny smile and softly lined face, she had a pleasant, nurturing countenance not unlike Flora's. PJ took to her right away, and she claimed to enjoy PJ's company.

Sybilla led an insular life mostly composed of PJ and her writing assignments. Her limited outside contacts consisted of the gallery owner who represented her photography, fellow *Thrive* employees and her editor. None of them were suitable childcare candidates. Nor would she even consider asking them. Work and parenting PJ left little time to develop friendships in Mother Lode, and she hadn't made the effort. So she was left to prevail upon Sonya's kindness. The next morning after getting the all clear on the trip from Jay, she called her.

"I'm so sorry to ask you to do this," Sybilla explained her childcare dilemma and the writing assignment.

"Don't you worry! I have that extra bedroom. PJ and I will have a good time. Besides, what an exotic adventure! Just imagine. It sounds like the movies," Sonya simpered.

"Well, if you're sure it's not too much trouble," Sybilla could hear the longing in the older women's voice.

"You know my life is just too tame these days. You go on. But I expect the full story when you return," she said. "That will be the exchange. I can at least live vicariously through you!"

They made arrangements for Sybilla to deliver PJ to her door in twelve days' time with a full complement of clothing to last him a couple of weeks if needed. When she tentatively broke the news to PJ about going out of town, she thought he'd fuss. Instead he clapped his hands, jumping up and down, to learn he'd be staying with Sonya. It gave Sybilla pause.

She would stay in the city a day prior to flying out. Jay intended to hold an in-depth meeting with her and Javier, who would accompany her, to flesh out known plans and anticipate problems. In the meantime, she compiled notes to take with her, got her photography equipment in order and began to pack. Looking at her closet she wondered what to take. What will March in the Mexican rainforest be like? Hiking boots and long pants for sure, shirts that covered her arms, rain gear, too. She thought about malaria shots and decided against it since she'd heard how ill they make you. She went out and bought bug repellant, the strongest kind you'd want in the jungle, and mosquito netting just in case. Javier was equally as exhilarated. They spent hours on the phone in preparation. Villahermosa, the capital of the State of Tabasco, was the closest international airport to Palenque. They'd scrutinized a map and determined they could probably drive from there to their destination in a few hours, assuming they didn't run into trouble. With some concern she read about the Zapatistas, the Indigenous revolutionary group who led an uprising against the Mexican government the previous year. The government had been merciless, massacring many of them. Their origins were in the very jungle where they hoped to go! But reports were that they'd been unsuccessful and had gone into hiding. Who knew? Maybe this trip will produce more than we dreamed if we run across them, too, Sybilla thrilled.

Then two days prior to her departure to *Thrive's* offices she got a late-night phone call.

"I'm so sorry!" It was Sonya, her voice quavering.

"Sonya, what is it?" Sybilla asked.

"Oh, I'm so sorry. I have to go to Tennessee! I can't take care of PJ! My mother fell and broke her hip. She's in the hospital. It's serious.

She's nearly eighty and I'm going to have to go take care of her!" A sob broke loose.

"Is she going to be okay?"

"They don't know. She's pretty frail. But I'll need to be there for however long it takes."

"You go! Of course, no worries here," Sybilla soothed. "I have someone else I can leave PJ with."

They said their goodbyes and Sybilla put the phone down slowly. The trouble is I don't have someone. Sybilla sighed. Now what? I'm going to lose my chance. Dejected, she went outside and sank into her usual lawn chair and raised her gaze to the stars then waited for clarity to be delivered. After an hour, she got up silently and went to bed, looking in on PJ along the way.

Early the next morning, she made a phone call. Having made the arrangements she intended, she telephoned Jay. He was in a meeting so she left a message asking him to call her back. Close to noon they spoke.

"What's up?" he said.

"I've had some complications here at home. Would it be alright if we had our meeting tomorrow by speakerphone instead of me coming in? That would help a lot."

"Anything I need to know about?"

"Nothing I can't handle, Jay."

"Okay. Call in at ten, and we'll have the meeting that way. We'll let Javier know. You'll just meet him the next morning at the airport?"

"Yes, that would work great."

"You've got it. Sybilla, I'm depending on you. Whatever you're able to find out down there, make it count. This is your story. This exposé could make your career as a photojournalist. And it would give *Thrive* a proud name alongside yours," he gave her those parting words and hung up.

I know, Sybilla whispered to the dial tone. She returned the phone to its cradle and went to stare fixedly out the backdoor at nothing, assessing once again. Yes, better to be forgiven than get permission ahead. She returned to her final preparations for departure.

— Chapter Thirty-one —

SYBILLA RUSHED TO the departure gate as quickly as she could, balancing everything. She was arriving purposefully late, just prior to scheduled boarding. She spotted Javier up ahead waiting for her, loaded down with his carry-on bags, glancing at his watch. Peering down the hall, he spotted her. The nervous look on his face turned to one of shock. She smiled in acknowledgment from afar and tugged at PJ's hand, "Come on. We have to hurry!"

The airline agent was already calling for boarding as they arrived. Javier threw her a questioning look and sat down on his haunches in front of PJ, "Now, who are you?"

"I'm PJ," PJ said, taking in the bustling travelers jockeying toward the flight door with curiosity.

"Glad to meet you. I'm Javier," Javier shook his hand and then said to Sybilla, "Can we talk over there a minute?"

"Sure. PJ you stay right here with our bags. We'll be right back."

"Sorry to be blunt, Sybilla, but what *are* you doing here with your child?" Javier's eyebrows knitted in open exasperation.

"Look, I know this may be a little unusual. But I didn't have anything else to do with him! It was either bring him along or not go at all. And I'm *not* giving up this chance!"

"What did Mr. Turner say?"

"He doesn't know."

"He's not going to like this, you know. Liability and who knows what other problems coming."

"I'm not going to tell him until we return. I need your promise that you won't either."

Javier's frown deepened. "I don't know. This isn't a good idea. We don't know what kind of conditions we'll be going into. It could even be dangerous with the recent unrest down there."

"Oh, everything will be fine," Sybilla said breezily. "After all, there are children everywhere. And those problems down there have been laid to rest. Come on, let's go."

The agent was calling their row, and Sybilla made a dash back to PJ. "You're going to love this, hon! Your very first time in an airplane!"

PJ beamed up at her, excitement dancing in his eyes. Sybilla adjusted the small backpack on PJ's shoulders, gathered up the rest of their bags and joined the line to load. Glancing back at Javier, she sent him a reassuring smile that she didn't feel. What are you doing? Have you lost your mind? The critical voice in her head chastised her, echoing Javier's words. She pushed it aside to focus instead on the adventure that laid ahead, the resulting article and potential acceptance as a serious photojournalist—and all that could bring.

They found their row. Sybilla strapped PJ into the window seat, folding their jackets under him as a booster so he could better see. Wide-eyed he missed nothing, from the other passengers filing by to the movements of the airline workers outside loading bags. This was the first time he'd been out into the wider world to any extent. Sybilla patted his leg, "Now you just be quiet. Pretty soon we'll lift off! Won't that be fun?"

The plane ride was uneventful, and they'd been lucky enough to get a nonstop. PJ behaved well, apparently mesmerized by cloud castles and celestial beings he kept pointing out. When the plane descended in Villahermosa and all the lakes and green came into view, he squealed with delight. Such lush landscape was new to him. It's all going to be okay, Sybilla told herself. He's going to do okay.

Balmy air hit them when they stepped onto the tarmac. Sybilla felt her skin thirstily soak it up. Since it was still afternoon, she and Javier decided they had time to make it to their destination. Emerging from the airport Javier signaled a driver leaning against his taxi. After the men loaded the luggage into the small trunk, Sybilla and PJ scooted into the back seat as Javier and the driver exchanged information in the front. Javier turned around, "The driver says it's about ninety minutes to Palenque. He's never heard of El Paraiso."

Sybilla was beat. All the tension and build-up over the last few days with things gone awry had taken their toll. She leaned back against the seat. Grateful the air conditioner was working in the high humidity, she closed her eyes to rest. PJ knocked out, too. She awoke to sounds of Javier and the driver carrying on a lively discussion, none of which she could understand. So instead Sybilla watched the passing rural landscape, increasingly green. Surprised to see all the stately Brahma cattle in the pastures, she noted the egrets that accompanied them, standing close by, some even perched on their backs. Curious, she thought. Periodically they passed through villages so small they were only designated as such by small signs that displayed their names. Young men stood by the road and held up bottles filled with a questionable cloudy liquid for sale. When they slowed down for speed bumps, children rushed up to the taxi brandishing soft drinks in plastic bottles or gigantic grapefruits. PJ had awakened by this time and waved excitedly to them. Finally, they were coming into the outskirts of Palenque, some tiny open-air restaurants, a garage and, surprisingly, a Volkswagen dealer with a few cars in the showroom. Traffic increased. There were a number of people on the streets going about their business. The car veered off to the right at a traffic circle with a huge warrior's head perched in the middle. Javier said over his shoulder, "He says if you go the other way it goes into the center of town. But the ruins are out this way."

Traffic dissipated quickly, and they were once again out in the country. She noted the small beaten trail by the side of the road, and with the exception of the occasional rustic dwelling and the Brahma cows in the fields, there was little other reference to human inhabitants. They had been climbing slightly in elevation. Ahead, she saw emerald mountains. Cracking the window, she allowed cool moist air to caress her face, a stark contrast to the hot dust of Palenque. An exquisite shiver ran up and down her spine. She was galvanized, anticipating much more than she could have imagined. This is so right, she told herself.

The driver slowed, not sure where he was going. When Sybilla was researching ahead, she couldn't find any reference to El Paraiso where Mitchell had directed her to go. So Jay told her to find a place as close to the ruins as she could. La Casa Mono popped up on the Internet and she liked the name: The Monkey House. A small hand- painted sign peeked out from the foliage. The vegetation had grown dense within a few miles from town even creeping out on the road. The driver turned the car onto the narrow lane that, within a few hundred yards, delivered them to some small bungalows and a tiny shack that acted as an office, almost hidden amongst the most majestic trees she'd ever seen.

— Chapter Thirty-two —

AS SILENT AS the desert was after dusk, the rainforest was equally humming with all manner of insects and amphibians clamoring to be known to the night. Darkness fell early beneath the canopy. The tiny restaurant at their lodging only offered breakfast. But Javier prevailed upon the owner's daughter Rosa to rustle up some dinner, and she'd obliged with a smile seeing how weary the smallest traveler was. They sat under the thatched *palapa* outside the open-air kitchen and wolfed down the meal with relish. Sybilla suspected the family had shared their dinner, simple fare of stewed vegetables, soup and tortillas. It was delicious. They had the luxury of being the only guests there. Even as tired as they were, none of them yet made a move to go to bed. Sybilla was making the most of the moment, storing it away in her memory bank, a sense of having firmly arrived even as the journey had just begun. She looked around, like a child in wonder. The trees fascinated her the most. Some had huge buttresses thriving with plant life other than their own: bromeliads perched on their branches, vines winding up their long trunks. They looked surprisingly like the houseplants she had at home, only much bigger. She imagined all kinds of other life hidden in the recesses. Indeed, one had a hollow at its base so big that an adult could stand up in it, shadows giving the impression of some forest sprite observing them from its post. Sybilla laughed a little to herself, I'm letting this place carry me away. But she noticed PJ had stopped eating and was gazing intently in that direction.

When Sybilla noted PJ's eyes drooping toward sleep, she finally called it a night. They left Javier to nurse his beer and headed off to their cabana. It was a simple room: two narrow beds, a rustic desk and chair, minimal facilities in the bathroom, but certainly adequate for their needs. Perhaps the best feature was the wide porch facing into the jungle. After getting PJ settled, she sat outside undertaking the ritual that gave her clarity.

Here her sight didn't fix on the sky, no visible channel extending there, but directly into the density just a few yards away, the close unknown.

When they checked in Javier had asked the old man at the desk if he knew of El Paraiso. Senor Ortiz gestured it was a bit down the road toward the ruins, close by. Sybilla was amazed at their luck. No, something is guiding me, she thought. Mitchell had only said two weeks, no exact time. While a part of her was tempted to rush breathlessly down to El Pariaso at once, a better head prevailed. She wanted to be in top form, contained but interested, when meeting Mitchell. She knew that his acceptance wasn't a shoo-in. She'd still have to prove herself worthy of his attention—and any potential connection to the Hach Winik.

After a long time, she went inside and slipped into bed. PJ was snoring softly. She lay there listening to a gecko chirping outside just under the eaves, nothing separating them but the mesh on the window, open to the elements. She drifted into slumber.

THE NEXT MORNING when Sybilla and PJ appeared for breakfast Javier was just finishing his second cup of coffee. They had slept unusually late. After Rosa took their order, Javier reported he'd already been out on reconnaissance.

"I walked up the road toward the ruins. Senor Ortiz is right. El Paraiso isn't too far. But it's not a hotel or restaurant. There's a track that runs into the jungle. A ways in there's a sign arching overhead. It looks like a family compound of some sort. I didn't see anyone around. Well, it was early," he took a gulp of coffee. "If you're up to it, we can walk down there or at least take a *combi* to the road entrance. On my way back I saw the vans had started running. They go between town and the ruins. You just wave them down."

He went on, "I tried to get what I could from Senor Ortiz about Mitchell and this man Ricardo Delgado. Apparently El Paraiso is Delgado's place. He's been here about twenty years and the locals like him. He was on a lot of the digs at Palenque but mostly retired now."

"I thought so since Diego referred me to him," Sybilla said.

"Looks like Delgado opens his compound up as a way station for colleagues passing through the area. Not only archeologists but anthropologists, botanists, anyone doing work in the field. Sounds like the place to be. From what I get, Delgado and Mitchell are friends going way back. Senor Ortiz didn't say more than that. So I guess we'll have to find out for ourselves."

Rosa came with breakfast, and they devoted themselves to fresh papaya, scrambled eggs and tortillas.

Sybilla had decided a *combi* was best, at least to deliver them closer, since PJ would be with them. A couple of dogs heard them coming down the overgrown track. Raucous barking announced their impending arrival at the entrance to El Paraiso. Sybilla was attempting to pull PJ away from the friendly animals when an older Mexican woman emerged from a rambling bungalow that sat back from the entry. She greeted them, smiling at PJ. Javier asked her if Davis Mitchell was there.

"Ah, yes. You're the ones who wrote to my husband Ricardo," she answered in perfect English. They made formal introductions.

"Please call me Isabel. Come in. I'm sorry that Ricardo isn't here right now. He'd like to meet you but he's in the Yucatán," she continued as they walked into the compound. They could see a large *palapa* surrounded by an informal flower garden in a clearing beyond the home. It had the look of a relaxed gathering place. Sybilla remarked on the beauty of the property.

"Yes, we are fortunate here. Now, you came to meet with Davis, didn't you? He should be back there," Isabel said. "If you follow that trail it will come to the creek. Just follow the creek toward the back of our land. You'll see his home."

"He actually lives here then?" Sybilla raised her eyebrows.

"Yes, he is an old friend of Ricardo's and mine. He's been here with us almost from the time we moved here from Quintana Roo. This was much better for Ricardo to work at Palenque then. Would you like for this little one to stay with me while you go visit?" Isabel offered.

"Oh, I couldn't ask you to do that," Sybilla replied.

"Really, it would be a pleasure. I miss my grandchildren and the dogs would like it, too. And you are going to talk business. I think this would be best," Isabel finished.

"Is that okay, PJ? We'll be back in just a while," Sybilla was met with vigorous nodding from PJ. He returned to playing with the dogs.

Javier and Sybilla picked their way down to the creek and followed its course another hundred yards until they saw a casita cloistered by foliage just on the banks of the water, an idyllic setting. They paused at the porch, listening for sounds from inside the house. Nothing. Sybilla shrugged to Javier and stepped forward. Before she could rap on the door, it suddenly jerked open. A tall man in a rumpled shirt and shorts barred the entrance, examining them with piercing, unfriendly eyes, hand firmly on the doorknob. He was barefoot. Several days' growth of white beard covered his scowling face. Grizzled hair sprung out from his head completing the impression of complete disarray and questionable sanity. Sybilla snatched her hand back and just stood there, nonplussed.

"Yes?" He scrutinized them with a stony stare.

Okay, he's going to make me work for it, Sybilla thought ruefully.

"Mr. Mitchell?" she stuck her hand out to shake. "I'm Sybilla Johns and this is my colleague Javier Alvaro."

"Yes?" He ignored her hand. She let it drop awkwardly.

"I'm very glad to meet you in person. You asked me to come. So here I am," she pulled herself up to full stature. "I've brought Javier as an assistant and translator."

Mitchell was silent. To Sybilla, the seconds stretched into hours. Abruptly, he stood aside and gestured that they should enter. She got a whiff of lingering alcohol and tobacco on stale breath. She noted that, for such an elderly man, his posture was unusually straight on his spare frame. Despite his disheveled appearance, Sybilla glimpsed the dashing figure he must have been forty years ago. They entered the front room that proved to contain a small kitchen and seating area. Mitchell waved them toward the easy chairs gathered around a low table and went over to the stove. "Want some coffee?"

"That would be great, Mr. Mitchell," she said to be polite. Javier nodded assent.

"Just Davis," he growled.

While he was busy at the counter, Sybilla stole a look around. Papers and books haphazardly covered a desk and she spied a room with an unmade bed through another doorway. But what held her interest were the old photos that covered the walls, some in frames but many just taped up. She could distinguish excavation sites, groups of men in front of relics, a number of Davis with Native people—and one especially of Davis sitting on the ground with a wizened elder wearing white. Crude masks and similar paraphernalia filled in the spots between the photos. It was like a museum.

He brought over coffee in chipped mugs. It was quite bitter, like it had been boiling on the stove for hours.

"Now what do you want?"

Javier sat back. They had prepared this introduction. Sybilla took the lead. She reviewed what she'd told Davis on the phone and then tied it to elements of her research thus far, ending with what they hoped to achieve: raising awareness in their readership and needling the Mexican government to take real action. "You see, we really think that if it's written in a way that exposes their part in this travesty, they can no longer just turn their heads. The Mexican government will have to take some measures to stop the loggers and somehow compensate the damage that's been done, both to the land and the people living there. Otherwise, they'll be shamed before the judgment of developed countries. But that's where you'd come in. If what we think is true, you have first-hand knowledge of the Hach Winik and the effect on them. If this is going to reach people, it can't be abstract. It's got to encompass personal stories by those who have been there, have seen it. And our magazine has wide enough circulation to get attention. Plus, my editor will make sure our article gets into influential hands," she took a breath. She'd been talking for nearly an hour through which Davis leaned forward, elbows propped on thighs, staring at the floor like they weren't there. He gave no sign whatsoever for her to play off.

"So interviewing you is important, and if it's possible to go to a village, that will add immediacy," she finished and looked over at Javier. He nodded slightly in encouragement.

Sybilla picked up her now-cold coffee and sipped. They sat in silence until Davis finally shifted in his chair and grunted.

He looked up, appraising her, "Okay."

She had to still her racing heart, "Okay? Do you mean you'll sit for an interview?"

"I mean I'll take you."

"You'll take us?" She had to quit repeating everything he said. *I sound like an idiot*, she chastised herself.

"That's right. You should hear it from their mouths, not mine. But one caveat," he looked straight into her eyes, "You've got to run what you write by me. I don't want some hogwash written by some journalist who *thinks* they've interpreted something correctly when they haven't. And it ends up hurting these people. You got that?"

His voice got threatening. Sybilla was taken aback, "Of course, I would check my facts."

"You run your facts and the slant you give them by me. Otherwise, forget it," Davis was firm.

"That sounds fine to me. I'd want to get everything right," she agreed.

"It's a rough trip out there, not much of a road. I'd need to make sure my Land Cruiser is up to it," he said.

Sybilla remembered an ancient Toyota sitting near the house overtaken by vines. She was dubious.

"I don't need a car much here. It's been sitting a while," he offered as though reading her mind. "I just need to crank it up. And you'll need to bring some gifts, out of respect. Basic supplies they can't get. Give it a few days. In the meantime, you go up the road and see the ruins. It will be important so you can relate."

Davis seemed to be warming to the idea, maybe even getting excited. Some of the heaviness lifted. Javier piped up, "Let me know whatever I can do to help."

"Right now I'm going to walk you back. I want to talk to Isabel," Davis said.

"Uh, there is one thing I didn't mention," Sybilla hesitated, nervous.

"Yeah?" he barked.

"My three-year-old son is with us. I didn't have anyone to leave him with at home. I'm sorry. I know this complicates things. He's up with Isabel right now."

Sybilla just knew that thoughts like 'Woman, what are you thinking of?' or 'Are you crazy?' were welling up in his mind. But he didn't give it away.

He blinked at her slowly and said, "It'll be good for the boy."

After all his gruffness, Sybilla couldn't believe he'd acquiesce so easily about PJ. Maybe I've found his soft spot, she thought. They all walked back toward the house and could see PJ lolling on the ground with the dogs and Isabel sitting on a chair nearby.

Davis crouched down in front of PJ and shook his hand. In his gravely voice he said, "Son, I understand you want to take a trip."

Sybilla put her worries behind her.

— Chapter Thirty-four —

DAVIS HAD GIVEN them a shopping list, things like boxes of salt, fifty pounds of rice, bars of chocolate. Sybilla couldn't imagine how the chocolate wouldn't liquefy by the time they reached their destination. He'd said they'd stop and purchase a live hen or two along the way. She wondered where they'd find room in the vintage Land Cruiser for all these items plus themselves, their equipment and bags, much less chickens. But they dutifully took a *combi* into town after their meeting and bought items at the local market while Davis attended to his vehicle. PJ was excited by the throngs of people, merchandise, noise and unusual smells. Stalls of produce, spices, *curandero* supplies, live fowl and colorful clothing commingled freely while lively recordings blared from the occasional music booth. They took their time to wander and left the burlap bag of rice until last. Burdened down with their purchases, Javier hailed the closest taxi to take them back to La Casa Mono.

Isabel had invited them for dinner. After showering off the sweat of their task, they presented themselves at her doorstep a little after six as arranged, early for the evening meal by Mexican standards but in deference to PJ's earlier bedtime. They weren't the only ones who had cleaned up. Davis was already there, lounging in a chair, drink in his hand. The contrast to their previous encounter with him was stark. Gone was the stubble. His wavy silver hair had been combed back, tamed into a mane that brushed the top of his shoulders. His clothing was pristine, light cotton trousers and shirt. But perhaps most startling, the scowl was gone from his face. Instead, a slight smile played about his lips, like in secret amusement. Isabel offered drinks and disappeared into the kitchen, source of the pungent aroma on the air.

"Well, my boy, how'd you like the market?" Davis patted his knee in invitation. PJ made a beeline, clambered onto his lap and started jabbering. Sybilla was shocked, given PJ's usual shyness with strangers.

154

He certainly hadn't taken to Javier that way, although Javier treated him kindly enough. Their conversation continued as Davis patiently answered PJ's questions and engaged him. Sybilla watched perplexed but also relieved. Davis' volatile nature was made apparent earlier, but she realized that, somehow, PJ's presence had turned into an asset rather than a liability. Having PJ along would leverage a more genial atmosphere for their expedition.

Drinks served, Davis turned to addressing what was ahead. "The Land Cruiser is running rough. I think I can take care of that tomorrow though. Be prepared to leave the next day. You need to know we have a long, slow trip in front of us. We'll leave before dawn. If we make good time it will take about twelve hours, maybe longer. I don't know what we'll find as far as the road. In some places, it's barely that, and we've had hard rains recently. There's no communication ahead to check. You should be prepared for anything, including having to camp overnight."

Alarm spread over Sybilla's face. Her imagination ran wild with thoughts of big cats and slithery things. She glanced over at PJ in concern.

"Yes, I know what you're thinking," Davis continued, "But I'm bringing what we need if that happens. We may camp anyway once we reach the village, or we may be invited to stay in one of the compounds. That's more likely. These people are my friends." Davis instructed them to bring minimal personal items but enough for a few days just in case.

"How open do you think they'll be to talk to us?" Sybilla asked.

"The Hach Winik are gentle people. Although they still carry a reputation for raiding other villages, mostly their own kind, for wives and such," Davis chuckled. "But those were the old days and a way of avoiding so much in-breeding, if you think about it. Other Native groups think they're cannibals. Of course, that's not true but probably a rumor the Hach Winik perpetuated just to protect their own. Such propaganda is frequent between tribes for that reason. Who knows if it was ever true? Unlikely."

Davis went on to reiterate some of what they already knew. Their brushes with outsiders, particularly lighter-skinned ones, had not been particularly beneficial over the years. Results had been a loss of land, disease and indignities. There had been some few gringos who had approached them, and they'd allowed in, who had taken what they wanted, documented their culture for their own benefit usually, and then were gone. There were few who really gave them respect and called them friend.

"They're a people literally trying to survive with a world closing in on them that's doing a good job of taking what's their birthright," Davis' voice had risen in agitation the longer he talked on the subject. PJ looked up at him. Davis glanced down then, realizing the charge he sent out and swallowed. He finished quietly, "To answer your question, I can't promise you anything. If you'd just wandered into their midst, they'd be polite but largely ignore you. I'm a friend and you'll be with me. That will probably give you an opening. I'll explain your intent, what you want to do. How it could be a benefit. Their numbers have dwindled dramatically over the last fifty years. If there's help for them, it'll probably have to come from the outside, by those who know how to navigate politics and big corporations. This is what it comes down to. Understand that's the *only* reason I'm taking you in. Not for the curiosity of your readers."

Isabel came sweeping into the room followed by her cook who was laden down with two platters. The spicy aroma made Sybilla's mouth water in anticipation. They sat down to a sumptuous meal of chicken mole, baked chayote, rice and tortillas to scoop it all up. Between bites, Sybilla cautiously introduced the subject of Davis' early days, to see if he would shed any light on his own background. After some silence, he told a story of himself as a young man of nineteen stumbling in from the jungle onto a small encampment of men in the midst of great temples shrouded by vegetation and time. The temples turned out to be Tikal and he later learned that the men were respected archaeologists of the day. He hung around on the edges until one of them saw the advantage of additional labor and handed him a pick. So began his life as an explorer. Warming to the subject, Davis held court and entertained them with a few more tales.

Sybilla's trepidation toward Davis began to slip away. A deep respect for that eccentric character was beginning to emerge instead. He's really someone who cares deeply, she thought. Whatever scandal happened back then to make him the way he is now...I can't help but think there's something there, that he's justified. He's not a mean old loon people make him out to be—or that he tries to be.

The room took on a romantic ambience of the like adventure tales told well produce. They were wrapped in a cocoon of enchantment that transported them back to the alluring heyday of archeological discoveries in Maya lands. But when Sybilla noticed PJ's head drooping toward his plate, she graciously thanked their benefactors for the meal and stories. They had their first ride in the Land Cruiser as Davis ferried them back to their lodging. Sputtering and hard seats aside, Sybilla thought it would do just fine. She breathed in the night air, taking the rainforest and all its sensations into the core of her being. A rush of gratitude came over her. Who gets to do *this?* She was giddy. It had been a big day.

— Chapter Thirty-five —

SYBILLA AWOKE IN the early morning hours to the rhythmic drip of water splashing on the floor next to the bed; a spot in the thatched roof had weakened. Sidestepping the puddle, she peered through the mesh window to find her vision quite limited. A deafening rush, torrential sheets of rain intervened, barely revealing the dark shapes of surrounding trees. I'm glad the casita is built up on blocks, she thought and returned to bed.

Later she re-awakened, this time relative stillness, the night creatures yet hunkered down from the deluge. Then in the distance a primordial roar. Drowsiness vanished. She propped herself up on one elbow, ear cocked. The sound had an undulating cadence that injected a signal to her limbic brain, and the hair on her arms prickled in goose bumps. Sounds like a tiger but surely not. She reached for her watch on the bedside table: 4 a.m. The rest of the night she laid, ears straining to determine the source's whereabouts. When the calls waned, she continued to imagine the unknown creature prowling somewhere close by and fervently wished the windows had strong shutters. PJ slept through it all.

Morning light brought the birds noisily celebrating a new day, freshly washed and bright. Sybilla skirted the trees that rained excess moisture from the leaves. PJ ran ahead splashing through the remaining puddles on the path. They joined Javier at the breakfast table.

"Did you hear that roaring last night?" she asked. "Any minute I expected a jaguar to jump up on the porch and barrel through the door!"

Javier chuckled and took a sip of his coffee. "Howlers."

"What?"

"I imagine that's why they call this place La Casa Mono. Howler monkeys. They're all over. Don't worry. The most they'll do is throw stuff at you. To me, their screams are comforting. Kind of like coyotes back home calling their presence to each other. Something enduring through time."

Sybilla looked at him in surprise having never heard him speak in such a philosophical manner. He was usually practical, all business. The place seemed to be having an effect on him, too. She laughed. "I guess that's a relief. Now I can rest easier. But I suppose there are still big cats out there somewhere."

"Maybe. Certainly less these days."

They ate breakfast hurriedly to make it early to the ruins. The *combi* emptied its passengers at the tourist market in front of the entrance. Rickety booths lined the small plaza. Traditional Mexican clothing and t-shirts hung from rafters of some stalls. Ceramic replicas of temples and Maya gods on parchment and leather filled others.

"I read that this was the actual marketplace back in the day," Javier offered. They made their way along the perimeter toward the entry.

"Look over there," Sybilla said in a hushed tone.

Two men stood in front of a stall next to the entrance. They wore the same white garment and shoulder length hair she saw in the old photo from Guatemala. Javier engaged them in conversation while Sybilla and PJ poked around their wares. Sybilla picked up a seed necklace, fingering the shiny smoothness of the large central pod. One of the men broke away from the conversation and walked over to her saying something in Spanish.

"*Lo siento! No entiendo*," Sybilla replied in her limited Spanish and smiled. I'm sorry. I don't understand.

He gestured for her to put the pendant on and held up a hand mirror. Head bobbing, he encouraged her.

"Lovely," she complied. "Yes, I'll just leave it on and take it." She rummaged through her bag for the pesos. In the meantime, he squatted down showing PJ a small contraption of string and wood that he worked until it spun on its axis, traveling across the hard-packed dirt. PJ clapped his hands in delight. "I see you're a very good salesman. Okay, we'll take that, too."

"Bol," the man touched his chest.

"Your name? Sybilla and PJ," she pointed to herself and PJ. His name tickled something in the back of her mind.

Bol seemed satisfied and started wrapping PJ's top in newspaper. Javier walked over with the other man.

"Sybilla, this is Nuxi'," Javier gestured. Nuxi' dipped his head and gave a shy smile. "I can't get everything he's saying because he only speaks a little Spanish. But they may be from the same village we're going to. He says they live on the banks of a big lake in the middle of jungle and come here periodically to sell crafts for the community. They're definitely Hach Winik. I mentioned Davis and Nuxi' knew him."

"How do they get here?"

"Sounds like they walk. He said it takes three days or more carrying their goods. That must be a tough hike. Looks like they're staying for a week hoping to sell everything before they go back."

Bol bobbed his head at Javier and waved his hand toward an elongated bundle of sticks on the table tipped in chipped stone arrowheads and parrot feathers, pantomimed shooting a bow and arrow.

"You'd better watch out. He did a good sales job on us," Sybilla advised.

Javier acknowledged him with a smile but shook his head no.

"Maybe later," Bol startled them both with heavily accented English and grinned as though he'd made a good joke. They all broke out in laughter.

"He must have heard that from tourists enough that it stuck!" Sybilla managed.

They said their goodbyes and made their way through the turnstile, formal entrance to the site. Sybilla was glad they'd come early. Not too many other visitors yet. Following the muddy path they were suddenly engulfed in foliage and immense trees, the earthy smell of decomposing plant matter intensified by last night's rain.

They approached uneven stone steps, obviously ancient, that they would be required to climb. She remarked to Javier. "Now these steps are nearly a foot high in places. I wonder why such small people would build such steep steps." She took PJ's arms and swung him up. "Hon, if you get tired, let me carry you."

Sunlight shone through on the path ahead, and they broke out onto the grand plaza. Sybilla gasped. On nature's dramatic stage, its veridian backdrop stretching to match the elevation, mist hanging in the air, evidence of a long-ago empire was displayed before them. Her eyes swept the scene: temples of various sizes, one with steps that went on forever, a long low structure with columns, carved exterior reliefs, strange symbols.

"I've seen pictures but nothing compares to this," Sybilla marveled. "Let's go sit under that tree. I just want to take it in." She pointed to a tree on the edge of the plaza with big blocks of stone seating. "And look, the tree has thorns on its trunk and those huge roots along the ground. This must be a ceiba! The sacred World Tree! I can hardly believe it. After all this time, all the hard work, here we are now experiencing the very things we researched. And we met Nuxi' and Bol!"

Javier nodded his agreement.

"Bol!" she sunk down hard on the stone. "I know where I heard that name before!" She glanced at PJ and abruptly became silent.

Javier looked at her in question.

"It's nothing. Just a name I came across," she waved it away. But it wasn't nothing, she thought. I remember exactly where I heard that name. It's Gabe's middle name, the one he couldn't place, that didn't make sense.

She became still with her thoughts. Sybilla had been successful in tucking away any emotions about meeting up with Gabe, the potential. Now they rose to the surface. She wrestled with them, trepidation and longing intertwined, further confusing her. What would it mean? Accusations swirled in her head. Toward Gabe: anger for leaving with no word since. Toward herself: taunting her own foolishness, selfishness, what it could do to PJ. To get away from the castigating voices, she suddenly stood up, grabbed PJ's hand and bustled ahead. "Let's go see what's here."

They wandered through the palace, the sprawling ruin at the end, but decided against attempting the climb up the Temple of the Inscriptions, it being too much with a small child. A guide pointed out the sacred spring as they crossed a waterway. Sybilla clambered down for a photograph. They found their way through the banana grove, a small trail leading them into a separate plaza, a raised stone platform in the middle encircled by still more temples. Mist hung heavier here truly giving it an otherworldly feel. And then not far away, the same as the night before, the howlers called, the sound traveling closer then farther away as they swung through the canopy. Sybilla looked around and discovered they were the only people there. It's like a dream, she thought. Then sprinkles of rain fell and quickly became more insistent.

"Maybe we'd better head back. It's way past lunch anyway. I saw a little place to eat on the way up," Javier said.

By the time they made their way back through the banana grove, the sky opened up. Javier swung PJ over his shoulder. Sybilla took off her shoes and they ran laughing, toward the entrance. Waving to Bol and Nuxi' as they sprinted by, they caught a *combi* just as it was leaving for town.

— Chapter Thirty-six —

DAVIS WAS TRUE to the message he left at their lodging the afternoon before. He arrived with the loaded down Land Cruiser about 4 a.m. His passengers were ready to go. Sybilla had been beside herself with excitement in the night, her mind too active to sleep. After awhile she arose to sit on the porch, listened to the umbratic symphony, and tried to tease out images of where they'd stay next. Finally, she went to do the last of the packing, quietly so not to disturb PJ.

Javier threw their packs in the back. Sybilla, carrying a sleeping PJ, squeezed in after and attempted to get comfortable. Davis barely grunted hello, perhaps it being too early for words. Save for the rattling of their vehicle, they pulled out silently onto the dark, empty road and headed toward their destination. The air rippling in through the window was cool and moist in the early morning hours. Sybilla pushed her face right into the wind, dog fashion, because it seemed the right thing to do, signaling to herself that she was ready for anything. They'd been driving for about an hour, climbing slightly in elevation. The terrain looked like a patchwork quilt, alternating between heavily forested areas and those bereft of trees. Sometimes they passed a pasture with a sole tree standing in the cordoned off land—a ceiba.

"You see all this land? Far as you can see it used to be rainforest. Now look at it," Davis growled, his first words since they'd departed. "Homesteaders moved in here, slashing and burning, using up the soil so there's nothing left, and moving on to repeat the same thing. No one stops it, and this is supposed to be protected land! A total sham."

Javier asked him to stop the Land Cruiser and jumped out to take shots. Sybilla took out her journal and began to jot down notes as Davis railed against a government that allowed such depletion and the detrimental effect on the people, aside from the environment. "Now you can't really blame it on those who've been displaced themselves. They're trying to survive. But they're overrunning this region and there's no control.

163

You can see it!" Davis waved his arm around. "The least the government could do is regulate how many people move into the area. And teach them how to farm their *milpas* like the Hach Winik, using a conservation method that doesn't kill the rainforest. Instead, they've set up a situation where the Hach Winik and homesteaders are pitted against each other struggling over the land. Very bad blood between them. All that aside from what the logging companies did, which started the whole thing. Mercenaries! Old T'uup said that when the trees are gone from the forest, the world will die and the Hach Winik before that. Their souls suffering such loss that they can't go on. The world will have collapsed. He told me that twenty years ago. It was happening before his eyes then. And mine."

Davis was getting increasingly cranked up, citing references, specific travesties that had occurred over the years. Sybilla wrote furiously, periodically peppering him with questions to encourage the onslaught. She gathered a treasure trove of notes to harvest later. "And T'uup, is that the elder you wrote about in your book?"

He affirmed with a nod. They had been traveling at the highest rate of speed the potholed road would allow. Davis slowed to a stop and pointed in the distance to a large bumpy hill in the middle of flat land. The trees remained intact on the unusual rise.

"See that? When you see a formation like that it's a good possibility that it's an unexcavated temple. Sometimes the locals know. Sometimes they've lost their knowledge." Davis continued educating them using the passing scenery to prompt his discourse until they came to a crossroads with a gas station in the middle of nowhere. "We'll fill up here, and services are over there. It's the last chance."

After a pause, they poured themselves back into the Land Cruiser. "There's one more stop I need to make," Davis remarked. A few minutes later they pulled up to a lonely adobe, nothing more than a hovel. Davis got out and talked to a man who stuck his head out the door. Both disappeared around the back and a flurry of cackling could be heard. Davis re-emerged with a cardboard box tied with twine under his arm. He opened the passenger door and thrust the noisy container into Javier's hands. "Here are those chickens."

Javier cast a glance back at Sybilla and raised his eyebrows, then tucked the carton under his legs as best he could. The pavement ended abruptly. The conditions of their travel changed accordingly. Open pastures disappeared. Dense jungle impinged causing the road to dwindle to a narrow passage, recent rains also having left their indelible mark. The Land Cruiser tipped precariously as they hit huge ruts, squawks punctuating the dips until the hens ceased commentary and took a nap. Gone was the breeze. Humidity rose. Sybilla resigned herself to a slow, sticky trip that was becoming longer in the process by PJ fussing his discomfort. The passing scenery, just several feet from their transport, became monotonous. She lost track of the hours. They only stopped to take the periodic pit stop and didn't linger. It clouded over in mid afternoon but the rain held off. Once they were compelled to cross a muddy creek running across the road, normally not present in dryer times. The passengers had to get out and wade through for a better chance of the Land Cruiser making it. PJ was delighted at the ride on Javier's shoulders while Sybilla scanned the water for slithery things that might be lurking. The back tires spun coming out the other side. But Davis, as a testimonial to his earlier word about being prepared, instructed Javier to locate the wooden plank on the vehicle's roof and wedge it under the tires. The wheels spun, splattering Javier with mud, then caught and rolled out. They resumed their journey.

As the sun began sinking, the lane widened slightly. A few small *milpas* appeared alongside, garden plots hacked out from the forest. They could see a body of water between the trees in the distance ahead. Rustic wooden shanties came into view. Then more. A group of men lounged outside a whitewashed hut, some in the traditional white gowns, others in jeans and t-shirts. Small children played in the dirt. A young woman walking by the side of the road turned at the sound of their vehicle. She sighted the driver and broke into a wide grin. The men stood. The children ran toward them jabbering. Davis waved his arm and called out something Sybilla couldn't understand, his face lit up. She felt her own giddiness erupting again. PJ hung on the open window staring. Javier was poised on the front seat, suddenly alert. The road ended. They had arrived in the village. Davis turned to his passengers and said, "Welcome to K'ak."

— Chapter Thirty-seven —

DAVIS SPRANG FROM the Land Cruiser and met the group of men as they walked toward him. They went through the greeting ritual of gestures and back clapping, boisterously talking over each other. Sybilla and Javier stretched from their long journey and stood by the car waiting. Still staring, PJ was glued to Sybilla's side. She was potently aware that she was completely out of her element and unsure what to do. As much as she'd anticipated this moment, she felt awkward. Her palms had gone sweaty, and she had a bad case of dry mouth. Finally, Davis seemed to remember them. He glanced in their direction as he spoke, voice tone earnest, and signed for them to join him. By that time their arrival had drawn the attention of other villagers who sidled over to see what was happening. More welcoming ensued. A few women had joined the gathering and looked with abject curiosity at Sybilla and PJ. A little girl broke free and tugged at Sybilla's hand. When she kneeled down to her level, the child plucked up a strand of Sybilla's blond hair, examining it closely. There was some good-natured laughing from the women. Sybilla joined in, and PJ waved shyly to the crowd, the ice breaker.

Davis discoursed for a while longer, making introductions and some explanation of why they were there. There were answering nods and murmurs signaling understanding. Finally, a woman who looked to be about forty called out to one of the men. She pointed to PJ and waved toward the sky. Sybilla supposed she was reminding them there was a child who hadn't eaten, and the night was coming fast. In turn, the man said something to Davis who dipped his head.

He turned to his fellow travelers, "Es is one of the T'uup's daughters-in-law. This is Chan Bor, one of T'uup's sons, her husband. I've known both since they were small. They've extended a kind invitation for us to stay in the family compound. Old T'uup is on some business at another village but should return, which is good. They say the *balché* may be ready soon."

Sybilla looked at him in question but was too tired to ask for an explanation. All she could think about was getting PJ fed and then passing out for the night. Her lack of sleep from the night before and the rough ride had caught up with her hours ago. She smiled her thanks to the couple. Young men magically appeared and relieved the Land Cruiser of its load. They hauled the bounty up an incline on a narrow dirt path that led to a cluster of unpainted wood-slatted huts topped with thatched roofs, enclosed by broken-down timber fencing. The travelers followed closely behind, and several dogs came to sniff them out. The porters entered one of the larger structures, which turned out to be the collective kitchen and general gathering area. Five women of varying ages were tending to pots over the open fire or making tortillas on a griddle. They looked up in surprise, which quickly changed to recognition and smiles. Several children were huddled in a far corner playing. Sybilla filed away her first impressions. The floor was dirt but packed hard and swept clean. The interior was utilitarian with the cooking area as the focus. Various implements hung in places on the walls, none of which stretched all the way to the ground or roof, in close convenience to the work area. Woven sisal baskets with several tiers hung from the rafters loaded with foodstuff, making it a challenge for an animal to get to them easily. There were a couple of long picnic-style rough tables and benches. Sybilla supposed the extended family must take their meals together there.

The most elderly woman wiped her hands on a towel and came to stand a few feet from Davis. Sybilla noticed that, even though her eyes showed much affection, she didn't take his hands or otherwise touch him. Two other older women joined in the conversation. Sybilla took the opportunity to note that the three women were dressed exactly alike: long, dark full skirts with white tunics covered by full aprons, many strands of colored beads hung around the neck and hair in one braid down the back ending with a complement of several toucan feathers. The two younger women, in ankle-length slim skirts and tight t-shirts, continued their labor but glanced up periodically. They wore their long hair loose pushed back with headbands. All were either barefoot or wore plastic sandals.

The women's attention turned in unison as Davis introduced them to his traveling companions. Sybilla felt their inquisitive eyes on her and PJ. She heard Es and Chan Bor mentioned, which produced nodding, more words, and guessed Davis was telling them of the invitation to stay.

He turned and said, "So, these are T'uup's wives. This is Chan Nuk and Nuk and Koh, the younger one. They've welcomed us here. And over there are Koh Elisa and Nah K'in, another of T'uup's daughters-in-law and the youngest, a daughter. Es and Chan Bor will be along in a bit. Some of the other family members may show up. A number of the married sons and their families live within this compound, too. The married daughters live with their husbands' families. But you can see that nothing is far away here."

Sybilla smiled at the women and said to Davis, "How many children does T'uup have?"

"Now that would be hard for me to remember. Maybe thirty or more but a number died early or in childbirth. Life is hard here. If a child lives past four, then there's a good chance for adulthood. But you see Koh is pregnant. She and Es are about the same age. And Es is one of Chan Nuk's younger daughters."

Sybilla was confused, "But wouldn't T'uup be ninety or so?"

"Yup."

"Good for him!" Javier chuckled. Sybilla was shocked into silence.

Nuk stepped forward, said something to Sybilla and touched PJ's arm.

"She's offering to take you to the toilet," Davis said. "And then to where you'll sleep with some of the children and women. We'll meet back here for some food."

"That would be great," Sybilla replied.

Davis turned to Javier, "They'll put you and me in quarters with the unmarried sons. We're not adults to them until we've married. A bit too late for me to grow up," he smirked with that aside. Javier raised his eyebrows, an expression that was becoming commonplace for him, and took in his change of status.

Nuk led Sybilla and PJ to the toilet, which was contained in a nearby outside room attached to their sleeping compartment. The bedroom consisted of several hammocks tied to the overhead beams and some mats on the floor. Toys littered the floor. Cardboard boxes stacked next to a wall appeared to contain clothing. Sybilla was glad they'd brought sleeping bags and intended to sleep on the ground. She could imagine getting all twisted up in one of hammocks or dumping herself and PJ on the floor in the middle of the night. While they'd been in the bathroom, thankfully with a flush toilet, someone had delivered her gear. She felt helpless without a common language or translator, but gestured to Nuk with her sleeping bag and motioned to one of the mats forming an unspoken question. Nuk nodded profusely and left them to return to the kitchen.

PJ had been quiet since their arrival in K'ak. He sat on the edge of the mat as she fussed with arranging their sleeping space. "Mama, where are we?"

Sybilla sank down beside him and put her arms around him. If it was a strange environment for her, it must be doubly so for him. "PJ, we're going to discover that together."

The next words he said startled her, "Will we see my daddy here?"

She didn't know what to say, any plausible words fleeing her mind. So she just gave him an uneasy smile in return for his steady gaze. An intelligence much older than PJ's years looked out through his eyes.

SYBILLA AND PJ rejoined everyone in the kitchen. The women carried platters of food laden with tortillas, beans, rice and squash to the table. Bowls were already stacked. One of the young boys got up from his place on the bench so they could crowd in next to Javier. Davis appeared to be catching up on news, involved with a few of the men at the far end of the table. Sybilla fell on the meal, famished. Even PJ forgot the unaccustomed surroundings in favor of food. As she ate, Sybilla watched the goings-on surreptitiously and decided these people were like most any extended family. There was good-natured joking, sharing of tasks, interrupting each other. She immediately noticed two things though. The children seemed unusually well behaved, and the men didn't lift a finger, except to eat. Sybilla made a mental note to ask about the division of labor later. It appeared to be strictly divided and guessed that, as a woman, her seat at the table while the men consumed their meal was strictly in deference to her guest status. She felt herself bristle a bit. Some things aren't so different, she thought, thinking of her own Southern upbringing.

Javier advised her where he was lodged, a cabana in the back of the compound with some of the older boys. There was a separate entrance, he supposed so the teenagers' comings and goings wouldn't disturb the rest of the family, and a path that led into the jungle where a large field was cleared out. There they grew all the food they were eating tonight, except the rice, which they bought. One of his roommate's had proudly shown him the *milpa*.

Davis interrupted their discussion, "Looks for sure like the *balché* will be ready tomorrow. Chan Bor checked it on his way here. They think T'uup will arrive some time late tonight. If he does, then he'll start the ritual early tomorrow morning or the next day. So we should be prepared in case. Get a good night's rest because it will go on most of the day at least, maybe into the evening. This will be a good time to get some of your questions answered. It takes little prompting to get the storytelling started, especially with *balché* in hand."

"What ritual?" Sybilla asked.

"Best that you should witness it. For now just know that it's a prayer ceremony, feeding of the gods. A communal offering for those who still keep their traditions. There aren't as many. But that's another problem," Davis shook his head slowly. His face showed a measure of pain.

They turned in soon afterward, the women not allowing Sybilla to help clean up. The temperature dropped a bit so that she was happy for the cover of the light sleeping bag. She curled her body around PJ who dropped off immediately. Sybilla lay awake in the dark for some time, listening to the other occupants getting settled and nearby jungle noises. She wondered what tomorrow would bring. Her last thought before she succumbed to sleep was of Gabe, and she unconsciously sent out tendrils through the village, searching for any hint of his presence—present or past.

THE NEXT MORNING Sybilla awoke to an empty room. The place where PJ had slept at her side was still faintly warm. She heard chattering in the nearby kitchen and threw on her clothes to join the others, guessing that one of the women brought PJ along. Passing through the doorway, her eyes darted around until she located her child. Surprisingly, he wasn't with Javier or Davis. He sat quietly at the feet of an older woman she hadn't seen before, while activities to ready breakfast were carried on around them. Sybilla greeted PJ and took his hand, at the same time nodding her thanks to his caretaker. The woman held her eyes, an unusual directness she hadn't seen thus far in her limited experience with the Hach Winik. It was as though the woman was looking into her very interior. Sybilla was taken aback.

She settled PJ at the table, and they accepted bowls of some kind of gruel. Bananas were piled high in the center of the table. Sybilla felt the Native woman's appraising eyes still on her and PJ. She noted that he returned her looks between bites. Davis was nowhere to be seen, but Javier sat just on the other side of PJ.

She leaned toward him. "Do you have any idea who that woman is over there? I don't remember her from last night. And she keeps staring at me."

"I'm not sure. Probably a relative who's curious. She showed up about an hour ago and brought the wives a basketful of something that looked like wild greens, maybe herbs. Then she sat down and has been there ever since. One of the wives brought PJ in. I guess you were still sleeping. He noticed her right away and immediately sat down by her where you found him," he said.

"That's strange," Sybilla glanced again at the woman, who was still calmly gazing at her and made no attempt to look away.

"I thought it was odd, too. I mean, PJ hasn't seemed scared since we got here, more shy. But he certainly hasn't joined in with the other children, aside from any adult," Javier offered.

"Maybe Davis knows who she is. Where is he anyway?"

"He's back with Old T'uup. Apparently he got back late as expected. Someone drove him in one of the village trucks."

Sybilla remembered seeing a pick-up truck that had seen much better days parked off to the side when they rolled into the village. That one and the one that carried T'uup must be the communal transport.

"I wonder why Nuxi' and Bol had to walk to Palenque with all the crafts. Seems like they could have taken the truck," Sybilla mused.

"My question, too. But Davis said there are only a few men here who know how to drive. Nuxi' and Bol aren't one of those. T'uup and two of his sons needed to attend a meeting about illegal logging in one of the other villages anyway. And they keep one truck available at all times for emergencies. There's no medical clinic here," Javier explained. "Although, if there was a serious accident I don't know what they'd do. You saw the condition of the roads and it's hours away from any facility."

"I guess they'd do what they've always done. They must have medicine people like other tribes," Sybilla said.

"I suppose," Javier started to say something else but was interrupted by Davis entering the room.

An elder accompanied him who had the most remarkably deep-lined face. It bespoke of his advanced age but didn't at all correlate to his coal black hair and twinkling dark eyes. Even though he barely brushed five feet, the way he carried himself caused him to appear much taller. In fact, he seemed to fill the room with crackling energy. Sybilla had only witnessed that once before in her young life. It was when the President of the United States made a brief campaign stop in Johns Wake when she was fifteen. He wasn't the president then but a candidate. She'd been roped into being a server by her mother during the dinner the local Democratic Party committee had in his honor. When she handed him his plate of fried chicken, she felt his charisma move over her like a balmy breeze soothing her soul. It hadn't taken much to know that man was a leader and their future president. Yet, here we are in the middle of a jungle, in a primitive shanty with a dirt floor where they cook over an open fire, and this ancient, barefooted man oozes the same qualities, Sybilla thought. Her mind did a little tilt.

"T'uup Garcia, may I present Sybilla Johns and Javier Alvaro," Davis said in Spanish. "And this little guy is PJ." T'uup smiled at them benignly and touched PJ on the head. Davis switched to T'uup's language and continued on for some time, periodically gesturing to Sybilla and Javier. T'uup, in turn, would acknowledge them with a nod or the same benign smile.

Nuk brought bowls of the mush over and the men sat down. Davis reached for a banana and said in an agitated voice, "T'uup has been telling me about the big meeting he just came from. The three main villages were represented, and there are a few families in outposts around a couple of the lakes that came in for it, too. The illicit logging operations are becoming bolder. They're getting closer and things have turned dangerous. He says last week one of the families went to their *milpa* in the morning to work. They were almost there when they heard chainsaws start up. When they got to their field they found some trees on the south end already cut down. The loggers must have already been there for at least a day or so. The family didn't hear them before because the *milpa* is a good distance from their home. When the father and sons started waving their hands for them to stop, one of the loggers started shooting at them! They had to run for their lives! The communities have elected T'uup's two sons to go meet with the regional Mexican government officials to get it stopped. So they'll leave day after tomorrow. T'uup decided to wait and hold the ceremony until tomorrow so they can plan about the meeting. But the *balché* won't wait more than that. So there will be prayers said for the protection of the trees, the *milpas*, also for his sons making that journey." Davis shook his head in disgust. Sybilla could see his rage beginning to bubble again.

One of T'uup's wives called over to him, and T'uup broke away to see what she needed. The logging discussion came to a temporary end.

The woman who had been staring at them took T'uup's place at Davis' elbow and greeted him profusely.

"Ah! Chax Nuk!" Davis exclaimed and exchanged pleasantries with her in Spanish for some time. Then he shifted to English. "Chax Nuk and I are old friends. She is one of just a few Hach Winik women who speak Spanish. At one time she and her husband lived in the town of Palenque. They used to visit me there. But they returned to K'ak some years ago when her husband became ill. She's a widow now and lives on the edge of the village. She knows how to work with plants from the forest and people come to her for cures, even those from other villages. Sometimes she helps the women in birthing if it becomes difficult. So she has a status in these parts that's unusual for her gender."

It was Sybilla's turn to assess Chax Nuk while Davis introduced her, a handsome woman with regal bearing. Sybilla's keen eye noticed that her braid was unadorned, the only difference in Chax Nuk's dress from the other women. "Please tell her that I'm very happy to meet her. I wonder if she might talk to me later about the plants she uses."

An exchange occurred between Davis and Chax Nuk. He bowed his head slightly and said, "She'd be fine to talk with you about the plants. She's also offered to squire you around. Since she speaks Spanish you can converse through Javier. That would free me up some to visit old friends. Not that I'm going to run off by any means. And she says she's quite taken with your boy."

At that point everyone looked at PJ who had his eyes locked onto Chax Nuk. Sybilla said, "I think the feeling is mutual. Tell her thank you. That would work very well."

Koh approached Chax Nuk and engaged her in conversation. Sybilla took that opportunity and asked a question. "Davis, all the other older women have feathers on their braid. Does it mean something that Chax Nuk doesn't?"

"Yes, it does. Young men give a feather as an offering, a proposal of marriage for a daughter. If the mother accepts it from him and wears it then she's signaled agreement to the marriage. The number of feathers shows the number of married daughters. Chax Nuk has no daughters."

"That's such an interesting practice. Does she have sons?"

"She has no living children. They all either died in childbirth or didn't make it to adulthood. That may be why she's devoted herself to her craft. I know that her uncle was an adept, and she apprenticed herself to him years ago, unusual for a female that he formally accepted her in that role. But she can be quite persuasive," he smiled.

"That's so sad. Her life must be difficult as a widow here. She's all alone? No one to help her?"

"As I said, she retains an unlikely role and stature within the Hach Winik community. For most widows it would be quite hard. However, the people exchange food and other goods for her services, or even help in her small *milpa*. That's where you should ask her to take you. She could take you on a forest walk, too, but she's transplanted some of the herbs into her plot."

Javier and Sybilla nodded to each other in agreement. Sybilla said, "That would be perfect for our purposes! Would you ask her? Also if it's okay to take photos and record her?"

Koh's consult with Chax Nuk had ended, and she was waiting politely. Davis made the inquiry, "She'd be glad to if you'd like to go now. And no problem with recording or photos." Sybilla and Javier charged off to collect their equipment while Chax Nuk took PJ's hand.

Chax Nuk led them along the main path through the village, the first time Sybilla got a larger look at the rest of the settlement. It was mostly identical to Old T'uup's place, compounds with several of the same rough planked huts with enclosures to keep the chickens from escaping. There was no indication of any other livestock, not even horses. She noted the meeting hall where they first saw the villagers. Next to that looked to be a small store. A glance through the doorway revealed shelves sparsely filled with items like canned tuna, powdered milk and the ever-present soft drinks.

They turned onto a lesser-used trail heading toward the lake. The sun had not yet intervened, and it was still shrouded in morning mist. Sybilla remarked on its mystical allure. They all stopped to admire the view.

Javier translated, "Chax Nuk says there is a place very sacred to them on the other side of the lake, a cave. It's the home of one of their gods. She goes there to make offerings. The mists hide it from those who shouldn't go. Even in full sunshine it can't be seen by them, and it's protected by caimans, too. She says when she travels there she knowingly steps from this world into another dimension and may not be able to return. But so far Ah K'ak liked her offerings and released her to come back."

A small hut was ahead set back from the lake and, with the exception of its breathtaking setting, resembled the others. Chax Nuk led them through the gate and around to the back where there was a garden plot with beans, corn, squashes and other vegetables. But there were also medicinal plants. She led them on a tour, lovingly touching the leaves of one plant and then another, all translated through Javier.

"This one is anise. Good for digestion. And this one the same, lemon grass. You boil and drink as a tea against an upset stomach. Here is wild clove you chew for muscle cramps," she continued with her tutorial mentioning mulberry, wild lime, ginger and others as she moved along. She finally stopped in front of a tall stately specimen and fingered its leaves reverently. "I don't know the name of this one in Spanish. She is sent to us by Äkna', our Mother Moon, and she lifts the spirit and opens the way."

A sad look came over her face. "I am very worried what these loggers will do. If they remove Hachäkyum's forest all these plants that heal us will be no more. The doctors have their medicines but mostly they don't work so well. They don't have the life force of the plants and this is what calls upon the life force in us. The plants talk to us this way and convince us to be strong. That is how healing takes place through them."

She turned back to the stately plant and chanted softly for a few moments then carefully detached one of its long slender leaves. She took Sybilla's hands, enclosing the leaf between her palms. Once again, Chax Nuk held Sybilla's eyes with her gaze.

A look of confusion came over Javier's face. "She says to tell you that the one you searched for in the night is not here."

Sybilla froze, still holding the frond as she received it. Chax Nuk turned, leading PJ back in the direction they had come. Javier followed. After a while Sybilla tucked the leaf into her bag and retraced her steps.

— Chapter Forty —

THE NEXT MORNING Sybilla arose just after dawn. When she entered the kitchen with PJ, she found Javier and Chax Nuk there waiting for them. Old T'uup had already gone, Davis with him. Koh was dishing up some bowls of the same watery gruel as yesterday offering them to those few assembled at the table.

"Chax Nuk says that PJ should eat but those of us who are going to participate in the *balché* ceremony should eat lightly," Javier advised. "Then we need to go down quickly so we don't miss anything. Old T'uup left before the sun came up to prepare."

"That's fine. I can go without eating for a while," Sybilla snagged a bowl for PJ. "Why don't we go? I can take this for PJ."

The previous day they'd had a sneak peek at the advance work involved. Chax Nuk took them down a path at the back of Old T'uup's compound leading away from the homes and *milpa*. They followed her through brush and high grass until they came to a young ceiba tree. Sybilla commented, recognizing it even in its much smaller version due to the thorny trunk. Chax Nuk explained that T'uup planted it a few years back to act as a guardian to his god house. They began to descend. Below was a cleared-out hollow hugged on three sides by the hill, bordered by thick rainforest on the other. Its only contents were two thatched *palapas*, one three times as large as the other, and a long dugout canoe held upright by a complement of sturdy sticks. The area was deserted with the exception of Nuk and Chan Nuk who were occupied in the smaller structure. Nuk was vigorously grinding corn by hand at a well-worn worktable while Chan Nuk held large banana leaves above an open fire making them pliable. Next to the fire ring sat a huge Dutch oven half-filled with leaf-wrapped packets. They greeted the visitors and went back to their work.

Javier translated, "This is a sacred place, Old T'uup's god house. The women are making tamales for tomorrow. These are ceremonial offerings but we will eat them, too. You'll see tomorrow. Over there is the *balché* fermenting for the last four days. It's made from bark, honey and water." Chax Nuk had pointed to the dugout overlaid with large palm leaves and tied securely with vines.

Sybilla walked over to the remaining *palapa*, peered in and started to take a step inside but felt Chax Nuk lightly take her arm and draw her back. "The women aren't allowed inside. We must stay over here by the kitchen. But maybe you can be a little closer tomorrow. We'll see."

Javier spoke to Chax Nuk then said to Sybilla. "Sorry about that. I asked if it was okay for me to step inside and take some shots. She says there's no restriction on me because I'm a man. I thought it might be a good thing, to get some shots without the people."

"Sure, go ahead. That's a good idea," Sybilla replied. "And we've got to respect the customs." Even if I don't agree with them, she said under her breath.

Javier walked around quietly snapping, pausing every now and then to throw questions at Chax Nuk. She patiently tutored them while Sybilla held out a recorder to catch her words. The god house poles were situated according to the Four Directions. The wooden shelf that hung from the eaves on the west side contained thirteen terracotta pots, each one portal to a god. If the god wanted to participate in a ceremony, its receptacle would be brought out. Netting similarly hung was filled to overflowing with gourd bowls, the *balché* drinking vessels. Some baskets and a conch shell sat underneath, kept off the ground by a wooden plank. Otherwise, the god house was sparely furnished. Only a few low, wooden stools or logs were grouped around a cold fire ring.

But this morning a fire crackled in the chilled air. A few men in traditional dress were already present; they'd drawn the stools up close and huddled to catch some warmth. Their normally white shifts were dotted with red dye. The god pots had been placed in the middle, arranged in a line on the ground facing east, with palm leaves spread out in front. Old T'uup was carefully laying six-inch rings made of woven vines on top. Davis sat on a log directly across, next to another frond display. There rested a large terracotta footed vessel with the drinking gourds, freed from their netting, clustered around it. When his traveling companions approached, Davis greeted them and called to Chax Nuk as she joined Nuk and Chan Nuk in the god house kitchen. He wore a white bark headband dotted with the same red dye.

"Sybilla. Javier. Come on over," Davis held out his hand to PJ and curled him into a hug. PJ laughed and remained balanced on Davis' lap.

"Sybilla, it's not usually done, but T'uup has given his permission for you to sit on the perimeter of his god house. He's fine for you to record anything you want to. And photos are okay, but he doesn't like video. He's agreeable to this only because of the article you'll be writing. He wants the word to get out about the logging companies, the dangers to his people and the complicity of the government. But I still want you to keep our agreement. I want to see what you write before you send it off to publish." He looked at her meaningfully.

"No problem," Sybilla replied, "And please pass on my thanks for this accommodation."

As if he understood every word, T'uup looked up from his preparation and smiled in their direction. Sybilla and Javier laid down their equipment outside the god house within easy reach and settled themselves in the corner as best they could. Sybilla noticed the men were barefoot and removed her shoes. Old T'uup reached up into the central eaves and brought down a large square paddle that looked like something a pizza maker might use. He sat down on his haunches and began digging a gooey substance out from yet another gourd with his fingers. Rolling pieces between his palms, he placed them equidistant on the board, so that it looked all the world like he was readying a baking sheet loaded with cookie dough to pop into an oven. T'uup held the paddle aloft and began to chant, swiveling to each of the Four Directions. More men and a few young boys wandered down, the men finding seats in the god house, the young boys hanging around just outside. With the exception of T'uup's wives, Chax Nuk and a few young women of the family who remained near the kitchen, females were patently absent.

PJ had clambered down from Davis' lap and joined Chax Nuk. He sat at her feet happily eating a banana she'd given him.

T'uup completed his chant and carried the laden paddle over to the god pots, and removing the sticky globs one by one, placed them on the black mounds in each god pot until all was shared between them.

"What's he doing?" Sybilla asked Davis.

"That resin is copal, *pom*, one of the headiest scents you'll ever smell. The gods like it. As the smoke ascends it turns into tortillas, food for the gods. You'll see that the god pots have different features to distinguish them from each other but the mouths are all open so they can be fed, aside from the *pom* that goes into the interior."

Sure enough, Sybilla could see an exaggerated lower lip jutting out from the simple features that adorned the outside of the pots.

"Old T'uup will bring the *balché* over and fill the drinking gourds there then make the offering to the gods," he gestured to some baskets filled with leaf-wrapped tamales, the same they'd seen being made the day before. "He'll offer them the tamales, too. Now you'll see that all the gods wanted to be involved today. Not one of them stayed on the shelf. There is much at stake, and they know it. Old T'uup will be asking for help to protect the forest and all creatures that live within it, their *milpas*. He'll ask the gods to intercede on their behalf, that his sons will be heard by the government, that all are safe and may live in harmony. So over there is Hachäkyum who created the Hach Winik and there Äk'inchob, his son-in-law who protects the *milpas*, and there Äkyantho'. He must be included to have any effect. He's the god of foreigners and commerce, so he speaks their language," Davis continued until he named each one and their role, pausing before he ended. "Ah yes, and there is Äkna'. T'uup said he had to give her special prayers and reassurances. Our Mother sometimes gets a bit jealous. He had to get her permission to allow you this close—and to ensure that you wouldn't distract the male gods. So please be unobtrusive."

Sybilla looked at Davis to see if he was kidding. His serious look told her: he wasn't. T'uup finished placing the *pom*, looking strangely like caramel-colored topknots on black beanies resting in ceramic bowls. He carried the large footed vessel over to the *balché* canoe, one of his sons in tow. They carefully untied the vines that held the palm fronds in place, pushing them aside enough so that the elixir inside was exposed. Sybilla wandered over and saw a muddy-colored liquid with some questionable looking debris floating on top. Old T'uup draped a large handkerchief over the top of the terracotta container. His son dipped a drinking gourd into the canoe and emptied its contents onto the handkerchief, which acted as a strainer. A good thing, too, from the looks of it, Sybilla thought, noticing the small drowned insects and sticks left on the cloth. The process continued until the container was nearly full to the top. T'uup made a big show of attempting to pick it up himself until his son helped him. The two grunted with their burden, returning it to its designated place with the empty drinking gourds. The others continued their conversations with each other, which seemed to include much joking.

Sybilla was fascinated with Old T'uup's actions. He picked up the conch shell and, turning again in the Four Directions, blew into it several times, producing blasts that called the gods to the ceremony, Davis told her. That done, he took his time doling out an amount of *balché* to the gods' drinking gourds then used a rolled up palm leaf as a dropper, dipping it into the gourds and dribbling *balché* into the mouth of each god pot. The gods must have been satisfied because he took a break to fill up the remaining gourds. He began passing them out to the men who took big gulps. Sybilla felt Davis nudge her arm.

"T'uup wants to know if you'd like some," Davis said. He was holding a gourd out to her expectantly. "You won't offend him if you don't want to. He's being polite. As a woman, you don't need to accept."

"Why not?" Sybilla said, "I've come this far. I'll try it." She bobbed her head in thanks to T'uup and examined the contents carefully to check for floating things. None discovered, Sybilla tentatively brought the bowl to her lips and sipped. She did her best to keep from screwing up her face. Luckily, only Davis was watching her, anticipating her response. Javier was preoccupied with his own bowl, taking long drinks.

"Ewww. It's oily or something. Tastes like kerosene smells!" Sybilla pronounced.

Davis chortled, "I guess it's an acquired taste. No need to drink it if you don't want it."

"No, I'll hang onto it and give it a chance," she replied. Old T'uup called over to the women, and a young boy carried a few gourds of *balché* to the kitchen. The wives threw back commentary, laughing. All very informal, Sybilla noted to herself. Checking on PJ, he appeared to be carrying on a conversation with Chax Nuk. She was nodding and replying as though they spoke the same language. Very strange, Sybilla thought but turned her attention back to T'uup who had resumed feeding the gods. He gouged his thumb into a tamale and deposited the bounty into the mouth of a god pot, repeating the process until all had a portion. Then he offered the baskets to those assembled. When it came to her, Sybilla looked for a smaller one and plucked it out, not sure she could choke it down. The banana leaf packet had blackened from steaming. She imagined its hidden contents unappetizing and wasn't feeling too adventuresome after the sip of *balché*. Sybilla opened the banana leaf to find a compact tamale, the texture slick and plastic-like. Breaking off a small piece, she popped it into her mouth and chewed warily.

"Why this is delicious! A bean tamale?" Her features reflected her pleasure. Sybilla took another nip of *balché*, and this time found it not so bad. "I guess the *balché* could grow on me," she said to the air.

In the meantime, Old T'uup lit a firebrand and stooped over one god pot then the next lighting the *pom* until all were blazing. The god house filled with *pom* smoke. It entered Sybilla's nostrils and registered profoundly in her brain. In that moment, she felt transported to another dimension, no longer the cautious observer but fully present in the midst of the happenings around her.

As if on signal all the men rose as one, holding small palm fronds, and lined up behind Old T'uup, including Davis. Only Sybilla and Javier remained seated in the god house. She noticed that Davis had freed his mane so that it hung loose. She didn't know if it was an optical illusion, but tendrils of *pom* smoke seemed to capture strands of his hair and float it playfully in the air around his head. In her fantasy, she saw it as the gods' version of a welcome mat. Indeed, even though Davis was Anglo he appeared as natural and comfortable in that environment as any of the Hach Winik. Her respect for him grew again.

T'uup alone chanted as the men moved along the line of god pots, the palm leaves they held, taking on a life of their own, undulating through the *pom* smoke. Suddenly the limitation of language fell away. The alternating tones of T'uup's prayer, exaltation to mournful loss, acted as the backdrop to ancient story and entreaty. Sybilla became the human being created by Hachäkyum and his wife, She of the Sacred Breadnut Leaves. It was she, Sybilla, who planted her feet on the earth and found it firm, who felt the rays extending from Hachäkyum on her skin, who walked through the lush jungle and heard the comforting calls of monkeys and birds, saw corn growing in the *milpa*—and knew that all was well; food was plentiful. She rejoiced in her soul. And it was she who found herself just as suddenly in a wasteland. Gone were the trees, the ground opened in parched chasms. No birdcalls giving comfort to her walk, only bereft silence. No corn in the charred remains of the *milpa*; nothing grew. Sybilla felt the hunger of her stomach as it embraced her backbone. She heard the internal keening of her spirit. Then all was black. She felt herself floating, no foothold, no foundation. Slowly, the sounds of Old T'uup's chant returned, the language foreign. She was aware of her toes scrunched up in the dirt, the tears still wet on her cheeks. She opened her eyes and saw that the men had returned to their seats and were picking up their *balché* bowls to quaff their thirst. Davis examined her intently then held out a palm leaf. She took it and covered it with her palms, gazing at the god pots as the remaining *pom* burned itself out. Finally, she glanced down at her recorder. Somewhere along the line it had stopped. But Sybilla didn't care.

— Chapter Forty-one —

SYBILLA KNEW SHE'D been uncannily affected by her experience in the god house. She wasn't able to explain it logically and kept any thoughts to herself. She retained a close eye on Javier who, like her, had never participated in such a ritual as far as she knew. But he appeared as he always did, nothing unusual. She, on the other hand, felt like she was walking through a different world than she was used to, not the one she habitually observed from a distance that gave her the keen photographer's eye. She even found it difficult to speak, words seeming too crude, too disruptive. Since Old T'uup's prayer the day before she had the perplexing sense of having lost her skin, as though she was an intrinsic part of everything. It was disorienting, the connection startling, and frequently so uncomfortable that she wanted to run and hide. But at least for the moment, her skin refused to recreate its membrane, the one that encapsulated her from the outside world. So over the next day, instead of her characteristic note-taking, she merely sat in the kitchen with the women and children and let the nature of their lives permeate her. She wandered with PJ and Javier by the lake's edge and lingered, soaking up the ethereal qualities that housed the sites sacred to the Hach Winik. And she really saw Old T'uup, not as a diminutive curiosity but the powerful leader of his people that he was, whose lineage stretched back to ancient times. It was in this state that Chax Nuk approached her, took her hands. Sybilla looked down in surprise. Something passed between them; her hands tingled and felt suddenly warm. Chax Nuk calmly held her eyes. This time Sybilla didn't look away disquieted. Instead, she returned her gaze. Emotion washed through her. Tears welled up and slipped down her cheeks, not because she was sad but because she felt seen, maybe for the first time, truly. In that moment, Sybilla realized something. When she thought Chax Nuk had been staring at her like an unwelcome snoop, she'd really been sending her acknowledgment. It was Sybilla's own discomfort with herself that had been the barrier. She looked back at Chax Nuk then and saw the invisible thread that ran between them. Sybilla had no idea why or how it was woven. But she knew.

Chax Nuk called over to Javier. He was sitting a distance away with Old T'uup and Davis, who was holding PJ on his knee. Javier wandered over. Chax Nuk spoke to Javier quietly, gesturing periodically toward PJ. Javier's eyes widened in surprise. He paused before turning to Sybilla, as though he was unsure of what he'd heard.

"Chax Nuk says that your boy is special, that he was born of the sun but must be taught the swiftness of the deer. Already he looks for this teaching even as young as he is. But his teachers are absent. There is a portal that comes. He must be protected, and he must be watched over."

Sybilla listened. A few days ago such a proclamation would have been nonsensical to her, even terrifying, the words of some lunatic talking about her son. But somehow, coming from Chax Nuk, it was none of those things.

Javier continued, "She says she must go home with you. She says that she, Chax Nuk, will watch over him."

Sybilla glanced over at Old T'uup. He was too far away to have heard the conversation. But he gave Sybilla an imperceptible nod. She heard Flora's voice from those many months ago: ...*there will be another one who comes*. She thought about the heavy load she carried: the unceasing demands of her work, being a single parent, loneliness. Unhesitating, she said, "Yes, you must." Sybilla took Chax Nuk's hands again to seal the agreement.

It was only much later that she regretted their pact.

Preston

Chapter Forty-two

PRESTON WAS GENTLY shaken out of his reverie of the past by a paw delicately placed on his arm. He opened his eyes to find Gato sitting beside him on the bed staring into his face intently. He was still holding the smooth stone and the blue feather loosely in his hand that he'd found in the tin treasure box in his closet.

"Yes?" Preston ran his hand over her bony back and scratched her ears. But Gato shook him off as if to say: We don't have time for this nonsense. She continued to stare.

"What is it, girl?" Gato was demanding when she wanted to get her point across. Preston heard a high-pitched sound, not unlike that of a circling mosquito close by. Gato twitched her ears and diverted her attention to the treasure box from his childhood. It was where he'd left it on the other side of his bed, its lid off. The tin seemed to move. Gato slunk around him and took up a post beside it—on high alert. Her eyes grew large and dark, looking for prey. A paw snaked out and swatted the box.

"You're crazy, girl. There's nothing in there." Gato tentatively dug into the contents with her paw until she came into contact with a small leather medicine bag, the kind that's worn around the neck. Suddenly, Preston heard the tone again, and Gato jumped back like a shot. "Whoa! Maybe I was wrong! Good find. I'd almost forgotten this."

He fished out the soft pouch. It vibrated in his hand, and the almost inaudible tone instantly switched from intermittent to what Preston could only think of as excited chatter, like someone who has held silence too long. He lifted the flap and slid out the stone inside. This one had ridges. "Oh yes, girl. I do vaguely remember this. I don't know where it came from, but it sure is talking." Gato had inched up until she was almost nose to stone, giving it close scrutiny.

Preston sat holding the smooth stone in one palm, the ridged stone in the other, and became aware of the difference between the two. The smooth stone brought the sensation of cool water running over him, taking away any impurities. The ridged stone resonated through a steady heat that found its way into his very core, an infusion. It's just like the sun, he thought. Indeed the ridges were shaped like the sun, oddly enough. Both were equally powerful but distinct from each other in their emissions.

"I think they both have stories to tell, don't you? This Water Stone and this Sun Stone?" he said to Gato who still had the situation under surveillance. She blinked at him slowly as if in agreement. "Okay then. I'm going to listen."

He slipped the Water Stone into his pants pocket and returned the Sun Stone to its pouch, hanging it around his neck. Preston carried the blue feather over to his bureau and placed it among the found nature objects he had in an altar of sorts for safekeeping, not wanting to risk damage. Over the next days the stones became his constant companions. He only removed them to shower. Even when he went to sleep at night, the Sun Stone remained around his neck in its pouch. He placed the Water Stone under his pillow. Preston felt comforted and sensed that the imperceptible tales they transmitted held memories that he didn't know he had, unconscious knowledge of times untold, like an elixir that ran through his bloodstream inducing hope. Messenger maintained a presence but offered no counsel, his very quietude echoing the deep truth delivered.

— Chapter Forty-three —

IT WAS NOT UNUSUAL for Preston to spend time outdoors. He was drawn to nature and felt more at home in wilderness areas camping and hiking solo than he ever did walking city streets in a crowd. In fact, he avoided the congestive energy there. It seemed to choke out his very lifeblood. When he was an adolescent Sybilla had talked about moving them to Phoenix because it would be more convenient with her work and jetting off regularly. But in the end she said she liked coming home to the quiet and didn't want to uproot him from the only home he'd ever known. He was begrudgingly appreciative. As Mother Lode had begun its inevitable growth, Sybilla was astute enough to buy up places on either side of them as they came up on the market. Her increasing status as a photojournalist provided the means. The land was more valuable than the houses on them. She had one leveled but fixed the other one up to quarter the changing stream of housekeepers throughout the years. When she was on assignment, the housekeeper would sleep in a small room near their kitchen to oversee Preston but return to the house provided upon her return.

Sybilla upgraded their home and added natural landscaping on the expanded property. Her handiwork created a sweet private oasis sheltering them from the surrounding out-of-control development. But she'd never touched the back corner of the yard. Preston had vague memories of that spot containing Mama Luna's garden, and it was there he had a compulsion to spend time. He was attracted especially in the evenings. It began after he'd rediscovered the stones in the tin box and kept them on his person. He was thankful that the desert stretching to the north was still protected land, although he feared that some developer would make a deal with the state, and the pristine landscape would be wiped away forever. But for now there was an unobstructed view to the mountains in the distance.

He sat under the stars in the midst of the long-gone garden. Coyotes called in the distance. The medicine bag began to vibrate insistently against his chest. He drew out the Sun Stone and held it in his hand, listening. Such occurrences had become commonplace. Usually it was the Sun Stone but the Water Stone had its moments of garnering attention as well. In the quietest moments of the day he'd notice and pause for whatever message was there, normally nonverbal, something vibrational. But tonight was different. The message was verbal, a lilting chant of sorts that he couldn't decipher. It's unlikely anyone else could have heard it. As loud as the Sun Stone might get, he received its missal through his own resident interior. Imagery engulfed his visual field. The sterile dirt he sat in was exchanged for garden soil. A tall willowy plant was before him. Long ago memories surfaced and washed over him. The incomprehensible chant was suddenly clear.

Chan K'in. Chan K'in. Chan K'in. And he understood that the Sun Stone was calling his name, his True Name: Little Sun. He felt stirring deep inside. A feeling emerged every bit as physical as if someone was gently tugging him by the shirtfront. He followed the lead and moved to a place several feet away where a sweetish smell was strong. Preston stepped a few feet beyond, and the feeling and scent disappeared. He stepped back, and it was more potent than ever. Light was limited under the moonlight. Crouching down, he ran his hands over the ground but felt nothing of significance. He picked up a nearby rock and scraped the earth. The chant calling his name intensified. Something is there, something for me to find, he thought.

But the surface was hard and didn't give up its secrets easily. Preston sprinted to the garage and came back with a shovel and began to dig in earnest, albeit cautiously, exactly within the perimeter containing the pungent smell. The shovel hit something about a foot down then gave way. He drew out the blade carefully and started sifting the dirt with his hands. He pulled out small sections of saguaro skeleton, chunks of charred wood, a few stones that weren't native to the area. He set them all aside. Then his fingers felt something smooth with sharp edges, a dirt-caked shard of terracotta pottery. This must be what I hit, Preston noted. Gingerly, he dug at the loosened earth with his fingers and quickly came upon the remaining vessel. He held it up to better see and could have sworn that a ray of starlight extended downward to aid him. Breath left him in a rush. He'd been holding expectancy, a part of him already having remembered. Tears slipped slowly down his cheeks. Sadness and jubilation mixed in equal parts. The Sun Stone sang. The Water Stone joined in.

He sat down in the midst of the debris he'd cast aside and cradled the ruined pot. It was blackened inside from many fires—and still held pieces of unburned resin. From this receptacle had come the ephemeral fragrance of incense, reaching up through time. It had marked the spot he was to discover. A reflection bounced off a white object in the hole he'd dug, as if a star ray had again reached down in the dark to guide his attention. Preston leaned over and withdrew a white plastic container encrusted with soil. It was small and oblong. He cleaned it with his sleeve and flipped open the top. There were kitchen matches inside. With shaking fingers he withdrew a few. Dry. He struck one against the rough exterior of the terracotta vessel. Its small fire lit the night. He touched the match to the resin—and it instantly flared, perhaps unwilling to contain its own message any longer. The tendrils of heady smoke found its source, and his limbic brain released memories in a flood.

Once again he was a young child sitting in the dirt. The cactus skeletons weren't debris at all but part of an elaborate outdoor altar of found nature objects all encircled by stones. And next to him sat a man. He reached over and tended a small fire. He leaned back. His big hand patted Preston's small bare leg, and when he gazed down at him with his ice-blue eyes they were warm with love.

The resin had long burned out. But Preston sat for an indeterminate time savoring the sweet agony of recovery: what was lost and yet found. He finally got up. But before he turned to go into the house, he surveyed that corner of the yard, seeing beyond its present barrenness to the time when it held a sacred garden—and before that a hallowed portal.

PRESTON OPENED HIS EYES the next morning to Gato sitting close by patiently staring at him. Then he remembered the events of the night before and swung his legs over the edge of the bed, instantly awake. He threw on the clothes he'd deposited in a heap before jumping into bed.

"Girl, if that pot was still there and the matches, too, I wonder what else I'd find," he addressed Gato. She trotted ahead of him making a beeline to the kitchen clearly conveying: first things first.

Mama Luna must have put her garden in right over my dad's site. I wonder if she knew, he mused plopping Gato's bowl down absentmindedly. No feedback from Gato who had her mouth full.

It was early yet. The sun was just making its journey upward to peek over the mountain. He strode to the back corner of the yard and surveyed where he'd dug. The vessel and matches were inside on his bedroom bureau for safekeeping, but the cactus skeletons and rocks were where he'd left them. He picked up the spade and continued his excavation, this time carefully so as not to damage anything. Periodically, he traded off and used a hand trowel to comb the soil after it had been loosened enough. His efforts were quickly rewarded. Over the next several hours he turned up a variety of skeletons: cholla, prickly pear and more of the saguaro, along with dried seedpods, bleached out branches and a few skulls. One was coyote for sure and another so tiny he thought it might be hummingbird. But perhaps the most meaningful item was an intricately woven pouch the size of Preston's hand. Once the colors must have been bright but faded blues, orange and yellow survived. It had a few holes, unraveled places, likely where a desert rodent had tested it out as a meal. Inside were more chunks of resin like those he'd burned last night. He imagined his dad must have touched the bag many times in an attitude of reverence, extracting the incense that would carry his prayers in its smoke. Preston sensed residual traces of his father as he fingered the cloth, and the pouch became as important to him, a ritual item of communion. He would use its contents sparingly with only the purest intent.

With each item he unearthed Preston felt a quickening, an affirmation as to just how paramount it was for him to follow these clues into the treasure trove of the past. He knew without a doubt that this was his birthright. And I had it stolen from me, he thought angrily. He had a realization that Mama Luna never would have so haphazardly buried the site with its ceremonial contents disrespected in that way.

"Sybilla must have demolished it after she ran him off," he said to the air. His face hardened into a scowl. Preston was very glad she wasn't at home now. She would have interfered. She'd returned from the Middle East long enough to see him graduated from college and then flew back to resume her work. She wasn't due back for at least another month. In the meantime, he'd been free to ruminate and consider his future. Sybilla hadn't put any pressure on him then, although she put forth the idea of graduate school. Preston had shrugged it off as meaningless. He didn't want to bide time any more. This is my journey now, he decided. And I've got deeper teachers. He touched the Sun Stone and Water Stone, reassured. But he'd noticed that Messenger had removed himself since the Stones reappeared. He felt a pang and briefly wondered if Messenger had left him after all these years. Maybe I've graduated in that way, too, he contemplated the possibility. Deep down he knew that Messenger would be there in a pinch.

Over the next day Preston recovered everything he could from his father's deconstructed sanctuary. The dig expanded. He made an unanticipated find buried in the common area overlapping Mama Luna's garden and his father's site: a woven strap that could only be one of her own. His heart lightened even more. Now I have something from both of them, he thought, and tied it around his head. Its tail ends hung down brushing the back of his neck.

Preston was finally satisfied that the dig had ceded all it contained and covered it back over with the dirt he'd removed. He began to make forays into the wild. He carried back items similar to those he'd found of his dad's and particularly ironwood, acacia and juniper branches he'd scavenged from the desert and mountain floor. He piled them where the dig had been. Those that were twisted and ravaged most pleased him. When he had a good selection to work with he began to construct a wickiup, meticulously interweaving the stash from his father and those newly acquired from his forays. In this way Preston began to reclaim his lineage, also weaving in what he symbolically represented as solely his. It gave him grounding. Preston was awed. How could such a simple process of recreating this space have this effect on me? I guess it really means something, puts things in motion. Yes, it does indeed. He felt the habitual itchiness that ran just beneath his skin gradually being replaced by bubbles of excitement.

He put final touches on the wickiup, a fire ring just outside its entrance and a larger stone circle enclosing it all, thus making it evident that here lies a sanctuary. It made an unmistakable statement as a work of natural art but more than that: It was a sacred place. It held memories and secrets to be revealed. But that night when he sat before the fire, feeding it with herbs, he had the strong sense that something was missing that he should have in his possession at that moment. The Sun Stone began to chant. With invisible hands, it tugged at his shirtfront in the same way that guided him to his father's terracotta vessel—and set the stage for his discoveries. He knew enough to follow its lead.

Strangely, it brought him to the garage. He flipped on the light. It wasn't the neatest. There were shelves that went from floor to ceiling with things crammed in haphazardly, stacks of boxes in front of that, gardening implements here and there, Things had just piled up over the years. It hadn't even been touched when his mother did the renovation. He had no idea what all was there. And yet, the Sun Stone did. After pausing, he wrestled boxes away from the far corner, which allowed him to stand in front of a length of shelves. He was astounded when his hand reached out, under some power other than his own, fished behind some old paint cans and plucked out a stack of newspapers. Too thick to grasp at once, half of them fell to the floor. There among the fallen newspapers was a dingy white cloth folded in a square. Preston bent over to retrieve it. He rubbed his hand over the scratchy texture. Again, as in the last days, tears welled and slipped down his cheeks. He recalled a distant time.

— Chapter Forty-five —

PRESTON SOUGHT CONSCIOUS awareness. He wanted his daily thoughts informed by remembrances and teachings from long ago. He wanted to embody their guidance, have the dots connected, intuitively. This much he knew: He was teetering on a precipice, about to swan dive. These last years he'd been biding his time for this time, for a journey that would determine his make-up and his destiny. But there was a gap. With only a vague sense of the destination and little of the landscape, he had no map to get there, no idea where to begin, or how to go back in time so that he may return to the present renewed.

He took to sleeping in the wickiup. He let Miriam, the current housekeeper, know so she wouldn't worry if she came over to check on him in the night and found him gone. Miriam had been with them for five years, and even though he was long past needing supervision, she still fussed over him. Preston knew she'd worried about his increasingly dark moods over the past year. He'd done what he could to hide his unrest, but she had noticed. He was glad she cared.

Even though fall had arrived by the calendar it was still hot in Mother Lode, too hot really to go outside until well into the evening when the temperature began to drop drastically. By then the nightly ceremonial fire he built was not only tolerable but welcome against the frosty air. Preston kept his sleeping bag in the wickiup to stave off the chill after the coals died down, always careful to shake it out before sliding inside just in case some unwelcome bedmate had found its way to shelter. Sometimes Gato joined him curled up next to his belly, soaking up the toasty warmth produced by dual body heat.

After getting over the shock of finding the white cloth those weeks back, he'd examined it closely. That's when he realized it was really two oblong pieces sewn together with a head hole in the middle. It looked like it had once been sewn down the sides to make a gown of sorts but the threads had all unraveled. He took to wearing it poncho-style but only in front of the fire at night. Somehow it seemed disrespectful to wear it at other times based on its meaning to him. Anyway, it was scratchy. When he wore it as he did, in the ritual space, he intended to connect with the knowledge it held, to allow it to permeate his very skin. Messenger had long ago taught him that vital energy never dissipated; the pattern was held in the ether for all time and could be called upon for purpose. He hoped for clues as to his father's whereabouts, virtually anything relevant in the way of teachings and guidance. But he grew frustrated. On one hand he was consoled, but on the other hand he grew impatient. Night after night he sat, fully intending his wish and nothing emerged short of a few breadcrumbs dropped on the trail of retrospect. They led him nowhere. He had fleeting memories, snatches of images that didn't make sense: flying out into the cosmos, big dripping leaves, or his father's arms wrapped around him, bundling him in the same white gown he now wore. Worse, the Sun Stone and even the Water Stone had become mute. There was no sign of Messenger still.

The hollow place in his heart started reminding him it was yet there. He felt the underlying yearning of loneliness. The edginess lurking under his skin spiked periodically. He shrank from the discomfort. No, I'm not going there again. He was firm. And yet the old familiar feelings became more demanding. Preston was locked in a struggle.

But one night in front of the fire Mama Luna's words came back to him: *Chan K'in. You call this name when you need to see. You look in the middle place and you will see what is so. This is the way of those who know.*

He threw some of his father's precious resin in the fire and began to chant his True Name. Did he imagine the flames started to jump a bit higher? In affirmation, the Sun Stone and Water Stone broke silence and joined him. The chorus attracted Gato who emerged through her cat door and made a direct path to Preston. She settled herself in the bowl left by his crossed legs and laid her chin on his knee. He called his True Name lyrically, softer then louder, until it cocooned the entire sanctuary—and only that reality existed. When he finally slowed to silence, a tremendous power, an energy unlike anything he'd ever experienced thrilled his body, indeed filled the cocoon. It surged and pulsated—and he could do nothing but surrender to it.

After a time he was drawn to lie prone. He crawled the few feet away to the wickiup and into his sleeping bag, although it seemed more like he was transported there, not under his own powers. Gato followed and looked strangely like she'd regained five years of cat life. He resisted closing his eyes until he could no more.

Roaring, like a wind tunnel, awakened Preston. He felt strange. He was floating, or so it seemed. A strong field inserted itself between him and the ground, keeping him slightly suspended. He was electrified. The interior of his sanctuary glowed. Mist swirled beyond. It was like being in the eye of a storm. He lifted one hand and held it up in front of his face. A jagged force field surrounded it, cartoon-like. The roaring intensified until Preston couldn't bear the sound. The familiar scenes that kept reality in place split wide open. In the black space revealed, something propelled itself toward him with comet-like speed. The immense head of a terrible snake hung before him, taking up every bit of his visual field. It appraised him. Preston forced himself to gaze back, taking in the abyss that stood for the serpent's eyes, the forked tongue flicking in and out, seeking to hypnotize. In that moment, its monstrous jaws opened wide—and an unseen force projected through, slamming itself between his brows. Preston fell into nothingness.

— Chapter Forty-six —

THE SUN WAS HIGH when Preston awoke the next morning. Bright rays peeked in through gaps in the wickiup where the wood didn't quite come together. It was already a hot box. Preston felt around for Gato, vaguely wondering what happened to her during the events of the night before. With some relief, he heard a yowl, and Gato stood framed in the entrance complaining to him about his laziness. He unfolded his body and headed toward the house, answering Gato's impatience to being fed.

There was no doubt in his mind that the visitation on the previous night had been real. He had the evidence when he touched his forehead and found it slightly sore. Although he'd never had anything with such tsunami force occur that he remembered, Preston accepted things that went bump in the night, and even the day, as normal. He preferred to acknowledge that he had certain gifts of perception, as Mama Luna's voice in his head reminded him. Certainly it was better than wondering about his sanity. He had Messenger to thank for schooling him and wondered again where he went. Just when I really need you, Preston thought. But maybe not so much. He felt opened. But how or what exactly that meant, he didn't yet know.

He waited until the sun was long gone, and the moon was well risen. The night had cooled and his fire was lit. He squatted Indian-style before the flames in his sanctuary. Rocking slightly on his haunches, he reviewed the day. He'd known that serpents held a special role in mythological stories throughout the world. Today he'd been compelled to learn more. There's no way the one he'd experienced was a myth, and he hadn't dreamt it either.

Perhaps because Mother Lode drew those with more eccentric tastes, especially in the last years, their small public library was replete with a collection of obscure, esoteric literature. Preston spent the afternoon poring through the material and came away quietly validated. From ancient times, the serpent predominated in a majority of world religions as a sign of communication with the gods and ancestors, dispensing wisdom. He found that snakes commonly appeared to people in states of altered consciousness. In some tribes live snakes were used in initiatory rites. It was only in the Bible's Old Testament did the serpent become demonized, something to be slain, a symbol of ill enticement. Preston stared into the fire and continued his rocking, entranced. How things get twisted, he mused. Yes, I'm being enticed, more like invited to remember what runs in my veins. But how? I'm only getting pieces. And Sybilla either doesn't know or won't tell me.

Then he recalled Mama Luna's long ago instruction on the "middle place." By now he felt rooted. No longer rocking, he was stock-still like some massive tree that reached into the earth and up to the stars. His eyes began to travel along a pathway, a farther point to a near point, repeatedly. He de-focused his eyes. There was pressure, almost pain, on the spot between his brows where the force hit him. The discomfort gave way to tingling, then to a whirling sensation that widened beyond the breadth of his head.

Preston heard Mama Luna's voice in his head encouraging him to let his eyes get very soft and to see the middle place where it gets even softer. His eyes continued traveling back and forth until…yes, he did see the middle place. It attracted his attention until he finally let himself rest there. It billowed and morphed into something finally recognizable. He was drawn into a scene of some world other than his own, yet vaguely familiar. Snippets of imagery fed to him over the last weeks filled out. The large dripping leaves came from densely packed trees, vines hanging from high branches. The buzz of insects and cries of birds reached his ears. Fingers of moist humidity brushed his skin. Tree branches shook, and a monkey showed itself, hanging by a very long tail. It looks like pictures I've seen of spider monkeys. The thought went winging through his mind. Then he noticed brown human faces framed by long, black hair merged amongst the trees, barely visible. They seemed to be staring curiously back at him. Preston was mesmerized by what lay before him. It's like we're in a house, each in opposite rooms with only a hallway between us. He thought idly what they must think from their side viewing his world, it being quite different. *Good thing it's limited to my backyard.*

It never occurred to Preston that his experience was anything other than reality, just perhaps not most people's reality. He was considering how to project himself through the space that separated them when a voice jarred him, every bit the same as someone shaking his body physically. He took a sharp breath in, exhaling a rush of frustration. The seam that had opened immediately stitched closed. The spider monkey and the people instantly dispersed. The rainforest vanished. What remained were the constants, what he'd placed there himself over the last couple of months: the wickiup, the fire ring, the stones.

He turned to the voice that called him. She stood halfway between the house and his sanctuary. "I'm sorry, Preston," Miriam repeated, "Your mama is on the phone from Afghanistan."

Great timing, he groused angrily. As he trotted inside to take the call he considered asking Sybilla once more about his dad. They spoke briefly. The line was bad. She told him she'd be home in two weeks, earlier than expected. He told her he was going to be traveling for a while. He didn't know exactly where.

"Okay, you deserve that," Sybilla's voice faded in and out. The last thing he heard before the line went dead was about asking Miriam to take care of Gato—as if he needed reminding—and to check in periodically. Preston put the phone down slowly.

He stood in the doorway looking up at the stars. He'd decided not to ask Sybilla anything. "I have to find this place myself," he murmured. "This is my journey. I wonder if the stars will guide me." He knew Messenger had purposefully stepped back. Preston no longer needed the same kind of teacher. But he did need the guidance that came from paying attention to whatever cues came his way. Preston felt the now-familiar vibrations where the pouch hung against his chest, followed immediately by the resonating response of what was nestled in his pocket. "Allies," he pronounced.

Chapter Forty-seven

SPIDER MONKEYS. RAINFOREST. That could cover a lot of territory, he considered. South America? No, that didn't feel right. Honduras? No. Guatemala? He felt a flutter of excitement in his mid-section. Mexico? Another flutter. That still covers a lot of ground. Preston said each out loud, testing, comparing the sensations they each produced. But he could tell little difference, if any. He finally decided that Guatemala would be his landing point. It had a large rainforest in the northern region. Besides, he remembered the pictures he'd seen of the big temple at Tikal overlooking miles and miles of jungle. He wanted to climb to the top and see that green expanse.As quickly as he made his decision, Preston did some research and booked his flight for a week away. He needed enough time to tie up a few loose ends since he didn't know how long he'd be traveling—or if he'd be back—and certainly wanted to be long gone before Sybilla's new arrival date, particularly if she came any earlier. The closest airport was in Flores, supposed to be no more than a couple of hours from Tikal. Having reserved his flight, the meaning of the journey he was launching began to sink in. He felt no trepidation.

His flight left in four hours and, on a good day, it took nearly an hour to get to the airport. Today Preston wanted no traffic snarls in the city. The night before he'd loaded his gear into his backpack, including a small tent and sleeping bag in case he needed them. There were just a few last-minute things to slip inside. He left it by the door.

Preston sat at the kitchen table drinking his coffee. He thought about all the changes that had come in this home over the years, how he'd thirsted for stories of the missing links. Gato had finished her breakfast and sat next to him daintily cleaning herself.

"Old girl," Preston's throat thickened. His eyes began to water. She jumped up on his lap. He didn't say more because some things needn't be said between good friends. He held her tight. She looked up at him. They remained that way for a while until Gato started squirming and leaped down. "Okay, I get it. Time for me to be on my way."

He brought his hand to his chest and then to his pants pocket. Satisfied that he had all he required, Preston allowed his eyes to sweep the room a last time then strode over and threw on his pack. He paused at the door, resting his hand on the knob in consideration. Then he purposefully stepped outside. In that split second, if he'd looked back, he would have seen Gato staring intensely, her body yearning toward him. The door clicked shut with a finality. He'd deftly walked through the threshold.

— Chapter Forty-eight —

EVEN THOUGH SYBILLA regularly traveled around the world, Preston had little experience in that area. Coming from stark desert, he was mesmerized by the green landscape and plentiful pockets of water as they flew over Guatemala. Since he left home bright anticipation buoyed him. During the layover in Guatemala City a fellow backpacker named Rob struck up a conversation saying he'd been knocking around Central America for the last three months. He'd just come from Tikal and was on his way to Copán in Honduras. He dispensed advice readily and talked a blue streak. I'm glad I'm not traveling with him, Preston noted. But he did listen and jotted down a few things Rob said that could prove useful later. Now as he flew into the airport just outside Flores, he saw the pretty little town with its red-tiled roofs situated on a small island in Lake Petén Itza, a short causeway connecting it to the mainland. He caught a taxi to the hostel Rob recommended. José, the desk clerk, was friendly. He heard lively chatter. A variety of languages and accents filled the air. There were a number of young people passing time in the courtyard garden, mostly from North America and Europe. Sybilla popped into his mind. She would have said it looked like a rest stop on the granola trail. He smiled shyly at a pixyish, dark-haired girl who'd managed to pull her colorful ragtag attire into something über-cool. She nodded at him and went back to her conversation.

Preston opted for one of the five-dollar-a-night hammocks the place offered. He dumped his pack in the locker and went out on the street. There was still an hour or so of light. The entire town could be traversed in a fifteen-minute brisk walk but he wandered the cobble-stoned lanes unhurriedly. When the sun started to set he found an open-air café on the waterfront and ordered beer and local fish. Marimba music could be heard from another establishment. He gazed out over the lake and marveled that he was actually there taking in its beauty. When he finally returned to the hostel, he fell into his hammock and slept soundly.

Preston left for Tikal well before first light. The mist was thick as he walked the path into the temple grounds, an unearthly reverence stilled the air. It's like I've stepped back in time, he thought. In the distance he heard roaring, and his skin prickled slightly. Visibility was constrained to just several feet ahead. Periodically, he noted shadowy movement and hoped it was merely other visitors. Dense forest was close. A sign materialized out of the fog directing him to Temple IV, the tallest in the excavated complex. The immense trees with roots snaking above ground like fingers fascinated him; he had to watch the trail carefully not to trip. Finally arriving at his destination, he considered the steep wooden stairs stretching toward the heavens. Their safety looked questionable. When he made it to the top he was breathing hard. It was worth it. Preston leaned against the roof comb of the crumbling relic, overcome with awe. The rainforest stretched for as far as he could see. The sun was just rising, its orange glow diffused, revealing other ruins standing tall through the canopy like so many sentinels. At this height, fine particles of moisture caressed his bare skin. He heard roaring, louder this time, and saw a migration of trembling leaves along the treetops, and knew it to be a howler troop on the move. The birds were waking up. He heard the raucous call of parrots interspersed with a melodic song like falling water and countless others he couldn't identify. He fell in love with the jungle.

Preston explored the complex until it closed for the night, only leaving for a short time to get some lunch at one of the park lodges. He was puzzled though. He'd made an assumption that messages from that Other World would pour in, but they didn't come. He sat on temple steps and actively sought direction, quietly chanting his True Name. Nothing. While he did feel a strong response to the site, it was more like stimulation that adventure brought. It wasn't the kind of resonance he experienced back in his sanctuary when he was testing where he should go. Maybe I'm off base, he mused. The Stones haven't said a word. Still, I can't believe that. My destination must be around here somewhere.

Feeling a bit lost, he dragged himself back to the hostel. By the time he got there it was quite dark.

Much the same travelers were sitting in pockets in the courtyard like they'd barely moved since the night before. He noticed the über-cool girl amongst them. Her lips curved in acknowledgement and motioned him over. Preston felt his cheeks color and chastised himself for blushing. Even though females had thrown themselves at him since before he was old enough to care, he didn't respond as he might. He'd get tongue-tied, uncomfortable because he wasn't good at social banter, particularly the kind between males and females. His shyness was mistaken for aloofness more often than not. Any connection that might have been made usually came to an abrupt halt. Because of that liability he'd had little experience with the opposite sex and made few friends his own age.

But I'm going to be different. That's what this journey is about. He forced himself to go over.

"Hello," he said.

"I thought you disappeared!" she spoke English with a heavy French accent. "I thought maybe the Maya ghosts carried you off!" She teased him and a deeper shade of red stained his face. He sat down in the chair next to her.

"Ahhh. No, I wanted to see the sunrise at Tikal," Preston dipped his head self-consciously and looked up at her through his long lashes, which had the unintentional effect of charming her.

"And you didn't ask me to go?" she flirted.

"Ah," Preston didn't know what to say.

"I'm Evie, short for Evangeline. And you are?"

Preston told her. Evie waved her hand to get the attention of the others in the circle, who were engaged in heated conversation, and introduced him. They nodded and returned to their debate. He was left with Evie, which he didn't mind at all.

"So what brought you here?" Evie asked.

"I wanted to see the Maya ruins," He could kick himself for saying something so mundane. But Preston wasn't about to launch into his story and his response was at least partially true.

"*C'est ça.* Yes, of course. That's why we all are here, is it not? But me? I also wanted to find some more inspiration for my work. I'm an artist, you see."

That would explain her clothing, Preston said to himself. She had his full attention, and he could tell she knew it.

"*Mais oui.* For the Maya, these things we think are legend aren't so. The stories the young ones are told come from beliefs about creation. They are taught early. These things are here today in their ceremonies, even in the way they dress. Everything has meaning," Evie launched into a long recital, tracing the ancient Maya creation stories and symbolism connecting it to Maya life today. She finally brought her monologue to a close. "So you see, these things are what lets them know who they are. I can take inspiration from them and see what it means to me, and how I do my art. My paintings and installations can come from a place that calls to people—because we all feel a longing to know who we are."

Preston wondered how, out of all the girls he could have met, he met this one. He considered again telling Evie the real reason he was there. But it felt too precious to share when he didn't know what it all meant, where his journey would take him or what might come of it. As much as he knew he'd made a decision, took a leap, he felt a bit fragile, tentative. If he grasped onto the not-so-random thoughts moving through his mind that told him there was nothing here—he'd made a mistake—he would be pulled back home, the hole inside infinitely more vacant. He didn't think that Evie would mock him, but she might turn his search into a tale of grand adventure, of Hollywood proportions, something to regale her friends with, lifting him to hero status as they passed him overhead by their outstretched hands. His imagination ran wild and he shrank from the possibility. But a voice of reason sustained him.

From long ago, he remembered Messenger advising him: *Keep those things that are just newly born inside you for a while, those things that are sacred, until they strengthen. If you speak of them too soon, the energy they contain will be scattered. They must be nurtured, just like a newborn, and be given a chance to find legs. Then will come a time for such things to be shared. But not before.* So Preston protected his newborn for the reasons that mattered and kept the focus on Evie.

"That's really interesting," Preston offered. "Have you been doing any art since you've been here?"

Evie pulled an oversized hardbound book out of her backpack. It turned out to be a journal of sorts. She shared a number of marker-colored, surreal drawings, her interpretations of different places she'd been, with notes jotted to the sides. "These will help me remember when I go home. I will start to paint, and I can step right inside the place, and then I will see what more comes from my notes."

"These are really quite good."

Evie gave the classic French shrug indicating that's just the way it was. "Yes, this is what I do. Now, have you thought about where else you will go?"

Preston allowed that he hadn't given it much thought, "I want to see what pulls me."

Evie looked at him curiously, "*Alors*, you must be sure to go to these." She went on to shortlist some of the Maya ruins.

But Preston knew about these big sites and was looking for something else. "What about where there aren't so many people, maybe more remote?"

Evie thought for a minute, "There are places…*oui*…but I haven't been myself. They are not so easy. Maybe no one goes. I think there is one some hours away, near a river between Guatemala and Mexico. But it is deep in the jungle."

Preston felt a slight flutter. "Do you know the name?"

Evie paused and pursed her lips, "Hmmm, that is it! Piedras Negras. It means black stones."

The Sun Stone vibrated in its pouch. Preston touched his chest unconsciously receiving the cue.

THE NIGHT DUTY CLERK at the hostel knew little about the site on the river Evie mentioned but thought José, whom he'd first met, might. The next morning Preston was waiting when José showed up for work.

"Yes, this is a place of great mystery for my people," José said.

"What do you mean?" Preston asked.

"The spirits are strong there," he replied cryptically. "My uncle helped with an excavation some years ago. But the jungle takes back what belongs to it."

He wasn't sure what José meant but asked in a low voice, "Is it possible to go there?" The fluttering in his midsection had resumed.

"People don't go. It's hard and maybe dangerous."

"No, not tourists. How can I get there?"

"I'm not sure this is a good thing. There are other ruins, easier places you can go."

"I must go. There's something for me," Preston's voice was firm with conviction.

José examined him carefully as though he'd just seen him for the first time. "I see. Well, it would take you a long day if you're lucky, probably more. You can only reach it by the river and you'd have to get to the water first. Very bad roads. If you have some money you could get a driver. Otherwise, a bus goes that way about six a.m. but makes many stops."

Preston had heard of the chicken buses and was dubious. But mentally reviewing what he had in his wallet he made a decision. He didn't know how long his money would need to stretch or when he would be in a place to obtain more. He asked José the specifics of where to catch the transport and said, "But there's still the problem of continuing on once I'm at the river."

José hesitated then said, "You would have to have a guide with a boat. I told you my Uncle Felipe worked there at one time. He lives close to that village at the river. But he hasn't been to that place for years and doesn't like it. You could ask him and maybe he would take you. But you'd have to tell him why you think you must go. If he heard your story and thought it important enough…well…maybe. He has his own story."

Preston determined that communication was spotty, the only means by radio to the community store. José agreed to call ahead to let his uncle know he was coming, to vouch for him. But said he'd have to plead his own case about the request.

"You know, there's no guarantee my uncle is even there or that he would get the message. And don't say anything about what you want except to my uncle. The people out there get suspicious of gringos. Maybe it's not so good."

Preston heard the concern in the clerk's voice but the more they talked, the stronger he felt about taking the risk. At this point the Sun Stone told him he had no choice. He'd already missed the bus, and José agreed to send a message to his uncle on his next break. Preston would depart the next day. He had nothing to prepare, and the rest of the day and evening free. So he set out to find Evie and invite her to accompany him back to Tikal, which she did.

THE BUS BOUNCED with each pothole—and they were unending. Preston's body absorbed the shock meant for the non-existent coil springs. He couldn't help jostling his neighbors crammed in as they were. A young father, who looked to be about his age, was next to him, a toddler on his knee, while the mother sat across, another baby in her arms. The couple had acknowledged him with smiles when they boarded, and the toddler stared at him openly with abject curiosity. The bus had been nearly empty when Preston boarded in Flores but now, six hours and fifteen stops later, every inch was consumed—and he fully understood why they were called chicken buses. The cool of the morning had quickly been replaced with blanketing humidity. No breeze provided a break. Travel was excruciatingly slow hampered by the road conditions. Dust billowed through the open windows when another vehicle passed, coating everything. Preston drowsed and daydreamed, bumped along. He'd reluctantly left Evie in her warm bed that morning and was somewhat confused by their casual encounter. I'll probably never see her again, he thought regretfully. I guess that's how things are on the road.

According to José, he estimated arrival in the waterfront village, called merely Frontera, in about an hour. Knowing that Preston had little Spanish, José wrote him a note and told him to give it to the storeowner who would, hopefully, point him toward his uncle's home.

"Uncle Felipe speaks some English, but you have to find him first," José warned that, where he was going, few spoke anything other than their Mayan dialect or Spanish. He'd know when he was supposed to get off because it was the end of the line. The road simply dead-ended at water's edge.

Preston climbed out of the bus, pack slung on his back. As the remaining passengers scattered, he stretched his legs and looked around. To say the place was modest was an understatement. The only thing that could remotely pass for the community store where he was to deliver the note was nothing more than a small shack with no windows but an open door. He headed in that direction and saw a short wiry Maya man who looked to be about sixty approaching him. "Hello? Perhaps you are the one my nephew sends?"

"Yes! You are Señor Felipe?" Preston was relieved. "I'm Preston."

"Just Felipe is good," he said. Felipe motioned Preston to walk with him to a bench under a nearby tree. They sat. "You are a friend of José?"

Preston explained how they met and the referral for a guide to Piedras Negras. A cloud passed over Felipe's friendly face. "My nephew did not tell me this. You know, this is not a place we go. The worlds come together there. Not even the ceiba tree can hold them apart. People can get lost. No, this is not a place we go," he repeated, shaking his head. "I am sorry you have come this far."

Preston's heart sank. *Without a guide, how will I get there?* Then he remembered José's counsel and the newborn inside him found legs. He knew this was not a time to remain silent. Over the next hour, he sketched out the reason for his quest. Preston sensed he could trust Felipe. Given what José said and Felipe alluded to, he had his own tale. So Preston told him about his father's disappearance all those years ago, the finding of the sanctuary in the backyard, his own visions of the people in white and the spider monkey. He finished by pulling the Water Stone from his pocket and withdrawing the Sun Stone from its pouch, telling Felipe what little he knew of the way they came to him but how they guided him and brought him here. "I have this empty place in me and it hurts," he had never spoken it before and his voice cracked, "I want to find my father. I think there is someplace…maybe it has to do with him. Maybe I'll find something." Preston could feel tears coming. He blinked them back.

Felipe had been listening intently, his eyes never leaving Preston's face. Silence was now between them. Felipe sat rubbing his chin thoughtfully. Then he patted Preston's arm as a parent might, in reassurance. The small gesture was kind, and Preston felt hope.

"Yes. Okay, young man. I see what this is to you. But you must know that there are places in the jungle where you cannot tell when you walk from one world to another. This place—the real name is Yo'k'ib'—that means Great Gateway. This is one of those places and that is why—no matter how the gringos try to uncover it—it is taken back from them. And sometimes it claims those who look for its secrets. This is why I have not been there in many years. I was almost one of those," he warned.

Preston's heart started to sink again. Felipe was turning him down.

"Young man, I do not say no. I hear what you have to say. Yes, I understand, and we will go. But you must know what this is," he was emphatic, "You must have a reason and I see that you have one. Well, maybe this is why you came for me. I think there is something of me still left back there. It is time I returned."

And Preston began to understand, in a way he hadn't before, something else Messenger had taught him. People's lives overlap. Words are exchanged. Events coincide. In this way an attraction—something of common need—occurs so that meaning and possibility connects them, irrevocably, through time.

— Chapter Fifty-one —

JUST AS THE SUN whispered its daily greeting to the sky they launched to stave off its rays beating down as severely. Felipe said they would encounter some rapids and so took the small motorboat with no cover, as opposed to his long motorized canoe with overhead thatch. Felipe said he used the latter to ferry the few tourists that came their way across the waters to Mexico. Preston had passed the night on a cot in Felipe's simple home. Since it would take them at least five hours to get there, they planned to stay overnight and spent the remains of the previous day gathering meager supplies to cover their needs. Felipe's wife Luisa made him feel welcome but was clearly worried when she learned about their intended trip. The couple excused themselves to talk away from Preston. However, the walls were plywood-thin, and he could hear Felipe's attempted soothing responses to Luisa's rapid-fire questions, rising in volume and heat as the conversation ensued. The encounter ended with a calm but firm tone from Felipe. Luisa attempted to tuck away her frown as they re-entered the room. Preston was chagrined to be the source of their disagreement. But, to Luisa's credit, the tension passed quickly. The rest of the night was pleasantly filled with a home-cooked meal and Felipe as translator covering safer topics about their lives.

Felipe and Preston were fortunate. A couple of hours into their river trip it became overcast, protecting them from direct sunlight. They caught a steady breeze as their boat cut through the wide waters making it an altogether pleasant journey. Preston was mesmerized. The small settlements along the shores quickly gave way to the occasional glimpse of a cabana or two between thickets that immediately turned wild just beyond. Then any sign of human habitation was gone. Among all the trees he saw, the ceiba stood out like none other, its majestic trunk strong and visible, full growth focused at the top, an oversoul plentifully dotted with flowers. Large buttress roots provided stability. It wasn't hard for him to understand why the Maya people identified it as the World Tree that held the dimensions securely separate.

For the most part their travel had been uneventful. The relatively minor rapids they'd come across were marked with regular waves and open pathways. Only once did it become dicey, but Felipe skirted the rocks and eddies like the pro he must be. Over the last hour dark clouds gathered overhead, the promise of a deluge soon. The sky rumbled threateningly. Luckily, Felipe announced they were within sight of their destination. He pointed to a rock outcropping just offshore ahead.

"On that rock there is a glyph that marks this spot as Yo'ki'b. The city is in there," Felipe waved his hand in the direction of the jungle. But Preston didn't see a thing, just dense rainforest. Large drops had started to fall, and jagged lightning split the heavens. They'd arrived just in time. As they beached the boat and came to a standstill, Preston felt the full effects of the rainforest's humid breath. At home they had monsoon season, its humidity a relief and torrential rains welcome. But it's nothing like this, Preston noted. Sweat mixed with the rain hitting his face. Felipe quickly secured the boat on the pristine shore. They grabbed their packs and trotted over to intermittent shelter under large vegetation fifty feet away. Preston followed Felipe's lead and sat on his haunches, his pack wedged under him to keep it dry. The sky had opened up, the torrent so thick they could hardly see the boat. Even though Felipe was in close proximity, Preston had to nearly shout to be heard as the rain crashed to earth.

"Do you think the boat is okay?" He was worried. The last thing they'd need would be for the boat to be swept away leaving them isolated without transport. It must be days of walking to the nearest village, if there was even a trail. And Felipe said no one comes here.

As if reading Preston's mind Felipe said, "No worries. It is safe. The gods are with us. They held off and let us get here. This is a good sign. The worst thing would be if we are in the boat now on our Sacred Monkey River. Look, the waves!"

Sure enough, they had become choppy and treacherous. Preston thanked the gods and touched the Stones. They were squatting under huge elephant ears, which were no longer providing much respite. Water came in steady rivulets falling from the naturally formed funnels by the weight of the downpour. Preston decided it was too late to pull his rain jacket out of his backpack.

"What should we do?" Preston shouted.

"We should go and find Yo'ki'b. Maybe it will be more dry. There could be some roof over us. We will see. It is many years since I am here. But we must be careful now in this rain," Felipe indicated a barely visible trail several feet away. "We could get off the path easy."

It was then that Preston noticed an unusual vapor developing, not on the shore but along the border of the jungle where they would enter. Was this a natural phenomenon? He glanced at Felipe who was staring hard in the direction of the path. He turned his eyes back toward the boat to reassure himself it was still there. That's when he thought he saw a figure standing on the rock that announced the mouth of Yo'ki'b. Despite the sticky warmth, Preston felt a chill.

Chapter Fifty-two

FELIPE WENT FIRST, and Preston followed close behind. They carefully picked their way along the path, so overgrown in places to be almost invisible. The jungle pressed up against them. Felipe hacked at vegetation encumbering their passage with his machete. Mist drifting among the trees hindered visibility and gave an eerie effect. The thick canopy had decreased the amount of rain able to reach them, but the downpour had let up anyway. Now a steady, light tap-tapping could be heard overhead. It was hard to tell how far they'd gone. The going was slow. They could see nothing but forest around them and a thin trail ahead. Felipe stopped, shoved his machete into the ground and used it to lean against. He was breathing hard.

"Felipe, let me do that for a while," Preston said.

"Well, I forget I'm getting old! Maybe just for a while. You're a gringo. You know how to use one of these?" Felipe joked.

"I think I can manage it," Preston said dryly. As Felipe handed him the machete, a long ago time with his childhood friend Smoky, the one Sybilla had called imaginary, arose. They were playing "swordfight" in his backyard. He realized that Smoky had been teaching him to be laser-focused in his attention. Strange that should come back now, he thought. The machete was heavy and unfamiliar in his hand, but Preston wielded it in front of him and they moved on. With the added exertion and humidity, water seemed to leap from Preston's body and served as a calling card for the insects that had started buzzing around them since the rain had lessened. He was distracted by a pesky gnat flying around his eyes and almost didn't detect slight movement just a few feet ahead. What he'd taken for a fallen branch across the path wasn't. It suddenly undulated, a flattened wave on the ground. Preston's reptilian brain recognized a cousin, even though camouflaged by the undergrowth. Adrenaline charged through his body, "Snake!" He jumped back knocking into Felipe who was right on his heels. They both fell down. Felipe scrambled up and shot back on the trail. But Preston was hypnotized. The serpent lazily coiled its thick body smack in the middle of the path. It must be seven feet long or more, Preston heard commentary in his head.

Seeing that Preston wasn't behind him, Felipe shouted, "Young man! You must come! A fer-de-lance! It will kill you!"

The viper swung its magnificent head slowly side to side considering Preston. How can its head be that big? Again, the commentary. And suddenly its jaws opened so wide that Preston deemed he had a glimpse of eternity. Time vacated in déjà vu. A rough shake of the arm brought him back. Felipe was trying to drag him away. "You must! You must!"

"No! It's alright!" Preston pulled himself out of Felipe's grasp and turned back in time to see the large snake slither gracefully into the underbrush. Gone. "Felipe, I was right. I was supposed to come," he said markedly, "We will not be hurt here. This is a place of my people."

He picked himself up from the jungle floor, attempting to brush the mud off his pants. Felipe shook his head, a worried glance toward the spot the fer-de-lance had been, "I do not understand this. These snakes...they are very aggressive. By all that I have seen in my life, you should be dead now from that snake."

"But you can see that I am not," Preston's voice was infinitely calm and matter-of-fact.

Still shaking his head in wonderment, Felipe took the machete from Preston's hand. "I will go first." Soon they could see a break in the trees ahead. It was lighter. They broke out into a clearing of sorts. The jungle had nearly been successful in reclaiming it as its own. Preston was dumbfounded;he was rooted to that spot. Just inside the clearing was a crumbling temple, its stones moss-covered and irregularly placed. Many of its rocks had fallen out of the mortar leaving gaping holes. It resembled humus on the rainforest floor, centuries upon centuries of life layered and decomposing, secrets with it. And there in the middle, emerging from that vault of mysteries was a massive stone mask, the nose flat, mere pinpoints. Its eye orbits dark and vacant. Its jaws open and gaping. Terrible beauty. One Preston found inviting.

The rain drizzled, plastering the hair to his head.

Still he stood.

— Chapter Fifty-three —

FELIPE CAME AND STOOD beside Preston. "You see this serpent mask temple. For us, the serpent is the messenger. It can go in and out of cracks between the worlds and makes no sound. It can stay hidden. But when we see it, something happens. Every cell in our body becomes electric. We know when we see the snake something may happen. That's why we become afraid…because of its power and its ability to kill us. We can fall into another world," Felipe's voice was barely above a whisper, "This is what I was telling you about this place. So you say we will not be hurt. But…still…we must be careful…yes…because it can happen."

Preston nodded. He knew from the moment they squatted on the beach, and he saw the spirit on the rock. The site was a potent vortex. He could feel its insistent draw. It would be easy to get sucked into its cavity. Do you ever get spit back out? He wondered. Maybe that's what happened to Felipe. But he didn't ask. He sensed that those were elements of Felipe's life he kept to himself or only let loose sparingly.

Felipe suggested they go farther into the lost city and see if they could find a place to set up for the night to keep them dry. The sky was again sounding off with promises of rain and it was nearly mid-afternoon. Night would come early in the rainforest. The mist was becoming thick. They stopped at a small stone enclosure Felipe identified as a steambath and told him about the sacred role the practice played in ritual cleansing, healing and childbirth—even today. They went inside, but the place was too narrow and full of bats to consider an overnight stay. They moved on. Preston marveled at every turn. Even though the structures were in decay, vines crawling through walls and plant matter dusting the floors, they vibrated grandeur but also some kind of warning. He could imagine what the city was like in its glory.

They approached a small ruin with steep, uneven steps leading up to a tier immediately outside an enclosure of sorts. The entrance and a portion of the platform were still protected by a thatched *palapa*, albeit one side fallen down. It looked more like a lean-to.

"This will be good for us tonight. It must be left over from the last dig. Some shelter anyway," Felipe said. "Let's look inside."

They dropped their packs just inside the entrance. The interior held a narrow hall with shallow niches cut into the wall. At each end was a small vaulted room with window slits. Its roof was intact.

"I don't know this one from my time. But it looks like a burial place, maybe some minor noble." There was little light. Felipe swung his flashlight around disturbing a few bats. "Look there by the wall. Someone left wood. Maybe they had the same idea we do."

They each gathered up an armful of wood and dumped it at the entrance. Felipe suggested they set up just inside the mouth of the ruin to keep dry from any rain. It offered some protection from night creatures. Later they could build a fire, too. Preston reluctantly agreed. He wasn't keen on sleeping in a tomb. But I guess they're everywhere, he said to himself.

Felipe sat down on the stone floor and took water from his pack. He drank and surveyed the area. "You can use your mind to see what it once was. As much as you see covered now was once a large city. We don't know how far it stretched but we do know much because of what our picks found. Let's rest for a few minutes, then I'll take you to see an important thing. Tomorrow maybe we can go deeper for a ways. But we also must leave. My Luisa...well, you see how she is about me being here." He went on to tell Preston something of his time working the site more than forty years ago. A well-known archaeologist of the time had rolled into Flores looking for workers to accompany him for a project. Felipe was newly married with a baby and having difficulties making ends meet. He saw a chance and took it.

"Yes, I was a very young man then, barely twenty. It was an exciting time with the discoveries we had. But hard, too. Some things happened," he stopped abruptly. Whatever the circumstances, they remained with Felipe. Preston understood not to ask.

Felipe hauled himself up and stretched. "Come, let's go while there is still light."

224

They set off. He led Preston into an open plaza surrounded by megalithic steps leading to tier upon tier of rubble and architecture in various states of collapse. They carefully picked their way up. The rain and moss rendered them treacherous. Once on the top, they gazed out over miles of jungle.

"This is the acropolis where they say the most important things would take place. So here is the palace. The rituals the kings wanted the people to see? They happened mostly here. And these other temples, too," Felipe informed him. "There are some more plazas over there and there." He pointed in the general direction. "And we don't know where else because nobody uncovered them yet. You see how hard it is to get here. So I don't know if it will ever happen. Except for the jungle covering over so much again, it doesn't look so different from when I was here. I don't remember everything. Forty years was a long time ago! But sometimes it comes to me in my dreams. I think that once you have been here, it doesn't let you go, not entirely. So young man, you should know this."

Preston nodded. He heard the veiled warning in Felipe's message. A feeling had stayed with him since they'd landed earlier that day. Somewhat foreboding, but he couldn't quite identify it, a premonition he couldn't quite grasp. He knew to use caution. They wandered through the acropolis and saw some intact mural reliefs with elaborate images and symbols. Felipe explained some of the meaning. Felipe maintained a life-long interest in the discoveries related to his ancient heritage. Preston thought that unusual for a man living so simply in an out-of-the-way settlement. The sun was close to the horizon, and the howlers had begun to call in the moon.

"We must get back so we don't get lost out here. Come. There is something I can show you on the way," Felipe said. He guided them to the opposite side end of the platform. They descended the steep steps slowly. When they reached the bottom, Felipe appeared to be looking for something and walked back and forth along the base.

"Ah! Here it is," he pulled back some vines to reveal an opening, pitch black. "We will just step inside a ways."

Preston followed. Felipe flicked on his flashlight and stopped several feet inside the entrance. The passageway descended rapidly. Stones had fallen from the walls. It was clearly unstable. There was a chill extending from its depths and the unpleasant, musty smell of decomposition assaulted their nostrils.

"These tunnels are like a maze and believed to connect the whole city underneath the ground," Felipe was whispering, "If it wasn't so dangerous we could see how big it is just by following the tunnels! And there may be things hidden here against their enemies, too. We don't know."

Preston was uneasy. The walls of the passage seemed to be closing in. Something bumped up against his arm. He quickly brushed at it hoping it was merely a bat. But when he pivoted he saw nothing and bolted outside.

Felipe chuckled and followed him, "Yes, I know it is a creepy place. But I show you anyway."

They found their way back to the campsite. Their packs and wood were where they left them, nothing disturbed. By the time the sun went underground they had a fire going. Dinner was comprised of tamales made by Luisa and fruit. After they'd eaten Felipe pulled out a small flask of alcohol.

"Have you had?" Felipe asked.

"I don't think so. What is it?" Preston said.

"This is *quetzalteca*," he replied, "I thought we could warm ourselves a little." He offered the bottle.

Preston took a swig and immediately coughed, nearly spewing the liquid. "Whew!" he sputtered.

"Yes, it is a little strong. But maybe you'll like it!" Felipe laughed.

And after the first attempt, Preston found that he did. They talked for a long time about their lives, what more Felipe knew about the site. Preston shared more about his quest.

"You know what you said about your vision of the people in white?" Felipe said. "There is something. Something. I can't quite remember. Maybe it will come back to me. But now I think we should sleep. We must get up early tomorrow."

They crawled into their sleeping bags and let the fire go low to burn itself out. Even though Preston's eyes were closed, his ears were open.

The insects played a symphony to the night, a musical contrast from the intense silence of his home landscape. He heard periodic rustling and hoped it was just monkeys moving through the trees or birds with insomnia. His mind refused to go to blank but, again and again, went over their day, then random thoughts. In the distance he heard a woman scream. But that's impossible. Then he remembered the mountain lions at home sometimes sounded like that. There must be a jaguar stalking out there. His skin tightened. He pulled his arm from the sleeping bag. The reflective numbers on his watch told him it was past midnight. He closed his eyes again hoping sleep would come.

Preston felt himself falling, rapidly down a long tunnel. It seemed to go on forever, a bottomless pit. Air rushed past and adrenaline kicked in. He clawed at nothing. Just as suddenly the fall ceased. He hung suspended as though caught in a sticky web. In the abyss he sensed movement around him, coming close and backing off. Nearly inaudible whispering peppered the atmosphere, but he couldn't make out the words or language. Nevertheless, cognition permeated his skin, truth ingested. He smelled earth, and fear dissipated even though he couldn't wrest free of what held him. Instead, he had the feeling of having come home with no choice but to languish there.

Then just as suddenly he was propelled upward, front-first through the long tube along which he'd come, propelled by some immense hand at his back. He passed indistinguishable figures and pinpoints of light. The shaft narrowed until finally he was expelled. A multitude of leathery pink petals softened his landing. Dawn was coming to the rainforest. Preston looked over to see Felipe just sitting up from sleep.

— Chapter Fifty-four —

THEY LISTENED TO the birds stirring and ate a scanty breakfast of fruit and tortillas. "We can go farther in for a little time, but then I think we make our way back to the boat," Felipe reminded. "I think it will be okay. It will be faster returning with the current."

They packed up their gear and headed back the way they'd come the previous afternoon. Felipe recommended going to the edge of the excavations to see what they may discover—if they were even able to penetrate the density beyond. On the far side of the acropolis, there was a large toppled slab of limestone with an intricate relief face up to the sky. Age and moisture had worn away much of it, but a figure clothed in elaborate costume and symbols could be made out. Felipe told Preston that it was probably a king, and the imagery likely told about his life. Not long after they took a break for water. The humidity was already increasing as the sun traveled into the sky. As he tipped the bottle to his lips, Preston felt a strange sensation in his chest but not physically troubling. He could tell something was being activated. The feeling was reminiscent of the time he'd been pulled into the garage and found the white cloth. It was building, and the Sun Stone entrained with its vibration. Both Stones had been silent since Preston had arrived in this lonely place. He'd begun to think he'd miscalculated earlier signals to come here until his waking dream—he didn't know how to classify it—last night. Now he was reassured, merely stood still as the whirling in his chest gained intensity.

"Are you okay?" Felipe was looking at him oddly.

"Yes, just give me a minute," Preston was afraid that, if he moved, the sensation would go away, and guidance would be lost. It felt like a tornado was building in his chest, without debris, solely energy. He could literally feel the vortex magnifying, flipping horizontally, its apex extending out beyond his body. Then the pulling began.

"Come on! Let's go!" It was literally impossible for Preston to refuse. Something else had taken over. He found himself crashing through the jungle where there was no path. Thorny saplings slapped at his arms and face, and wet undergrowth slimed his pants.

"*Que pasa!*" Felipe was alarmed but followed Preston's lead attempting to keep up with the much younger man. "We will be lost!"

No answer from Preston. Finally, the trees opened up overhead. Preston came to a sudden halt, gasping.

"*Dios mio!*" Felipe let out as he came up behind him. Before them was a gargantuan hole in the ground at least several hundred feet wide. They couldn't see the bottom. "*Cenote!* You call it a sinkhole! What you have found!"

Preston didn't dare get any closer to the edge. Even at twenty feet away, the pull of the vortex was so strong he almost lifted off his feet. Blood pounded in his ears. The very atmosphere crackled. The Sun Stone chattered, jumping up and down against his chest. The Water Stone felt like it would leap out of his pocket. "What is this place?"

"I do not know of one so big anywhere, this passage to the Underworld!" Felipe was breathless, "Now I know where the danger came from. It comes from here. We didn't know. I think no one knows… except maybe those who never came back. They are the ones who found it. Now I know what haunted me in my dreams."

Preston's brow crinkled, "I don't know how long I can stand here."

"Yes! We must go!" Felipe face displayed a sheen of sweat.

They started to turn when Preston's eye caught color, barely visible in the underbrush, at the edge. It was out of place.

"Wait," he walked over and knelt down. He had the absurd desire to leap out into the abyss. It was almost overwhelming. He brushed back the growth to reveal what had caught his eye. Terracotta, partially covered in moss, much of its surface blackened. It was a vessel, half of it cracked off and gone. Preston felt like he'd been hit in the chest, his air knocked out. He sat down abruptly. It was the same kind of vessel he'd found in his sanctuary at home. He leaned over and picked it up. His entire body tingled. Tears filled his eyes. Silently he carried it over to Felipe.

"Ah," Felipe breathed, "I have seen…" But he broke off because Preston had started off in another direction still carrying the ruined vessel, bypassing the *cenote*, heading into dense jungle again. By now Felipe didn't question and followed him. Maybe a hundred feet away they came to the mouth of a cave nestled into a sheer, natural rock wall.

"I need your flashlight," Preston demanded. Palming the torch, he led the way in. It smelled dank. The interior walls were black with smoke and slick with seeping water. Light shone there revealed odd petroglyphs scattered from floor to ceiling. Some resembled the bubble-headed ones he'd seen adorning sites in the Southwest.

"What you have found…" Felipe shook his head.

The passage got narrow and angled off ahead. The wall contained a recess—lined up in two haphazard rows were about twenty clay receptacles. These were whole. On the front of each one was a crudely-fashioned face. Preston was astounded. He started to pick one up.

"You must stop," Felipe cautioned, "I think I know what this is. I started to tell you before…that thing I tried to remember came back. The people you mention in white. I don't know much, but a very long time ago I think those people were here. Something happened. It is said they left and crossed the water."

Preston stared intently at him in the semi-darkness. "Go on."

"I don't know more. But these pots? When I was here we found one in a temple, and it was put in a museum. I think it is theirs."

"I do, too," Preston allowed. "I found one buried in our backyard. It was my father's. I can't even imagine what this means…" His voice choked.

"Well, I don't know. But this place? These are very old, and I think they are supposed to rest here, like a burial ground." Felipe was firm.

"What about this one?" Preston held out the broken vessel he still held in his hands.

"This one I don't know. But it was out there, and that's a mystery," Felipe said.

Preston held the pot with both hands and ruminated. "I'm going to take it with me. And I found what I came here for," he looked up at

Felipe. "I know you need to get back. Would you drop me across the river on the way?"

Felipe put a hand on his arm, "Yes, young man. I will do that."

PRESTON AND FELIPE found their way easily out of the jungle, like they were riding a laser beam clear to the Sacred Monkey River. Their boat was as they left it, tied up securely. It seemed that, just as when they'd entered, the gods ushered them safely out. And Felipe had been right. It took less time going with the current on the return. Now they were standing on Mexican soil outside a small settlement whose main purpose was to service tourists heading upriver to Yaxchilán, the Maya ruin perched at water's edge on the Mexico side.

During the hours it took to get there Preston felt more and more resolute. Between the Stones on his person and the terracotta vessel in his pack, the visceral guidance he received was non-stop. He silently thanked Messenger again for tutoring him all those years to be aware of cues. Was it really that easy? And he knew for the first time that it was—when you're clear and on the right track. Even when things may get dicey somehow it still seemed like he would maintain a flow. So when he was reviewing the options with Felipe about where he may go once in Mexico, and the name Palenque came up, he knew that was it. Felipe had asked him: Didn't he want to see Yaxchilán since he was so close? He'd answered no, but maybe he'd return at some point. Right now he wanted to ride that laser beam all the way to Palenque and wherever it would take him from there. Besides, something was niggling at the back of his mind about the place, but he couldn't bring it forward.

"Felipe, I don't know how to thank you," Preston choked up. After securing the boat they'd gone to eat at the open-air snack bar. Now it was time to part ways.

"Young man, you are the one I must thank," Felipe held both Preston's shoulders firmly then clasped him in a tight hug. "Without you I would never know the source of my dreams, all these years. That I'm not a crazy one. For this, even though she didn't want me to go on this trip, my Luisa will be grateful, too. I can grow old in peace," he laughed and wiped the tears from his eyes. "We both found something in the lost city. We are connected for all time."

Felipe gave him a final pat on the shoulder and turned toward the shore. Preston watched until Felipe got into his boat. He felt warmth for the older man that he might have carried for a grandfather if he'd known either of his. With a final wave, he slung his pack over his shoulder and walked toward a couple of beat-up looking vans at the side of the road. One of them would take him into the town of Palenque, about a three to four hour trip.

They rolled into town in the late afternoon. The van deposited him and the other three passengers at a station a couple of blocks off the main road. It was murderously hot. A fellow backpacker started to climb into the van he'd just vacated, apparently going on the return run to Yaxchilán.

"Hey!" Preston said. "You know a good place to stay?"

The backpacker turned out to be German and spoke precise English. He told Preston to catch a *combi* and head out toward the ruins. There was a place that had *palapas* and he could rent a hammock if he didn't have one, or there were a few rooms.

"A *combi*? What's that?" Preston asked.

"You know, a van. They run back and forth between town and the ruins. Ten pesos! Catch one out on the main street." The German swung into the transport. The van rumbled off with a belch of exhaust.

He sighted a sign that said Internet and thought to drop Sybilla an email. He felt a little guilty because he hadn't been in contact since he left home, and she must be home by now. So he fired off a noncommittal message telling her he was having a good time and was in Palenque. Then Preston followed the German's lead, trouped up to the main drag and was quickly able to flag down a *combi*. The only other passenger was a Mexican woman who looked to be heading home from the market. She was weighed down with a shopping bag. Preston was relieved when they were quickly out of town and appeared to be climbing slightly in elevation. It immediately cooled down. He held his face at the open window letting the breeze dry his sweat. He admired the lush beauty of the landscape and tingles of excitement ran up and down his body. Soon he could only see the trees lining the road. They were entering forest. The vehicle slowed to a stop dropping him under a sign that said Mayabel, identifying the compound he'd told the driver. He saw two girls who were walking by the side of the road turn into the narrow lane that led into the place. He followed them into an open-air restaurant covered in thatch and approached the Mexican woman behind the counter. He'd opted for the luxury of a room and a bed since they were cheap enough, dropped off his pack and returned to the restaurant. He'd wolfed down the best guacamole he'd ever had, along with a quesadilla. Now he sat with his back against the stone half-wall, his torso lounged along the booth, nursing his second beer, delivered ice-cold, taking in his surroundings and the other travelers. He noticed the girls looked to be cut out of the same mold as Evie. Evie, he thought. Tikal was so long ago. Hearing howlers close by, Preston was strangely comforted. Nothing could be more perfect.

— Chapter Fifty-six —

THE NEXT MORNING Preston was up early. He sat outside on his little porch and watched dawn come to the day. Looking skyward, he saw shafts of diffused light through the treetops. The morning air was cool and sweet on his skin. The insects were quieting down, and the birds were taking over. Preston felt calm in a way he couldn't remember in his entire life. The edginess that made him want to jump right out of his body was just no longer there. He realized that it had been vanishing bit by bit. Instead, waves of peace had taken over, ushering out any habitual discomfort. It's been happening ever since the *cenote* and I picked up that clay fragment, he thought. He went back inside and pulled it out of his backpack, then resumed his place on the porch holding the terracotta pot in his lap, contemplating his newfound tranquility. It wasn't something that made him want to get lost in the clouds but rather instilled an inner power and laser-like direction. Preston longed for Messenger. He wanted to share this self-knowledge with the teacher and friend who had been leading him to this point.

There were no amenities in his room, and he was forced to wait until the restaurant opened to get morning coffee. He gave his order at the window and took up the same position in the booth from the night before. Preston nodded to a guy he'd seen on his first visit and checked out the other travelers, fascinated by the combination of clothing and adornments some of them were wearing. One had braided his long beard and had feathers stuck in it. I guess I'm a throwback, Preston chuckled to himself. His customary wear had always been basic: t-shirts and jeans.

One of the cooks called out his name through the serving window. He collected his coffee, eggs and tortillas. There was a dab of refried beans on the side. He devoured it all not realizing how hungry he was, and was just thinking on ordering another plate when a friendly British couple slid into the booth next to him and spoke.

"Didn't we see you in town yesterday?"

"I don't know. But I just got here last night."

Todd and Carol introduced themselves. "Been up to the ruins yet?"

"Not yet, but I'm headed that way. How far is it?"

"It's just up the road a bit. First time here?"

Preston nodded.

"Then instead of going in the front like all the tourists do, there's a trail you can slip in the back way and make your way up. It's fantastic! You get to feel a little what it was like for old Maudslay when he was there," Todd advised.

"And that way you'll come upon the Queen's Bath!" Carol was exuberant, "It's brilliant! The waterfalls! There are some quieter pools down below it. You should slip under the railing and take a dip. We do if there's no one around. Skinny-dip! You can just imagine the queen there and her attendants. If you go early enough you can probably do it."

"I'm on my way then," Preston stayed long enough to get directions to the trail. He was told there was a marker of stones about a quarter mile up on the left. He'd have to watch for it, because it wasn't obvious. As he was going back to the room to collect his backpack, the Water Stone vibrated wildly in his pocket. He reached his hand in and cupped her. She didn't calm. "What's going on, girl?" Preston muttered under his breath. The Water Stone answered with more pronounced knocking against his palm.

He turned left out the entrance of the Mayabel. There was a well-beaten dirt path alongside the road. He passed by a rancho and a small girl observed him through the fence, fingers in her mouth. Preston gave her a big wave and smile. His excitement was growing. It was hard to contain the compulsion to fling his arms overhead and announce his joy to the cows and egrets in the pasture. He even surprised himself.

There was a narrow dirt lane off to the right and a small peeling sign stuck in the ground next to it, almost unnoticeable, covered by vining foliage as it was. It read La Casa Mono. He walked on. Preston glanced at his watch. It was close to eight, still pretty early. He passed two more tracks going into the jungle. He was compelled to stop at the head of one. Something pulled him, again the niggling at the back of his mind. But he assuaged his curiosity by saying to himself maybe he'd check it out later. Knowing he must have gone at least a quarter mile, he crossed over to walk along the left side of the road where there was no path. He started watching for the marker in earnest. Todd had said, just off the road's edge. Five minutes later he spotted it. If I hadn't been looking I would have missed it. Hidden, yes, Preston thought.

Just beyond was a thin ill-used trail not unlike the one he and Felipe had traversed in Piedras Negras, just not as overgrown. He entered the jungle and quickly left civilization behind, another world entirely but one that was becoming familiar. Howlers roared nearby and then moved off along the canopy leaving a trail of shaking branches. Preston imagined they were leading him.

He tromped on for another forty minutes and began to think he might be lost. It was disorienting at times. Vegetation sometimes crushed up against him. He was careful of thorny branches. There had been a junction with another trail, no bigger than the one he was on, snaking off on its own. But someone had placed another pile of small stones along the mother path, headed up a steep hill, showing the direction to the ruins. That's if I'm on the right trail to begin with, he worried. But I can always turn around.

Preston was glad he hadn't though. In the next ten minutes the path widened slightly and joined with one that was wider still. He came to the first of the ancient structures, broken down walls with little intact. He wasn't sure they were temples, maybe living quarters away from the acropolis, potentially a steam bath, too. Then Preston realized he was hearing water, lots of water. The Water Stone hadn't stopped singing since that morning and now was pulsating powerfully against his leg. He slipped his hand in his pocket and cupped her again. What are you telling me, girl? he asked silently. Something is definitely up.

The Sun Stone was relatively quiet against his chest, entraining to the vibration every now and then, perhaps in a show of solidarity, but seemed to be in the role of witness. This was the Water Stone's time to speak. Preston felt the familiar tugging at his chest and, where he might have lingered to explore these first ruins, he was compelled along the path and, leaving them behind, an astounding sight came into view. With a quick intake of breath he let loose a low whistle. The Queen's Bath, it was a series of waterfalls, white water forcefully merging, sending spray into the air, emptying in a roar into the churning water below. It finally flowed into quieter pools—perfect for bathing. Just as Carol said, he could readily imagine the queen and other women languidly moving in the more shallow waters, maybe sitting on the smooth rock banks combing their hair.

He noted the railing meant to keep people out and slipped under it. No one was around. He only heard the sounds of the birds and waterfall. Preston kneeled on the bank and plunged his arm into the water. Cool and refreshing. He walked over to an overhang closer to the waterfall, an alcove hidden from the path. He slipped off his shoes and shirt and dropped them there. The Water Stone rattled violently in his pocket.

"You want out, don't you girl?" Preston whispered, "Well, why not?" He took her out and held her in one hand while he wriggled out of his pants and underwear, stepping out of them neatly. He stood at water's edge his lean body naked in the mist, rays of light descended through the canopy. Catching moisture in the air, a rainbow formed in front of him. He was enraptured. If he'd seen the Creator, he couldn't have experienced such infinite power more. Maybe it *is* the Infinite Power, he said to himself. He opened his hands, raised his arms, and still cradling the Water Stone safely in his palms, presented her to the waters. He was exhilarated beyond his belief, and tears coursed down his cheeks. He stood there for several minutes just so, a timeless image, if he could have seen himself, of a young god not quite foreign to those lands.

When he brought his hands down he held both the Stones together, the Sun Stone still in its pouch around his neck, his guides and allies for long before he could remember and felt a solid feeling of security, another new companion to the peace he was finding. Preston noticed a narrow shelf that ran along the rock wall and went behind the waterfall. The Water Stone chattered loudly. Okay, girl. We'll see what's back there.

He walked carefully. The ledge was slick, and he didn't know how deep or rocky the waters were below. The closer he came to the waterfall, the louder the roar. The waters plunged so closely that he had to edge along with his back against the rock wall not to be knocked off balance. The Water Stone was clutched in his hand, the pouch too small for both Stones. But finally he was behind the fall, and the shelf was more generous. Water crashed barely two feet away and sprayed him profusely head to toe. His body was electrified, consumed with an unimaginable energy. He brought the Sun Stone out of the pouch and covered both Stones with his palms. He held them thus. They both sang away. "Okay," he said quietly to them, "If that's what you want."

He opened his hand slightly to show them the power of the waters— and the Water Stone leaped. Preston cried out—but she was gone.

He stood in shock, the Sun Stone still exposed to the waters, resting in his palms. Then anguish engulfed him. He clutched the remaining Stone to his chest. What have I done? How stupid to take such a risk? He cried out inside. But he realized there was no point trying to search for her. He placed the Sun Stone back in its pouch and, after a few minutes, inched along the wall and returned to the ledge at the overhang. He sat on the bank, legs immersed in the water, staring hard into the bubbling waters, still in shock. His emotions were confusing. He felt abandoned, very old feelings surfaced that he knew all too well. At the same time, guilt rushed in that he'd taken such a risk with something precious to him.

The reassuring weight of the Sun Stone remained against his chest. Then as clearly as if someone was sitting next to him, he heard a sweet, bell-like voice speaking into his ear: *Thank you for bringing me home.*

That's all. Just those words...and Preston's spirits lifted.

— Chapter Fifty-seven —

AS PRESTON CLIMBED the steep trail from the Queen's Bath leading up to the main complex, he felt more and more like he was entering another dimension entirely. The short switchbacks revealed gnarly stalactite-looking formations hanging at the edge of the next level, encrusted with dirt and moss, slick with moisture, looking all the world like miniature caves with hidden treasures and whatever elementals graced that land. Early morning haze still hung heavy in the tall trees, and when he finally made his way among the ruins, Preston turned this way and that, just like a child, absorbing it all. The sun had not yet succeeded in banishing the mist touching the highest pyramids delicately in acknowledgment. It all left him thunderstruck. He was especially drawn to a diminutive pyramid with worn narrow steps. He climbed them and sat against the outside wall and gazed out beyond the Temple of the Sun, north to the main plaza with its palace and the commanding Temple of the Inscriptions. He learned the names of the structures by eavesdropping on a guide talking to a couple standing nearby. His strong attraction had been to the Temple of the Foliated Cross where he now sat. Preston could literally feel the powerful past of the site, and he knew without a doubt that some aspect survived. His eyes defocused. His gaze went soft. And when that happened he began to see not-quite-formed images of brown-skinned figures—not of the present day—going about their business below him. Then it was gone. He couldn't hang onto it. But he stayed in place, soaking up what was unseen, until the sun reached its zenith and too many tourists for his taste trekked up and joined him. He arose from his position, gave a mighty stretch and clambered down the age-worn steps, no less slick in their dried state, to the grassy square below.

Preston drifted through the palace and the remaining temples that were open before following the path toward the entrance most visitors used. Exiting, he found a square lined with booths selling souvenirs, drinks and snacks. A cold drink sounded good. He walked up to a young girl and purchased a cold bottle of water out of the cooler. As Preston stood there assuaging his thirst, he casually took in the square bustling with incoming tourists and vendors attempting to get their attention. Suddenly he was riveted.

Over in a quiet corner near the entrance stood two Native men and a small boy in front of a stall. They had long dark hair to their shoulders with bangs cut straight across the brow. They were wearing white cotton shifts that stopped at mid-calf and looked all the world like hospital gowns. Preston took a deep breath and crossed the square. The boy noticed him approaching. He smiled shyly and raised his wares toward him in offer, a bow and arrows.

Preston grinned in return saying, "Hola!"

As he got closer the boy ran up to him and the men nodded. One spoke to him in Spanish.

"*Lo siento! No entiendo mucho,*" Preston said. I'm sorry! I don't understand much.

Smiling, the men gestured for him to enter their stall. Preston examined the contents with great interest: seed jewelry, hand-rolled cigars, small clay animals, some bow and arrow sets. There were a few photos hanging against one wall. Two were of others in the same dress, one with a very old man leaning against a staff. The remaining image was a beautiful lake surrounded by dense forest and mist hanging low. Preston took his time going through their booth while the men stood patiently at the front. The boy stood close by, all the while looking intently up at him. Preston glanced down periodically and smiled. Finally he chose a string of small brown seeds and a pocket-sized terracotta animal that could have been an anteater. The boy beamed at him as he pulled pesos out of his pocket and deposited the money in his waiting hand. The men nodded their thanks.

Preston was stumped. He simply couldn't leave now without conversing with these quiet men, and didn't want to take the chance they wouldn't be there if he returned later. Raising his finger in a signal to wait, Preston walked over to some guides who were hanging around hoping for business. He came back with a young Mexican man who spoke English.

Preston didn't even know where to start and didn't want to put the Native men off with his mounting exuberance. He contained himself and said through the translator, "I am wondering about your people. Do you live around here?"

"No, not here. We live inside the rainforest."

"Really? Is it far?"

"Not so far. Maybe four hours if you can get a *combi* going near. But it doesn't go all the way. We have to walk maybe another hour."

Preston thought he would jump out of his skin with excitement. "What do your people call themselves?"

"We are the Hach Winik. The True People."

— Chapter Fifty-eight —

EARLY THE NEXT MORNING Preston checked out of the Mayabel and caught a *combi* in town that would take him as close as he could get to the Hach Winik's village. Over the last few hours he'd been mesmerized by the changing landscape but saddened, too. He knew from the conversation yesterday that, even though Hach Winik land was supposed to be protected, loggers and squatters had cleared a major portion. So much of the rainforest even from ten years ago no longer existed.

The van rolled to a stop at a desolate spot in the road. The driver turned to Preston and pointed to the dusty lane leading off to the left. Preston nodded his thanks and got out. The *combi* roared away throwing up clouds of dirt, leaving him to face the unknown alone. Not quite, he thought, and fingered the Sun Stone through the pouch. Preston was reassured even though his internal barometer was confusing him. He felt a keen sense of foreboding. At the same time, giddiness ran through his veins. Hoisting his pack he began the hike. The road stretched for as far as he could see. It was in bad shape with huge potholes, some spanning the width of the road, muddy at the center, speaking of impassable times. The forest was dense right up to the edge, refusing to give up secrets of what was beyond. Considering the chance of jaguars and who knew what, he hummed a tuneless song and kicked rocks every now and then, hoping that the same was true for any predators here as it was at home: They want nothing to do with humans, so let them know you're around.

He'd been walking about thirty minutes when he paused. Nothing stirred. It was dead silent. Even the birds must have sought shelter somewhere. The sun beat down, and the humidity had risen dramatically. There was nowhere inviting to escape the heat one iota. Preston pulled his bandana and water bottle from his backpack. Wetting the bandana, he tied it loosely around his neck looking to get a bit of relief. He was zipping his pack when he heard an inviting sound in the distance. Looking back the way he'd come, a pick-up slowly lumbered toward him. As it got closer, he made out figures standing up in the truck bed. Some wore white. Preston waited and the driver halted abreast of him. Sticking his head out the window, he said something in Spanish. Preston replied with the trusty phrase identifying him as a gringo who didn't understand the language. The man shrugged and gestured down the road in front of them. When Preston nodded that he was going that way, the driver invited him to climb aboard. Exchanging smiles of greeting, one of the passengers gave him a hand up. The back was overloaded with supplies of various sorts, and he edged to a place behind the cab where he could hang on. Preston stabilized himself against the constant rocking of the vehicle as they traversed the uneven road. He was grateful for even the small breeze created by their slow passage. Twenty minutes later he saw signs of a village: plantings of corn beside the road, some kind of huts well ahead and a young boy. One of the men in the back with Preston waved and yelled something. The boy took off running, calling and disappeared into the trees, perhaps a shortcut to the community.

By the time they entered, people had started to gather in a knot near the road outside a large shack. Others were streaming down paths leading to the central group. Laughing children and barking dogs ran beside the truck ushering them along. Preston scanned the village. It was hard to tell how large the community was. Trees hid much, but it looked fairly small. In the distance he could see water, probably a lake. The truck came to a stop, and people surged around. Preston pitched in handing boxes off to hands that reached up to take them. His old shyness returned in spades. He attempted to allay it by focusing on the task at hand. He could feel curious eyes on him. Not unfriendly, just interested.

But finally there was nothing left to do but climb down from the truck. He stood there, slightly smiling, uncomfortable. He leaned down and made a show of fiddling with his pack to buy time. The villagers busied themselves with the supplies. Suddenly in the dead-still day he felt a puff of wind in his face, not unlike someone blowing air from a short distance. It caused him to glance up. And when he did a chill ran over his body. His eyes went directly to an elder woman wearing a long white smock over a dark cotton skirt standing to the back of the crowd—and her eyes held him. Throwing up her arms, she cried out. Recognition quickly overtook him as the crowd of people opened between them. She rushed toward him.

He didn't have to hear her call out, "Chan K'in!" He knew who she was.

"Mama Luna!"

— Chapter Fifty-nine —

THAT EVENING MAMA LUNA and Preston sat in her small home by the lake having finished a simple dinner of thick vegetable soup with a side of stewed squash and tortillas, made by Mama Luna over an open fire. Their plates were pushed back. They had been talking for hours, catching up through the years.

After their joyous and tearful reunion, Mama Luna introduced him to the village at large in her own dialect and spoke for a minute. Several people exclaimed in surprise. Approaching, they examined him closely, afterward erupting into smiles and greetings. Preston was somewhat perplexed by their responses, and Mama Luna had yet to explain it to him. She'd said a few more words and then invited him to follow her toward the lake where she lived.

"We have plenty of time to speak of many things, don't we? Ah! It's been so long since I speak English! It is strange in my mouth," she chortled. "Come. We go to my home. You will stay with me."

The lake a short distance away drew him powerfully. But he dutifully followed her into her simple dwelling. They passed through a small anteroom with burlap bags full of plant matter lying against each other. Drying stalks and roots hung from a rafter. The comforting scent of flowers and earth faintly perfumed the air. A small wooden work stand was close by, and shelves lining the walls held crocks and jars filled with medicinals. A wave of nostalgia engulfed Preston as he remembered times from his childhood: Mama Luna plucking plants from her garden or bustling in the kitchen preparing some concoction to heal him of a fever. Gratitude rushed in for this kind woman who had graced his early years. He simply loved her and hadn't realized until now how much he'd missed her. He noted her frame had filled out slightly and her regal face had added some wrinkles and softened over the jaw line. But her beauty maintained, maybe increased. He wasn't sure about her age but had to put her toward seventy—and not one streak of gray in her black hair.

"We will move these things to one side," she'd gestured to her apothecary. "You will sleep here." Later he helped her make a pallet of sorts.

Now they sat by candlelight speaking between long silences. The bond was such between them; there was no need to fill the space with extraneous words. Once the sun said goodnight she lit several tapers. It surprised him that she had no electricity, especially since poles ran through the community. But she said that she preferred it that way. It was bad enough that she had to hear the radio blasts of community announcements, or worse yet, preaching of that new religion, uninvited into the air she breathed.

"You saw the ones not wearing our clothing? These are the ones that have left us. These missionaries that come in are very pushy, and they make lies so my people will convert. They say that it is our fault when our corn doesn't grow so well or when someone dies. They say this is so because we are on a crooked road with false gods! Not on a straight road like theirs. They promise big corn, food, medicines. Well, I haven't seen it. But people believe. And they are losing the old ways. They don't even use their birth names! These converts call themselves now by Spanish names," she shook her head slowly. "Chan K'in, this makes me very sad. But I continue and help the ones who want it. I know this is my place to be."

Mama Luna reached out and squeezed his hand. Preston was incensed. He'd heard of such things happening throughout the regions he'd been traveling, in fact all over the world: disrespect for the Native traditions that honor community and the environment.

"Why doesn't someone stop it? Do you have village leaders?" he asked.

Her face was doleful. "If Old T'uup was still with us, it would not be. But he went to join the ancestors more than ten years now. He held the threads very strong. He could weave them in beautiful ways to hold the faith of the people and tell the old stories that make us who we are. But none of his sons wanted to take his place. It was very sad for him. You see, it is a big job that is not easy…to hold that place…to hold it

247

without thinking of yourself. But when he left us, these missionaries knew it. And they came at once, in groups, telling lies. This hurts me in here," Mama Luna touched her heart.

"But Mama. I think I remember Sybilla calling you Maria, is that so? And to me you were always Mama Luna. What is your birth name?"

"Yes, my birth name is Chax Nuk."

"Chax Nuk," Preston tried it out on his tongue. "Why didn't you go by it when you were with us?"

"Well, your mama had a hard time. She would call me Maria because my birth name was too strange. And this was okay. I accepted."

Preston glowered, "How could she do that! It's so disrespectful! The US government did that to the Native people at home. So names like Washington Johnson or John McCormick were forced on them. How absurd! Sybilla *knows* not to do something like that!"

"Ah no, you are my big one now. You must forgive your mama in the ways you think she hurt me…or you. There were some things that she did not know. She was never prepared for some of the things that happened. How could she be? Your mama has a good heart, and she has always loved you very much. Many times things were hard, and she was scared. Yes?" She gave him a knowing look.

"Well, I don't know. Maybe," he was reluctant. "But what about calling you Mama Luna? I should call you by your birth name."

"No, it is special between you and me. It is a name I told you for me. You can call me Chax Nuk if you want. But it is the way you say Mama or Mama Luna that makes my heart soft."

Silence stretched between them until finally Mama Luna said, "Come outside. I want to show you something."

She led him down the path toward the lake until they stood on the shore. Again, Preston felt a draw to the place. The night had cooled and a bright three-quarter moon had risen. Its rays seemed to extend to the mist hovering over the lake as though cast by its spell. The effect was preternatural.

Mama Luna spoke quietly, "I knew you were coming. I saw you before, and I knew it was the time. So I have been watching for you to come down the road."

Preston swung his head toward her but said nothing. He was not astonished.

She continued, "There is a thing that is important to you, knowledge that you must have. I know this, and I will give it to you. It is why you have come. It is this thing that has guided you, even if you didn't know it."

She paused. Preston took the opportunity to speak of the Water Stone, and he pulled the Sun Stone from his pouch.

"Yes, many years ago I drew her from the water and asked her permission to bring what she carried to you, to remember this land. She was very patient, you see," Mama Luna smiled. "And she did her job very well. In some time I will go to this special place, her home, and make an offering in thanks for your safe journey here."

She touched the Sun Stone lightly, "And this one, he has a very sacred role. He will help you to always remember who you are. He will stay with you." She closed his fingers around the Sun Stone and held them there. Warmth engulfed his hands and the Sun Stone, nestled by his palms, reinforced by Mama's own, became electrified. The moment seemed to stretch on forever.

Mama Luna withdrew her hands and said, "Tomorrow we will rise early." She pointed across the lake, to a point obstructed by the night mist. "There is a very sacred place that I will take you. It is there I will give you what you must have."

They took their time on the silent return to Mama Luna's home. Preston felt like he was in a dream. He had the uncanny impression that he was floating.

— Chapter Sixty —

THE NEXT MORNING when Preston helped Mama Luna clear away the remains of their simple breakfast, corn gruel and tortillas, there was a call from outside. She wiped her hands on her apron and went to the entrance. Answering, she motioned someone to come inside. A young man in traditional clothing entered, nodding a greeting to Preston. Preston gathered from their conversation that Mama Luna invited him to some breakfast, but he turned it down.

"Chan K'in, this is Chan Bor. He will take us now in his canoe to cross the lake. Shall we go?" Mama collected a small bag, and Preston grabbed his pack. He wasn't sure why, but it seemed he should bring it.

They veered onto a different path than Mama Luna had taken him the night before. There at water's edge was a heavy dugout, obviously old and well used. It was narrow, and there wasn't a comfortable way to sit. Preston followed Mama Luna's lead. Kneeling, he sat back on his heels. Chan Bor had rescued a long handmade oar from the nearby reeds and stood at the back. Rhythmically dipping the oar into the waters, he guided the canoe toward the other side, still hidden by fog.

It wasn't until they got toward the center that Preston realized just how big the lake was. He was able to see small coves along the edge that, in some cases, led to other waterways beyond. He imagined that the lake stretched on through the reeds and water lilies to a series of lagoons. After twenty minutes or so of gliding along, they bumped up on a narrow beach. Chan Bor jumped into the shallow water and pulled the dugout onto shore. He gave a hand to help Mama Luna. Preston climbed out after her. They exchanged some words and Chan Bor settled himself on a nearby stump.

"Isn't he coming with us?" Preston asked.

"No, he will stay here. This a very sacred place we go. Mostly only elders go and not even so much now. But I have received the permission of Our Mother Äkna' who graces me, and then Our Lord Ah K'ak, especially because it is his place."

She started down a barely visible, muddy trail with Preston close on her heels, the mist closing in around them. He looked back once. The trail had disappeared.

He had the sense of being watched, and a few times he thought he saw figures out of the corner of his eye. When he looked directly, they dematerialized. He asked Mama Luna about it. She stopped and turned to him.

"Yes, it is so. There are many here, the Ancient Ones. This is a place that opens to all time, between the worlds. It is easy for them to come here. And so this is a place where the knowledge will always live, no matter what else happens to our people," she gazed into the barely visible trees. "Old T'uup and I would come here together, and our ancestors would tell us many things. And we listened because we could guide the people. Sometimes I see my old friend here. In this way I know he is still with me. There were some times when we brought special young ones here for rites. But it has been long ago since the last." She looked up him with sorrowful eyes and resumed picking her way along the path. A chill snaked its way up Preston's spine.

Finally they came to an escarpment where the trail dead-ended. In front of them was a cave. Mama Luna stopped. She spoke in a low voice directing her words toward the mouth of the opening. Preston didn't have to know her tongue to recognize a prayer.

"Come," she motioned. The entrance was low and narrow. Preston had to stoop slightly. The air was dank and smelled like something very old, not unpleasantly so. Just as when he and Felipe found the hidden cave in Piedras Negras, there was evidence of many ceremonies left by the blackened walls. But he saw no petroglyphs here. At the point where they were losing outside light, the cavern walls suddenly widened to reveal an inner chamber—and Mama Luna halted. She knelt to open the bag she'd carried and brought out a few small palm leaves, a small terracotta pot with a crudely fashioned clay head perched on one side and chunks of resin that looked the same as that Preston had found buried in the back sanctuary at home. Motioning for Preston to sit, she prepared for ritual. Mama arranged the fronds on the chamber floor and placed the pot on top. Searching in her bag, she extracted small kindling sticks and matches. Neither of them spoke. Once the sticks were burning, Mama Luna placed a silver dollar-sized chunk of copal in the flames. Its intoxicating perfume permeated the air, and a further sense of the Otherworld entered. Mama chanted the strange, lyrical word-swallowing song he remembered from childhood, an entreaty to the gods. Finally she rocked back and sat on her heels arranging her long skirts around her.

"This is the place of Our Lord Ah K'ak. In this place of protection I tell you what is yours to know, so you can hold the threads that are yours to hold. In this way you can weave your destiny."

Preston looked at Mama Luna expectantly. She took his hands and squeezed them lovingly. Releasing him, she began to speak.

"When you were very young you came to these lands with your mother. Do you remember?"

Preston nodded slowly, "I don't have exact memories. But some places seemed familiar, but I didn't know why."

"Yes…you were very young, barely a few years. So your spirit remembers. And, of course, your soul knows." She told him the story of a young Sybilla, unsure of herself, showing up in the village with another journalist. "She said she was here to do a story but really she was looking for your father, the one we called Bol. Just like I knew you would come down the road, I had this knowledge that she would come."

She paused, "Do you remember Doña Flora?" He shook his head and Mama Luna continued, "She was the midwife who birthed you from your mother. And we had a connection out of time. You see, she raised you to come into the world and I raised your father. That is how these threads go."

Preston's eyes widened, "What do you mean you raised my father?"

"We say raised because in our prayers you are called to travel up the World Tree and be delivered like a flower in this Middleworld. Like that I was the midwife for your grandmother. Your papa brought his first breath into my hands."

In shock, Preston had no words. Mama Luna turned to poke up the coals and added another piece of copal. "In this time as you were born, Doña Flora and I could see into each other's world and we could see how some things would happen. It is both the gift of this work that we could share such things but also sometimes a sorrow. People have their destiny and the way they travel to it. So we could only guide in some ways. An easy way is not many times the best way. And it would be out of our hands.

"Well, your grandmother, she called herself Graciela, came into the village one day much like your mother and then you after that. But it was even more rare back in those times to see strangers, and she was a gringa. A brave young woman in many ways, and I think you call it 'a free spirit.' Your grandfather—he was called K'in—fell in love with her at the first sight. He thought she was Our Mother in the body. He loved her so much. So she moved in with his family, and they stayed with each other. It was different for her, our ways, but she worked with her mother-in-law to cook and even in the *milpa*. And then after a time a life was going to come. Your grandmother shouldn't have taken your papa away after he was born. She didn't understand. There was a special ceremony that had to be done."

"Why?" This revelation, dropped in his lap at once, was overwhelming for Preston, hard to take in. But Mama Luna's words, as unlikely as they sounded, had the resonation of truth.

"You see, your papa was a twin, and he was the second one to enter. But his brother was blue. He had the roots of the World Tree wrapped around him. He held too tightly to the other world and could not breathe in ours. He fell back. Your grandmother almost followed him. She was screaming with grief. I think it was only because your father was in her arms that she didn't go, too. We didn't know for some days what might happen. She stayed in her bed. She wouldn't even let your grandfather hold your papa.

"Then she must have heard the elders and me talking outside. We were very worried. We knew that if something special wasn't done, then your father's twin would make that attachment so strong that your little papa and maybe your grandmother would be pulled into the Underworld with him. Something must be done to cut that connection just like the cord of the placenta. But your grandmother misunderstood. She thought that the elders were going to kill your papa. And maybe in the old times that would have happened, because he would almost have been lost anyway. There must be many strong prayers and smoke. It is very hard on the elders and even the community. They have to fight off strong spirits. Your grandmother screamed at the elders to stay away. And in the next night and everyone was asleep, when she was barely able to walk herself, she took your papa and walked into the jungle. We never saw her again. Your grandfather was heartbroken. And not a year later, he was bitten by a fer-de-lance and died. Some said your grandmother sent that snake. But I don't believe that."

Their eyes brimmed with tears: Preston's for hearing of his father's tragic beginnings and Mama Luna's for reliving the times she related. Emotional exhaustion was making in-roads for them both, but Mama Luna pushed on to finish the story.

"Yokha'. It means Place of Flowing Water, a most sacred place for us. But it is also a dangerous place. I saw when you came to enter there and Hach Kan—the True Snake—gave his permission and guided you in your visions," she said.

It suddenly dawned on Preston that Mama Luna had indeed witnessed the meandering path he'd taken. She's talking about that huge snake that crossed our path before we stepped into Piedras Negras, he thought, and he recalled the bizarre dream that night.

"Many, many years ago my people lived across the waters in that place Yokha'. But before that they lived deeper in the jungle. One day the leader of my people had a dream about people coming from far away to a place on the big waters. He asked the village seer to help with the dream. That one said it was a sign that our people would move to that place, and it was good. The leader believed him. They left their old home. And they made their home Yokha'.

"But that seer was wrong. The people from far away were the conquistadors. Our ancestors welcomed them, wanted to trade. But the conquistadors killed them. Those spirits you felt there? They were our ancestors. The ones who got away came here to settle afterwards. Before they left, they told the story on the walls of our sacred cave there. And they left the god pots of those who were killed. This new place our ancestors named K'ak after Our Lord of Fire so that if anyone came to threaten us again, there would be a wall of fire around our village to protect us. That is how we have survived all these years. But now many intruders are coming close. I don't know if Our Lord can keep us from harm much longer.

"Your father lived in Yokha' with the ancestors there. He was haunted by them and he was haunted by one other. His brother. He had already found us when your mother came. But he could not stay with us long until he would go back to Yokha'. That's where he was when your mother brought you here. I could see it would not be good for her to know this. Bol was already not of this world, and this would have caused your mother and you much pain. You see, your papa was special. And he needed a teacher when he was very young to show him how to travel these worlds. But it was too late for him when he finally found us. He was tormented. And we prayed to Hachäkayum and Ah K'ak to do something for his healing. Many times Old T'uup and I brought him here to this place where you sit now. No matter. It didn't work. Kisin wanted him too badly."

Heart in his throat, Preston barely whispered, "Where is my dad now?"

A tear slipped down Mama Luna's cheek.

She took Preston's hand, "Ah, my little one. My Chan K'in, he was lost to us."

PRESTON'S INSIDES CURLED. Anguish tore through him. The dream of finding his father, of standing before him, seeing those ice-blue eyes he was told were so like his own, looking back, had lived up until that moment. Now it was shattered.

"When?" he said hoarsely.

"I cannot tell you the exact day. You know the night before I left your home I had that bad dream—the one of the dark moving in front of the sun."

"The one of the eclipse."

"Yes, that one. I knew it was a very bad thing, and I was afraid for your papa. I did feel it was something about him. And I was helpless so far away. You and I made the prayers. I was sending them for him. And then your mama came. She didn't understand. She thought I was hurting you in your mind."

Preston vividly remembered the horror of that night. That trauma had remained lodged: the fright, the hurt—the abandonment. The thought that it all took place in the midst of something meant to save his father compounded his grief. His heart ached.

"It took me a long time to get back to K'ak. And when I did I knew it was already too late. Old T'uup told me that Bol, your papa, had stepped so much in the Otherworld that he could not stay long in ours. Your papa said his brother cried for him so loudly he never did sleep. Bol walked at night by the lake and through the village yelling strange things. His brother's spirit was strong pulling him. Old T'uup said he disappeared during that time I found my way back from your home," she paused and took a shaky breath.

"We came to this place, Old T'uup and I did, where we sit now. And we lit the copal and sent up our prayers. In the smoke we saw that your papa went to Yokha'. We thought to bring him back. But T'uup was too

256

old to travel like that. I took two of your papa's cousins, and we went over there. It took us some days to get there and cross the river. I had to do many prayers, too, because Yokha' is not a safe place for us. When we got there we didn't find your papa. There was nothing of him. And I knew he finally followed his brother and went to find the ancestors."

Both their faces were awash with tears. They held hands to comfort each other. Finally, Preston turned and reached for his backpack. He told Mama Luna how the pull at the *cenote* in Yokha' was so strong he just wanted to get away.

"But I saw something right near the edge. You could hardly see it, and it's like it had a hold of me. I had to see what it was," Preston said in a low voice. He pulled the remains of the terracotta vessel from his pack. He held it out to Mama Luna. "I think this is something of his."

Mama Luna took it in her hands. "Yes, it is of him."

Mama Luna and Preston returned to the lake's edge and found Chan Bor waiting for them. The clouds had grown pink in the sky. The sun was going down, and the moon had already risen. We couldn't have been in Ah K'ak's cave more than a couple of hours, he thought, confused. It was morning when we went. Did we step out of time? Halfway across the lake Preston turned and looked back. There was no trace of a far shore.

— Chapter Sixty-two —

THE EVENTS OF the day before had left Preston numb. When they returned to Mama Luna's home, he immediately fell on his pallet and slipped into a dreamless sleep. By the time he arose the next day the sun had climbed well into the sky. Mama Luna was nowhere around but she had left him some thick corn fritters filled with squash on the table covered with a cloth. He grabbed a couple and went outside. Back against the wall, he slid down on his haunches and mused.

It was a day like any other. Yet his whole world had changed. The story Mama Luna disclosed was one of misunderstanding, tragedy and loss. The night had provided a floating place—not only for his depleted spirit—but also a safe haven for meaning to find its level. Preston knew it would not settle within him completely for some time. But in his great loss he was finding solace and grounding, albeit fragile in the moment. The big mystery—the secret he'd always known was there—had vanished.

Preston spotted Mama Luna coming from the direction of the lake. He watched her approach. They greeted each other quietly, and she sat down on a flat rock near him. Mama Luna took up the threads from the day before as though the hours hadn't passed.

"I heard that you, your mama and the man had come, and I went by T'uup's where you were staying early the next morning. When I saw you, then I knew who you were. And you sat down right at my feet. I don't think even Old T'uup had an idea until I told him. But we agreed it was best to keep it from your mama. She never knew for sure that your papa was of our people, and I never told her anything that let her know. Now I could see something else right then. You had your papa's gift, and you must be protected. You remembered something of the other worlds and would keep them in you. You must be taught how to travel this path safely, things about the ways of the worlds. That's why I came home with you and your mama. T'uup and I thought this was best. You are one of ours. I was surprised it was easy for this to happen with your mama. Maybe she had her own reasons to agree. But I think she was very lost then and needed help. And so I made sure you learned some things you needed with these gifts you have. And your papa made sure, too."

Preston looked at her quizzically.

"Yes, your papa was there, too," she nodded but didn't explain. "Now he loved your mother in his own way, but he couldn't understand her. His love for you? It was greater than the world!"

"Then why did he leave me?"

"My Chan K'in. You have to know that he did that for you more than for himself. We are people who must know who we are, where our blood runs. If we don't, then we don't find our feet on the ground. Your papa felt that hole inside, that a part was missing in him, and he didn't want you to feel it, too. It was his plan to come back to you, and to your mama, in a complete way," she shook her head sadly. "But it didn't happen like he wanted."

Preston believed her words. They gave him comfort. He was even beginning to understand some of the confusion, disillusion and fear Sybilla must have undergone.

Mama Luna continued, "So I knew you would come back one day. We have done some things for your papa. But it is the son's place to make sure the way is open for a father. Come, we will prepare now."

They went inside. Mama Luna began to gather items and put them into her cotton bag. One was too big. "Here. You can carry this," she handed him a machete. With that, she motioned him to follow her. "Bring your father's god pot with you. There is something you must do. I will take you to a sacred place, and we cannot meet anyone on the way. So we must go through the forest. We do not talk until we are there."

Preston accepted her instructions and nodded his agreement. He understood the process of rituals and uses of silence. They entered the forest down near the lake. Mama Luna led him on a circuitous route of neglected trails branching off one from the other until, finally an hour later, having met no one, they arrived at their destination deep in the jungle. They approached a solitary rock formation, jutting twenty feet into the air, surrounded closely by trees and bushes; it was green with moss and small plants that sprang to life from unlikely cracks and depressions. Mama Luna pulled back branches to reveal an overhang running along one side, creating a depression four feet off the ground and extending equally as deep into the rock face. A troupe of god pots, neatly placed in long rows, filled the space. Faces of the gods greeted them. Many of the vessels were obviously quite old, a lesser amount newer. All held evidence of having been well used. Preston waited until Mama finished her prayer of respect then looked at her in question.

"This is where god pots are buried when they are not used anymore. So when a man goes to the ancestors, his god pots are put here by his sons. Sometimes the god pots are not needed because there has been a renewal ceremony, and others are made to take their place. But that hasn't happened in many years, since before Old T'uup left," Mama Luna pointed to a cluster near the front. "You see his sons put his there. Or when the men just don't do the ceremonies or make the prayers anymore, and their sons don't care, then they are still brought here. You see how many look newer? They are the ones who left our ways since T'uup is gone. So many."

Preston had a sinking feeling in the pit of his stomach, "Is that why you wanted me to bring my father's god pot? I just made his connection."

"Chan K'in, I am asking this out of respect for your papa. These are our ways, his way, and because you carry his blood, your way. What you have of your father is inside you. You don't ever lose that. Never."

Still he hesitated, once again tinged with grief.

"There are things he must have to rest and know the place he is to go. Or his spirit still walks, sometimes unhappy."

Finally he said, with tears in his voice, "I understand. What do I do?"

"Chan K'in, this is good. Over there are your grandfather's god pots. K'in. You make a little space and put it there," She rummaged in her bag, bringing out small kindling sticks, matches and a small nugget of copal; she handed the items to him. "You can put the sticks and light them."

Preston arranged the broken pot so it would safely hold a small fire and proceeded as she directed. Once the minuscule flames stayed lit, she began to chant asking him to follow her with the repetitive words, thanking the gods for their service in the life of his father. He made the copal offering. The prayer ended. They watched the smoke for a few minutes more, inhaling its sweet scent. Mama Luna turned and went back the way they'd come. Preston followed.

When they once again reached the lake, the sun was directly overhead. Mama Luna surprised him by saying, "There's another thing you must do now."

Without question he continued to follow her lead. Heading in the opposite direction, she picked up a trail that eventually led to a road he hadn't known was there, different than the one he'd arrived on just that short time earlier. Was it really only three days ago? Things have moved so fast.

The dusty road led into the village from another angle. They walked the other way. The sun was at its merciless stage. But soon they left it for yet another narrow path into the jungle and canopy cover. Within a few minutes they were in a clearing. And in that clearing were many open-air thatched huts, the majority no more than six feet long and a few feet wide, some much shorter, and seemed to be arranged haphazardly. Various things were hanging from the rafters; some held cooking utensils, baskets, strings of beads; others had knives, machetes, and hoes. The small ones appeared to have toys of various sorts. Preston quickly realized that they'd entered the Hach Winik burial grounds.

He heard Mama Luna sigh deeply, "You see these?" Her gesture swept some of the burial *palapas* that were in disrepair, caved in or littered with trash. Walking past, she shook her head, "These children have no respect for their ancestors to leave them like this."

Moving among the sites, she took him to an edge of the clearing to an unadorned but clean resting place. "We made this for your father those years ago. It doesn't matter that his physical body doesn't rest there. His spirit can have a place to return to until he can follow the ancestors for sure. But you can see that he needs to have certain things. Right here is his father, your grandfather. That little one there? His twin, your uncle."

Preston surveyed the spots, his emotions still raw from the earlier god pot rites. He sat down on his haunches and buried his face in his hands. His shoulders shook, wracking sobs broke loose. Mama Luna sank down beside him and wrapped her arms around him from behind. She rocked him gently and crooned like she did when he was very young, until finally he was silent. Still she held him.

After a time he broke away and blew his nose loudly on a cloth Mama Luna handed him. They both stood.

"What can I do for my father?"

"Chan K'in, when you are ready I have brought the things that he must have for his journey to the ancestors. And we will make the offering and prayers to open that passage."

"I'm ready now."

She pulled the remaining things she'd brought from her bag: twine, a drinking gourd, tortillas, corn still in the husk, matches, copal, a sisal basket, a few hand tools. "Chan K'in, you can make a fire there just in that corner."

Mama Luna sat on a rock and watched him. When the flames leapt she gave him the copal, and as the smoke enveloped them she began the prayer, pausing so that Preston could repeat each phrase in the dialect of his blood. He used the twine to hang the basket, placing the tortillas, corn, matches and chunks of copal inside. He carefully placed the machete he'd carried and the remaining items around the perimeter rafters. They both surveyed his careful handiwork. Preston was laying his father to rest, and amidst the grief—strangely—a glimmer of aliveness and hope washed through him.

Resolution.

THAT NIGHT MAMA LUNA told Preston that the community wanted to greet him as one of their own. His family wanted to meet him, some members of his *onen*.

"You remember when you were a boy and the deer came to you?" she asked.

"I do! And it came to me again not long ago!" Preston exclaimed.

"We say *keh* for this gentle creature. And the *keh onen* is your lineage, your people. We thought it is the best thing for you to have the privacy with me these last two days. But the *balché* has been preparing since the day you came. And tomorrow it will be ready."

The next morning they got up early and had a very light breakfast. Mama Luna rose from the table saying, "I have something for you." Disappearing into her room, she returned holding a folded white cloth. She pressed it into his hands, "You go put it on."

Touched, he gave her a bear hug. When he re-emerged he wore the traditional clothing of a Hach Winik man, jeans and t-shirt left in a pile on the pallet. They walked toward the village, taking a worn footpath that led toward the perimeter.

Mama Luna stopped at a large ceiba tree, "When you were here last this one was only this high!" She held her hand at five feet. "Now look!"

They descended the path and entered a clearing where nearly thirty people were awaiting them. Women and children were clustered around a small open-air thatched hut that held baskets of food, a cooking fire and other evidence of food preparation. The men and adolescent boys were gathered around the larger one. When Mama Luna and Preston approached, the people surrounded him talking excitedly, patting his arms. Children tugged on his sleeve. Preston grinned back in pure happiness. He'd never had such a welcome or the feeling of family around him. He allowed himself to take it in greedily. Mama Luna introduced him to his only surviving great-uncle, plus aunts, uncles and cousins. A man of about sixty motioned for him to enter the god house.

"This is Old T'uup's son K'in Bor. T'uup passed his god house into K'in Bor's safekeeping. You go with him now. I'll be right over here with the women by the kitchen," Mama Luna indicated the small hut.

Shyness overcame Preston, just like a few days ago when he arrived at K'ak. Mama Luna had sheltered him since his arrival. Now Preston was on his own. But he looked at the friendly faces looking back at him and put the inhibitions away. These are my people, he thought. He took off his sandals and followed K'in Bor into the open-air god house. There was a row of god pots on the ground in the middle with empty round drinking gourds in rows in front of them, along with a few large baskets filled with tamales. All had been awaiting his arrival.

K'in Bor indicated a log for him to sit on, and the other men and boys found their places near the central point. K'in Bor lit copal and performed a ritual dribbling liquid and placing small smears of tamale into the open mouths of the heads of the god pots. He'd collected the liquid from a large terracotta pot that held a questionable-looking brew. Once K'in Bor had finished he filled a drinking gourd and handed it to Preston. The other males passed their empty *balché* bowls to be filled. Preston lifted the bowl to them in acknowledgment, and over to Mama Luna who nodded at him in encouragement. He took a sip, and his taste buds gave pause at the odd sweet-sour libation. He took another and decided it could grow on him. He glanced over at a cousin about his same age, who raised his own bowl to him and smiled. The more Preston drank, the more he forgot himself and conversed in sign language, to the best of his ability, with those near him. He even took a short lesson in the Hach Winik language from a boy who came and sat beside him. So this is what it's like, he thought, chuckling inside. A real family reunion.

After a time K'in Bor blew on the conch shell and began a chant. They'd all been given a small palm frond. Now most of the men lined up behind K'in Bor. One touched Preston's elbow to join them. He followed along as, in turn, they moved along the row of god pots, copal smoke curling to the eaves, and dipped their fronds to each god. When Preston returned to his seat he gazed through the haze to a far corner of the god house that drew his attention. There was something there that he couldn't quite see. But suddenly he could see. There was his long-gone friend Smoky, but then he faded and the presence he knew as Messenger took his place. And then...he had a fleeting image of Messenger's "eyes," as ice-blue as his own, and the shadow of a smile.

Preston's breath caught. The impression hung in the air for a split second longer—then vanished.

— Chapter Sixty-four —

THE *BALCHÉ* CEREMONY went on for much of the day, an informal gathering with comings and goings after the initial offering. K'in Bor sat outside the god house on a log and told the creation stories passed down to him by Old T'uup. Most of the children and some adults clustered around him, probably hearing the stories for the hundredth time. But it was the first time for Preston or so he initially thought. Mama Luna sat next to him and quietly translated into his ear. A couple sounded familiar, and he asked Mama Luna about those. She confirmed that she had taught him those two stories all those years ago.

Finally the people drifted to their separate homes for good, some with the remaining *balché* that was shared out in big plastic soft drink bottles. Preston thanked K'in Bor and his wife Es Nuk for their kindness and work of holding the ceremony. He declined taking any more *balché*, having imbibed a lot already. Although he noticed the effects were minimal compared to the same amount of any other alcohol-type drink he'd known. He joined Mama Luna in heading home.

Later over their evening meal they reviewed the events of the last days. Preston expressed his gratitude for all she'd done for him, not only since he'd been in K'ak but his early years, too. She deflected it to a degree saying it was her love for him, but he also knew she heard and acknowledged him. It was just her way to be humble.

"Chan K'in, it is good for you to rest tomorrow. Just be quiet with these things. Then maybe the day after that I think it is time for you to return to Palenque. I see there is still something for you there."

He knew not to question Mama Luna in such things. The next day he spent long hours alone, sitting on the lakeshore digesting his emotions. Preston didn't try to figure anything out. He just sat with the experiences and new knowledge. At one point, he wandered up to the village store and chose a can of Fanta from its sparsely stocked supplies.

He greeted several family members he'd met the day before. So satisfying, Preston noted to himself.

Mama Luna had made arrangements for the communal truck to drop him at a main crossroads where he was most likely to pick up a *combi* going into Palenque. When he climbed into the cab early that morning he'd hugged Mama Luna and waved goodbye to those who had come to see him off. But he held no sadness. Preston knew that he would return and that he'd be welcomed back.

As he got out of the *combi* in Palenque he thought to stop by an Internet café before heading back to Mayabel. When he downloaded his messages, he saw one from Sybilla. He read it—and froze.

Dear Son,
Are you still in Palenque? There is something I have been thinking of telling you for a long time. That would be a good place for it. I am traveling tomorrow. I will be staying with an old friend who lives on the road to the ruins. If you head that way you'll see a sign on the right for La Casa Mono. If my memory serves me, the road to El Paraiso will be a few hundred yards past that. You can't see the sign from the main road but must walk down the lane a ways. Anyone in the area should know where it is. I'll be there waiting for you. Please come to me.
Love from your mom.

Preston looked at the date of the message. She must have immediately replied to the email he'd sent when he left for K'ak. He did the calculations in his head. She's been here for at least three days, probably four, he thought. Staring at the computer screen, he had all manner of confusing thoughts and feelings. I'm not ready for this. I don't want to see her. Why doesn't she leave me alone? The old resentments surfaced in a vengeance. He found himself ranting inside all the way to Mayabel. He sat on the edge of the bed of his room emotionally exhausted.

Then faintly he heard Mama Luna's voice all over again: *There were things your mama didn't know…she was scared…she was lost…your mama always loved you.*

He began to step into his mother's shoes, to understand how things had gone the way they did. He realized once more that the misunderstanding and loss hadn't been just his and his father's—but hers, too.

He knew the outcome. But she didn't. Preston went into the bathroom, turned on the shower and let the water wash away his resentments. He changed into the cleanest clothes he had and shut the door firmly behind him, leaving the room with resolve. There was no need to perpetuate the animosity of old grievances, especially over circumstances where Sybilla had little control or the knowledge to change what had ensued.

Preston turned left out the Mayabel and crossed the road to the well-traveled path alongside it. He came to the sign for La Casa Mono and was glad he'd noticed it from the other day, nearly hidden as it was. Farther down he came to another track but passed it by. He didn't think it was the right one. He remembered another a little beyond and the pull he'd felt. Sure enough, it was still there when he turned down the lane. Soon he came to an entrance with a freshly painted arched sign: El Paraiso. Two barking dogs ran toward him, but they were friendly. Preston stooped over to pet them. When he stood back up he saw his mother rushing out of the door of the bungalow, an elderly woman behind her. Sybilla ran toward him.

"Preston!" she grabbed him by the shoulders. "I've been so worried!" Sybilla cupped her hands around his cheeks and looked him straight in the eyes. Her eyes were tired, and Preston saw lines on her face he hadn't noticed before. She looked vulnerable in a way he'd rarely witnessed. She hugged him to her tightly. At first Preston went rigid but then consciously relaxed and hugged her back. When she released him, Sybilla had tears in her eyes. She wiped them away and stepped back.

"Preston, this is my dear friend Isabel. Do you remember Señora Delgado?" Sybilla introduced the silver-haired Mexican woman who had followed her out. She looked to be around eighty. Recognition tried to float up from Preston's memory bank. Isabel rescued him.

"Well, I met you as PJ. So you see it was very long ago. You cannot be expected to remember," she said in her perfect English and smiled. "Come. I will get you and your mother a drink."

Isabel settled them in the central patio, a bit removed from the house, surrounded by flowers. She brought the drinks and then tactfully excused herself.

Sybilla attempted to put forth her usual poise but looked more like a small girl about to make a confession. Preston was uneasy himself. He'd never attempted an intimate discussion with his mother.

"Preston," she started, "You know you always asked about your father..."

"I know," Preston said with conviction.

"You know?" her eyes widened and her eyebrows shot up.

He launched into all that had transpired over the last several days in K'ak. Then he went back and filled in the blanks from the time he found his dad's sanctuary in the backyard to his travels in Guatemala, until finally he came full circle to his reunion with Mama Luna. He left nothing out. Preston hadn't counted on Sybilla's response to what he told her. When he'd begun his tale she'd gone paper-white and was as immovable as a statue. At the point where he related the depth of his father's suffering, he witnessed her clear devastation. She looked like she'd been physically hit. At the news of his passing, she broke down in wracking sobs. She had to walk away for a long period of time. By the time he told her about his extended family in K'ak and their welcome, she offered a small, albeit grateful smile.

He finished two hours after he'd started, emotionally wrung out himself but light and calm. A load that had been weighing him down for as long as he remembered was gone. With the closing words of his story, he'd said, "Mom, I want you to know that I don't blame you anymore. I did for all these years, and I'm sorry."

Tears ran silently down Sybilla's cheeks. She hugged him once more and said, "PJ, I'm so sorry any of us endured what we did."

Preston allowed her the slip of his childhood name.

He stayed for the delicious dinner Isabel prepared. She insisted he call her by Isabel, fussing that Señora Delgado wouldn't do for family.

She regaled them with her husband Ricardo's early escapades—and those of his good friend Davis, both long passed. Sybilla chimed in with her first encounter of Davis and how scared she was. Before long they were all laughing. A spirit of adventure was in the air.

Against all attempts at persuasion, Preston insisted on going back to his room for the night but asked Sybilla to meet him at Mayabel for lunch. He knew he needed some time to himself before making a proposal to his mother, which had come to him during dinner as the obvious next step. But he had to get used to the idea first. Preston had a peaceful night.

The next day they sat across from each other enjoying guacamole, tamales and ice-cold beer. Sybilla's eyes were still red-rimmed, but she laughed as he revisited some of the more amusing pitfalls and adventures he'd had in his travels. He even dared to tell her about his encounter with Evie. He was as surprised about his disclosure as Sybilla was. And when he voluntarily called her "Mom" he liked the unfamiliar sound of it in his ears. She was obviously pleased.

Then he tentatively broached the subject of his proposal: Would she be willing to return with him to K'ak? Sybilla grabbed his hands in excitement. They spent the next hour making plans for a return the following day.

The threads that Mama Luna had placed in his hands were indeed now his to do with as he pleased. Preston wasn't wasting any time in weaving his own further story. He fingered the Sun Stone through its pouch and felt secure. Should he ever get off track he had a strong reminder to set him straight.

— Epilogue —

MAMA LUNA AND SYBILLA had embraced like old friends when she and Preston arrived in K'ak, the old difficulties forgotten. She was pleased that some of the people still remembered her. Sybilla found her own closure through their time there. After many years of hoping to regain something lost or imagined, she finally looked forward to a new chapter in her life.

A week later, Sybilla and Preston returned to their Mother Lode home together. It only took Preston a few weeks to track down his grandmother. Sybilla told him what little she knew of Gabe's background and family. One of her professional connections, who owed her a favor, had helped Preston input to the databases that might locate Graciela Cadell. The results showed a string of addresses. But Graciela had returned nine years earlier to the town where she'd grown up, and her phone number was listed. When Preston called her on the phone there was a long silence. She confessed to being shocked to hear that she was a grandmother but immediately invited him to come visit. Graciela asked about her son, but Preston put her off saying he promised to bring her up to date when he saw her.

Preston and Sybilla decided they would go together. Sybilla wanted a look at Graciela to see if she was really as eccentric as Gabe always said she was—and Graciela didn't disappoint. She looked like she'd just stepped out of the Sixties. Her little cottage was more like a museum, or maybe a warehouse, than a home. She greeted them extravagantly, checking them both out head to toe and offhandedly offered that the house doubled as her studio. That accounted for the odd paraphernalia piled on the floor or hanging from the walls, found objects from garage sales and the surrounding forest. Whimsical half-finished sculptures stood on tables. Mobiles hung from the ceiling. Preston couldn't help but like his wacky, artist grandmother. After the preliminary niceties and offer of food, Preston and Sybilla gently told her some of what happened to her son. They'd already decided between them not to let on about the breakdowns Gabe had experienced or why the Hach Winik thought it happened. No need to uncover old wounds more than needed. So they told her he had found his way to K'ak but had accidentally fallen into a *cenote* at Piedras Negras and died. Graciela had tried to hide it, but they both knew she was grief-stricken. As a mother, she'd always hoped there would be a day when she and her son were no longer estranged, and was still perplexed how it had happened. Preston and Sybilla stayed on a couple of days and met surviving family who were still in the area before bidding Graciela goodbye.

Preston worked on his mother for a few months until she finally gave in. They were going to Johns Wake for Christmas. Sybilla hadn't returned since she left with Gabe at eighteen. Preston had never met that side of his family. There was a stiff reunion. Sybilla had given him a sidelong glance like: I told you so. He'd watched in amazement. In no time at all, he saw his mother step into the old role of rebellious daughter to his grandmother's imperious pronouncements, even as decrepit as the old lady was. Preston decided that whole side of the family wasn't to his taste, but at least he made the connection. Preston was grateful to Sybilla for her big escape when she was a young woman. They'd managed to stay the minimum time it took to be polite—and then left for Atlanta to have a good time. At any rate, Preston now knew where his blood ran, both sides, and that's what mattered.

— Acknowledgments —

I EXPRESS DEEP affection for good friend Will Crim, my intrepid travel partner, for our many years' journeys in Mexico and Central America that served to kickstart my inspiration for this novel. Much appreciation to Alonso Mendez, who first provided me entryway to the highland and lowland Maya villages of Chiapas, Mexico, and arranged connection with spiritual leaders and healers. From these experiences came my initial inkling of the beauty, mystery and faith inherent in the Maya people. For Carol Karasik and Walter (Chip) Morris, I carry profound respect. Their dedication toward preserving the Maya traditions and culture is steadfast, and I feel fortunate for their ongoing involvement in my spiritual travel programs. Elements of shared rituals grace the pages of this book. The works of anthropologists Didier Boremanse, R. Jon McGee and Robert Bruce fleshed out aspects of the Lacandón Maya culture I hadn't personally witnessed and allowed me to fill in some blanks. To my readers Sue Woody, Patricia Bruneau-Gaber, Kathleen Sibley, Nancy Vandervoort and Janet Lincoln, I am indebted. Through their eyes, I tested the story and made significant adjustments. Sharon Brown, Jamie Reaser and Matthew Pallamary read advance copies of this novel and generously gave endorsements so important for the reach of a book. Many thanks to all.

— Praise for —

— Praise for —
Standing Stark: The Willingness to Engage
by Carla Woody

...Woody teaches us to soar to new heights of consciousness and open magical portals into our Core Selves. Miraculously, she also addresses terrorism, environmental destruction, medical dilemmas and other modern issues that distract so many of us from following our true paths. **Standing Stark** *is a magnificent adventure, as well as a fascinating read!*

—John Perkins, author of *Shapeshifting, The World Is As You Dream It, Psychonavigation* and *Spirit of the Shuar*

Writing from direct personal experience, Carla Woody tackles the mystery of life with sensitivity and an open heart. Most importantly, like an experienced teacher, she probes us to search deeply into the wellspring of wisdom buried in the inner recesses of our being.

—Kyriacos C. Markides, author of *The Mountain of Silence, Riding with the Lion* and others

This book is filled with wonderful stories that help to illustrate with great clarity our underlying relationship with spirit. I'm sure readers will gain insight from Carla's writing, as did I.

—Stephan Rechtschaffen, MD, Co-founder and CEO, Omega Institute for Holistic Studies

Carla's easy, honest style of sharing spins us through this story of a willingness to be fully human—the most sacred act we can ever achieve while being here on earth. She opens her heart to us page after page so that we, in turn, can experience feeling that wondrous gift of being wholeheartedly alive—in every moment—no matter what!

—Jacquelyn Small, Founder, Eupsychia Institute, author of *Awakening in Time* and *Becoming a Practical Mystic*

*Praise for **Standing Stark***

*In **Standing Stark**, Carla Woody weaves her personal story into a delightful tapestry of self-growth methods and tales of transformation. In reader-friendly language and with a flair for transforming challenging concepts into understandable ideas, Woody describes her unique path toward wholeness and fulfillment. In so doing, she helps her readers discover their own path through the sacred dimensions of life.*
　　—Stanley Krippner, Ph.D., Co-author of *Extraordinary Dreams and How to Work with Them*

— Praise for —
Calling Our Spirits Home:
Gateways to Full Consciousness
by Carla Woody

Calling Our Spirits Home is truly an enlightening guidebook for anyone looking for directions & tools for expansion, growth & transformation—Help yourself with this book and you will find your way home.

Malidoma Somé, author of *Of Water and the Spirit*

This is a pleasing and easily read story that tells what we must know and what we need to become to live in this new millennium. It is a spiritual map that offers paths to success in life. Take this book as your map and you will find the way that is right for you.

—Gay Luce, Founder, Nine Gates Mystery School

Calling Our Spirits Home is a beautiful spirit song that gently gathers the dis-integrated, frightened parts of ourselves into the warm unconditionally loving wholeness of a mother's embrace—a celebration of life, mysticism and magic emerging as a blossom from the consciousness of humanity after centuries of growing beneath the compost of an unbalanced, materialist world.

—Matthew Pallamary, author of *Land Without Evil*

— About the Author —

CARLA WOODY has been mentoring people for more than twenty years, helping them make the leap to an un-prescribed life—consisting of an expressive prescription of their own making. In 1999 she established Kenosis LLC to support human potential through spiritual travel journeys and programs integrating Neuro-Linguistic Programming (NLP) and sacred world traditions. She founded Kenosis Spirit Keepers, a 501(c)3 nonprofit organization, in 2007 to help preserve Indigenous wisdom ways threatened with decimation. Carla writes books and articles related to spirituality, natural healing and advocacy of Native traditions. She is also a fine artist and makes her home near Prescott, Arizona. Please visit websites: *www.kenosis.net* and *www.kenosisspiritkeepers.org*. You are invited to follow her blog at *http://thelifepathdialogues.com*.